LADY OF THE BRIDGE

by

Laura Kitchell

Lady of the Bridge
A novel

Copyright© 2015 Laura Kitchell
Print Edition
ISBN 13: 978-1517405793
ISBN 10: 1517405793

Cover Art Photographer: Allegra Christopher
Cover Design: Kristen Kitchell
Editor: Katherine Alexander

www.laurakitchell.com

DEDICATION and ACKNOWLEDGEMENTS

Thank you, Kathy, for your endless support and the work you put into making this book what it is. To Sara, for always believing in me and for your precious time and input. To my mother, for your gentle and sometimes not-so-gentle insistence that I continue to write and evolve. To Kristen, for your wisdom, creativity, honesty, and graphic artwork on this cover.

Most of all, to Steven, who showed me what love is.

A NOTE FROM THE AUTHOR

For those of you who enjoy historical fiction, you may find this one a bit different in terms of style. An historical novel set in western culture prior to the late 1800's typically should not contain speech with contractions. We must understand, however, that eastern peoples have spoken in an abbreviated fashion far longer, and especially so within the Japanese language. As such, I have endeavored to capture this through the use of contractions.

Also, you will find words in this novel that were not in use yet within the western world. The Japanese language has been vast since well before the fifth century and, therefore, had words equivalent to those I have used. As this story is not written in Japanese, I found it necessary to employ western words in use today that were not in use when this story takes place.

Chapter One

Sumpu, Japan
March 30, 1616

Upheaval.

It disrupted Princess Saiko's life and beleaguered her battle-weary country. When had she lost all choice in her life?

Saiko fisted a hand, wishing she had a bow and arrows. What she wouldn't give for a bit of target practice right now. She missed her younger brother in Mito. Yorifusa had taught her how to shoot. She'd gone to Mito as an untried, curious girl. While there, she'd become a woman with skills – skills that would go to waste once her father consigned her to live at the imperial court in faraway Kyōto.

Only days ago, she had lived free and independently, managing her brother's castle and learning the art of swords. Now, she sat in her father's castle under a cloud of upheaval in a pretense of calm. If she had come home to stay, perhaps she could enjoy some peace. Her return, however, was temporary. Frighteningly temporary.

Her father loved her. He never let her doubt his favor, but when he issued an order, he expected it followed. That her oldest brother carried the title of shogun didn't matter. Her father, Tokugawa Ieyasu, still ruled Japan.

Duty. The word had never left a bad taste in her mouth. Never been a burden. Now, she cursed it with every ounce of her being. What had she, the youngest child of Japan's most powerful man, done to deserve such a sour fate? Why had he chosen her to serve as consort to the emperor?

"It's not right," she whispered into the cool air of her chamber.

"Pardon me, Princess?" her pompous tutor asked, interrupting his droning instruction.

She merely shook her head, and he continued.

She wished she could slide open the shutters on her window, but the cold temperature outside would plunge her room into an unbearable chill in minutes. Only a brazier warmed her chamber, and its meager heat couldn't stand against the last of winter's icy grip. Besides, she had too many people in her room at the moment. It made no sense to subject them to misery.

Coming home reminded her how she, as a princess, should expect no privacy. At the emperor's palace in Kyōto, she would have even less.

Living in Mito had spoiled her. Saiko had worn *hakama* trousers, allowing her an ease of movement she could never have in the long silk of her kimono robes. She had ridden astride, learned archery and sword and how to fight with hands and feet. She'd come and gone on her own schedule.

She cast a longing glance at the window. Did it snow? Did the sun shine? She hadn't seen the sky in two days, and the confinement had her ready to come out of her skin.

Her tutor bore the sober expression of a man who had participated in one too many meaningless conversations. His dull eyes drooped a bit at the outer corners and seemed to fight the weight of his slumping eyelids. The whites had turned the color of bile, from age she suspected.

Saiko lowered her gaze to keep from glaring at him. He had talked about the proper handling of servants for too long already, and apparently had much more to say on the subject.

Her left hip had gone numb, and she fidgeted on her silk cushion. The seam of her sock scraped across tightly woven *tatami* straw matting, creating an unpleasant screech. On cushions near the brazier at the far end of her room, her ladies-in-waiting sat with heads together in soft conversation, their whispers barely registering. Their bright kimonos brought to mind spring flowers and made her yearn for warmer days.

Raising her hand, Saiko put a stop to her tutor's monotone lecture. "I'm humbly grateful for your wisdom, Hayashi-sensei. You'll surely have me ready for life in the imperial palace. As I've spent the last five years managing servants and the running of Yorifusa-san's castle in Mito, however, I believe this area of my education has been thoroughly addressed." With a serene smile, and feeling anything but, she stood. "Now might be a good time for me to get some air. I believe I'll take a walk in the garden." When he opened his mouth to protest, she shook her head. "Master Hayashi, your patience with me is admirable. Please take a rest and have some tea. Or perhaps, as my father's advisor, you have responsibilities that require your attention elsewhere?"

The sagging skin of his thin face and his protruding ears jiggled with indignation as he stood, but he simply nodded and bowed. When he straightened, his narrow, twelve-inch-high black lacquered hat nearly brushed the ceiling. He went to the brazier and gave his palms a warming then a rub. "I'll be gone a week. A few days to travel to Kotu, a day or two to conduct my business, and a few days to travel back."

Her three ladies ceased their whispers and cast him uneasy glances.

She frowned. "But Kotu is less than a day's ride on horseback."

"I travel only in my personal carriage. It's slow but more dignified than riding on a horse." He bowed then headed for the door. He sniffed. After another bow and a stiff rustle of his black minister's robe, he left.

She shook her head. How did riding a horse make a person undignified? Samurai, the most dignified in the land, rode on horseback. And how had he, an aristocratic sycophant, obtained a position of honor within the shogunate?

Shuffling to the door, she stayed her ladies with a gesture.

She slipped on socks then her platform *geta* sandals. She didn't bother searching for boots or a down-filled coat. A walk alone in the garden for a few minutes meant her sanity, and the potential chill outside couldn't deter her.

"But Princess..." her first lady protested, leaving the brazier's warmth to join her at the door. She had thin but not unpleasant features, and her warm, dark eyes almost always shined with some secret pleasure or joke she never revealed.

"I need this, Okiko-san." Waving sweet smoke from an incense burner over her hair and clothing to freshen her scent, Saiko shook her head. "I won't stay outside long."

Fisting her hands, she let the bite of her fingernails into her palms remind her not to complain. Wars had left samurai and their families lordless, homeless, and starving. Despite a growing peace, minor uprisings around the country still caused unrest and displacement, and the roads contained a steady stream of villagers who had lost their homes and livelihoods.

Saiko wore the finest silks, never went without a meal, and faced a world of opulent luxury in the palace of the figurehead emperor. True, she would serve as nothing more than a sexual servant to a man who no longer held any power or authority, but she would appear ungrateful and undutiful if she lamented. She bit her tongue as she left her chamber.

With the need for escape quickening her step, she emerged from the castle, ignoring every stare on the way.

* * * *

Attack-screams and the clang of metal filled Hosokawa Takamori's ears. Moisture laced the air inside Sumpu Castle's samurai quarters, a mixture of steam emanating from baths at the building's rear and sour sweat generated from practicing swordsmen. It stifled his senses.

He strode among the battling samurai, checking form and correcting weaknesses. Bare feet slapped pristine wooden floorboards, accompanied by grunts of effort and the rustle of fabric as samurai worked legs and arms.

This newly built facility gleamed with warm wood and clean lines. At various obscure points about the building, carvings sported Tokugawa dragonflies, and he had made a game of finding them. He offered a nod of approval to a man who executed a superior spin and block that countered an offensive that would have defeated a lesser opponent.

At the far end of the large *budokan*, his friend entered and stopped.

He suggested improvements to two more samurai as he made his way over. "Shosan-san, are you here to practice?"

"Marshal, I'll only practice if you let me spar you so I can wipe that scowl from your face." The short, muscular samurai tapped the end of his *wakizashi*, his mouth quirking to one side as humor glinted in his brown gaze.

"I'm not scowling."

His second-in-command's eyebrows lifted.

He attempted to stare his friend into intimidation, but the short samurai only smiled bigger. Takamori huffed. "I'm at peace."

Shosan barked a laugh. "If this is peace, turmoil must be utter chaos."

Tension tightened his gut and the muscles at the back of his neck. Hooking a thumb into the belt holding his *wakizashi* at his waist, he pivoted to stand next to his friend. Surveying his men in practice, he conceded, "I may be a bit on edge since coming to Sumpu."

"We all are. This practice helps, but we're men of war. What do we have to occupy us in this quiet place?"

Takamori shook his head. "I can't breathe."

"Exactly."

"No, I mean literally. I'm going to walk in the cold and clear my lungs. Take over for me. They're losing their edge."

* * * *

"Saiko-san," said Tokugawa Ieyasu, holding out a staying

hand as he left a group of elderly samurai and marched toward her. His boots crunched over loose gravel that separated a line of connecting structures that included her residence from the castle's extensive garden. "A word."

"Of course, Father." She let him take her fingers in his warm, callused hand.

He had worn the same rough, thickened spots for as long a she could remember, and they hadn't softened or reduced in size in his old age. Though he bore strength and authority in his straight posture, an unusual bruised shadowing under his eyes concerned her.

He patted the back of her wrist. "Your studies go well?"

"Yes, Father. Hayashi-sensei has managed to teach me a bit about protocol and imperial etiquette." She pressed her lips together to avoid complaining about the irritating tutor.

He chuckled. "I see your distaste. Bear with him, Saiko. Nobody knows these subjects better. I know you'll do well. You'll make me proud."

Anxiety shot a sharp pain through her head, and she blinked. "Is this entirely necessary? If you tell me I must, I will do my duty, but is there no other way?"

His eyes narrowed and hardened. "You must. Only a woman of my bloodline can create a bridge between Shogun and the emperor and end these civil uprisings that prevent the peace within our grasp. You are the only woman unattached and of age. You must."

His words slammed into her and stole her final hope. She somehow kept her spine rigid as he rejoined his men without a backward glance.

She should consider this arrangement an honor. Her father trusted her to represent the Tokugawa line. If she bore a son to the emperor, such a child could end the unrest and secure Japan's peace by binding the shogunate to the royal seat. So why did she struggle with the idea? Why did she alternate between anger and despair?

She checked over her shoulder to make sure Okiko hadn't

followed. Her two-story quarters occupied the middle of a structure among a grouping that formed the 'second circle,' a ring of buildings surrounding the inner citadel. At the castle's center loomed the main tower where her father conducted the running of Japan.

She sighed with relief as she stepped into the winter chill of the garden. The cold air had a clean, odorless scent so refreshing after the stale, stagnant air that permeated the fortress. It cooled her cheeks but didn't penetrate the three layers of thick silk she wore.

Despite the season, the landscaping held tremendous loveliness. Pale winter flowers bloomed, evergreens swayed in a slow breeze, and even dormant trees reached bare branches to the sky as if in celebration of the day.

Spring showed signs of life, though. Miniscule buds began to form on overhead branches, and a hint of green peeked through the straw-colored remnants of last year's grass. Drawing her fingers into the warmth of her sleeve, Saiko smiled. Spring was her favorite season. She adored the renewal and the colors.

She didn't share most everyone else's fatalistic view of life. Waiting for the next disaster. Ruminating on death. What did it accomplish? No, she wanted to savor every second and soak in the joy of her existence like her mother had.

Then again, Saiko would have more joy if she had *some* choice in her future. Was she so wrong to want romantic love? Why did duty have to preclude it? And why did her father not want for her what he'd had for himself with her mother? Her parents had been the perfect example of what love could be. Kind. Consuming. Forever. She wanted nothing less.

She strolled along a stone-laid path next to the happy gurgle of a winding brook that snaked through Sumpu Castle's south garden. Layers of silk and linen under her elaborate, flowing blue kimono continued to keep the chill at bay but wouldn't keep her warm for long.

It didn't matter. Every autumn, gardeners had placed a tall, lacquered wood cover over her bridge. It would block the breeze, and three lanterns inside would provide light and some meager warmth at the highest point on the arch.

Before she turned a corner where the path continued behind a hedge of evergreen bushes, she glanced back. Nobody followed. She hiked her hem to her ankles and hastened as fast as her *geta* sandals allowed. The exercise warmed her and made her smile. When her stone bridge loomed past a row of dormant cherry blossom trees, she slowed.

Her bridge. So beautiful. So peaceful. Rich wood planks carved with flowers and trees then coated with a hard clear lacquer formed the walls of the cover and glowed brightly in the muted winter sun. A cheerful red wood framed the long curved box at top and bottom edges and formed a crested roof decorated at each end with red dragons roaring silently to the sky.

Supporting it, pale stone sported enormous magnolia blossom branches chiseled into the side. It gently arched over the brook, and golden light shone from the opening nearest her. Despite earthquakes through the years, it stood intact.

She might never see it again after she left. Tears smarted. Other than the last five years spent in Mito helping her brother with the administration of his domain, she had lived here in Sumpu. This was her home, but not for much longer. A tightness formed in her chest, and she pressed a fist to the trapped sensation behind her ribcage.

Life had never seemed this unfair. Since returning less than a week ago, she'd had a chance to visit the garden only once. Sumpu Castle teemed with strange faces. Her father's veteran servants and retainers had gone to Edo to serve her brother, the shogun, and she recognized only a few who stayed at Sumpu.

She slowly headed for the warm glow at the bridge's entrance and what it meant to spend time inside the shelter. Freedom. Peace. If only for a few minutes. Saiko grasped the end of the handrail and swung into the bridge with a hop.

A man stood inside, and she yelped.

Dressed in shades of gray, he wore his long hair in a knot at the crown of his head. A slung *katana* long sword rested across the small of his back, and a smaller blade hugged the front of his neat *kosode* at an angle, proclaiming him elite samurai.

Barely moving, he cut a hard look sideways and gave her a once over. He drawled, "My lady."

My lady? Did he not know who she was? "Pardon me. I didn't realize anyone..."

But this was her bridge. Her father had ordered its building from Edo artisans the day of her birth. This man should apologize and leave. Not her. She released her kimono, and its heavy silk hem slid past her feet.

He traced artistic detailing of a tree carved into the wood and said in a deep, smooth voice, "I'm told this garden has seventeen bridges."

He had a nice voice. So what? "It does."

"Yet I'm drawn to this one. I haven't seen many stone bridges. I like its sturdiness. It promises peace and time alone in quiet solitude," he said, speaking her very thoughts.

She offered a mild nod. "Yes. It's the place I come the most. Though time alone is hardly possible with two of us here."

Keeping her gaze slightly averted in courtesy, she fought the urge to look him in the face. Study his visage. Search his eyes and any secrets he kept. When he sought the carving his finger traced, she took her chance.

He showed no hint of reaction to her sarcasm. Strength, unforgiving and unrelenting, lined each angle and plane of his handsome face. A scar, old if the brown shade of it indicated properly, tightened his skin from the corner of his left eye to the lobe of his ear. No doubt it marked a moment in battle. His dark skin attested to long hours outdoors. And though not considered an attractive attribute, on him his coloring added to his rugged, manly beauty.

Who was this man who made her breathe faster? Made her heart beat harder? Who was this warrior whose strength affected her physically without his touching a hand to her? The very thought had her stomach clenching with delighted anticipation.

He gave her his full attention, his black stare assessing and stern. Not decided on fighting him, she dropped her gaze. Would he try to demand she leave? If he did, she *would* meet his eyes in a confrontational glare and firmly put him in his place and off of her bridge.

He didn't wear weathered crags and creases upon his skin or the longer facial hair of samurai in her father's service. This man had smooth, clean planes. In his stare, however, glinted an edge of experience. He had seen battle. Horrors and pain. He was special. Different.

In a near whisper, he said, "Tell me about your tears."

Her tears? Wiping the tip of a finger across her lashes, she encountered moisture. She took a step closer and found the warmth trapped inside the bridge cover from the overhead lanterns. Something tentative in his demeanor had her less eager to see him retreat. "It's nothing. Just a moment of weakness. Are you newly arrived?"

"Yes, my lady. I fought with Tokugawa Ieyasu-shogun during the Osaka Summer Siege then stayed to maintain the castle's military defenses until his son assigned a *jodai*. When I returned, I reported to Sumpu to serve him."

"I'm told the Toyotomi clan is destroyed and their samurai with them. You must've fought well." She took a step closer.

"I was fearless." His statement held no boasting. "It's easy to be fearless with two hundred thousand samurai at my back."

"Tokugawa Ieyasu-shogun led the fight in the Osaka Summer Siege. Only the best serve him." Saiko ran a hand along the planks, enjoying the carvings' texture on her palm and fingertips.

She tingled at his nearness. Fine hairs stood on end along her arms and nape. When he spoke, his voice warmed her as if she eased into a hot spring. No man had ever affected her like this.

"Yes. I served the retired shogun at Osaka." He chuckled. "I use the word *retired* loosely, of course. His son holds the title, but we all know Tokugawa Ieyasu-shogun still rules from this castle. And you, my lady? What's your role here?"

She tried to read him, but his expression offered nothing in the way of his thoughts. Opening her mouth to tell him her name, she paused. She liked that he didn't know her identity. He talked to her as an equal – something she only experienced with her father and brothers.

In the distance, Okiko's call carried on the breeze. "I must go. I have duties and responsibilities, but I'll try to come tomorrow."

He gave a solemn nod. "I have duties, as well. I'll try to come tomorrow. I'd like to talk more."

She backed from the bridge, drinking in his rugged yet eloquent strength. "Tomorrow."

Swallowing against a lump of anticipation, Saiko turned and gathered her kimono in fists before running for the castle. Cold finally seeped through her clothing.

Her first lady met her and held the door. "You're flushed. Do you feel unwell?"

"I am too well, Okiko-san. Too well." Settling dignity around her like a cloak, Saiko entered her quarters with her head held high.

*   *   *   *

Standing on the bridge long minutes after she left, Takamori dared not hope. After all he had seen and done, could he find happiness? Could he find love? Battle and bloodshed had made him into a hardened, unfeeling warrior. Hadn't it? Yet when the gorgeous lady had drawn closer by inches, his entire body tightened in awareness. Maybe he wasn't as cold as he'd thought.

With his thumbnail, Takamori traced the Hosokawa family crest inlaid in gold onto the end of his *katana's* hilt. He hailed from an illustrious warrior family, one that had enjoyed favor by the Ashikaga shoguns because of loyalty, and who had served in influential positions within the government as a result.

He wanted most to honor his family, to do justice by his ancestors, and to have future Hosokawa generations remember him proudly. His acclaim in battle, and now his service as marshal to the powerful Tokugawa Ieyasu accomplished this. Yet he couldn't claim ambition in any sense. He had only ever wanted to serve and serve well. Now, he wanted...what?

He exited the refuge of the bridge from the opposite end and strode for samurai quarters. His thoughts warred with his desires. The lady had stirred something in him, and he wanted to see her again.

He tired of fighting. It no longer defined him. Since the Summer Siege, every minute he could spare, he read or wrote. He sought learning, betterment, a feeding of his mind and an appreciation of nature he had ignored until this blossoming peace brought by Tokugawa Ieyasu afforded him the gift of time.

As he approached the quarters, he admired the unusual architecture. The main entrance fronted a center section, which rose high like a temple. Square shutters ran in a line above the entrance's lower roofline which wore a sharp A-shape with a fancy crest and dragons arching in flight from each of the four corners. Two one-story dormitories flanked either side of the center section, sporting battlements along the tops and leading to the castle's outer protective wall.

Inside, the clang of swordfight echoed through the large entryway. Crossing to double doors, he entered the enormous *budokan* where the samurai continued to practice, bare-chested now, with their metal swords. No practice swords for these seasoned veterans. They blocked as well as they attacked, and occasional nicks served as reminders to improve speed and reflexes. Flashes glinted off of shiny blades from daylight streaming through high windows in the upper surround.

"Marshal," someone shouted, and practice stopped. Warriors, sweaty and huffing, faced him and bowed.

Returning the bow, he gruffly ordered, "Resume."

His second-in-command approached across hardwood

flooring and sent his *katana* into its scabbard with a crisp force that spoke of superb technique. What he lacked in height he made up for in sheer strength. His muscles bulged and gleamed with sweat. No man had ever taken Shosan down in hand-to-hand combat.

Despite the violence they'd seen and committed these past years in battle, his friend had clung to his humanity and humor. A gentle, teasing light shone from the wide gaze in his square face as he asked, "Did you find the perspective you sought?"

"I found a different perspective altogether, Shosan-san." Takamori took his two swords in one hand, untied his waistband with the other and peeled off his outer robe. Maybe practice would take his mind off of intelligent shining eyes, trembling lips, and skin so delicate and flawless as to make a woman from Edo's pleasure district jealous. Peeling off the upper layer of his innermost robe so it hung at his waist, he rubbed a hand across the skin of his chest. He winked. "Spar with me? I promise not to cut off your head."

Shosan laughed and put a hand on the hilt of his *katana*. "I don't know what you found in that garden, but this is a vast improvement over the growling bear you were when you left. Did you drink a magic elixir? Tell me where to find it."

Takamori dropped into horse stance and drew his sword. "Magic, maybe, but no elixir. And I'm going for more tomorrow."

Chapter Two

Fighting the urge to scream, Saiko pressed her lips together to keep from spewing words that threatened to escape, words outlining the injustice of this fate her father had assigned her. She resisted the urge to tell him what she had wanted from life. That would only cause them both pain.

Avoiding her father's glances, Saiko sat in the first seat of the table closest to the retired shogun's high table. Her father, though a warrior, understood finery. His great hall reflected his sumptuous taste. Purple damask covered every wall but the one behind him. That one gleamed, its shiny ink-like paint reflecting every light in the room. Huge pillars, glowing in gold, supported a ceiling two stories high. Each person in attendance sat upon a raven silk cushion and shared a low, black lacquered table with one other diner.

Large ink drawings framed in ebony hung at equal intervals against the damask. High on the rear wall behind him, seven sheathed samurai swords from various periods throughout Japan's history hung on display, one above the next and twelve inches apart. Everything implied elegance and cleanliness, even the pristine hardwood floor beneath her cushion.

Along a side wall, a bank of wooden folding screens painted in elaborate battle scenes blocked a multitude of doors. From behind them, a parade of servants bore laden trays. Her father received his meal first, then her middle brother and she were served.

The food provided a further tribute to perfect beauty. Not a single grain of rice strayed from round molded mounds presented in rice bowls the exact shade of purple as the walls. Vegetables formed lovely flower petals upon gold saucers. Even noodles in a rich broth seemed to perform a complex dance as servers gently placed the dishes before each diner.

Across the aisle, her brother sent her a questioning look, but she ignored him. She ate in silence, her chopsticks not making a sound. At her side, Okiko expelled worried sighs between bites of her own meal.

"He won't chastise you," Saiko whispered.

"But I'm your first lady-in-waiting. I'm supposed to care for you." Okiko's chopstick clinked a nervous clatter against the edge of her soup bowl.

Saiko cast a fleeting look toward the dais. "My father knows me. He understands that if I make a choice, there's nothing you could do to stop me short of pinning me to the floor." She bit back a smile, imagining her friend attempting to hold her down.

As dinner drew to a close, she rhythmically flexed tension from her hands. Her father studied her, so the time had come. Forcing her shoulders to relax, she calmly set her chopsticks aside.

"Daughter, I'm informed you took time alone this morning." His eyebrows slanted to form a fierce scowl. His hair, though completely white, hadn't grown thin, and his topknot could compete against any young samurai on his estate. His age of seventy-two didn't detract from his power or his ability to wield it. The glistening richness of his black *kosode* decorated with white hash marks added to his aura of power, especially in contrast to his pale gray *hakama* trousers and the glistening wall behind him.

Still, she loved the old man and refused to let him intimidate her. She stood and bowed low. "Yes, Father. Master Hayashi has been merciless in preparing me for my new life. I thought it wise to take a short break to give us both a rest so his great knowledge could sink into my tiring mind."

"I see." He cleared his throat then roared, "And you could not take a companion with you?"

Not a single rustle of clothing disturbed the silence in the huge room. Behind her, two aristocratic diplomats from Kyōto gasped, as they should. His show of anger was for their benefit, after all.

Saiko peeked at her father through her lashes, batted them briefly then bowed her head lower. "I find it easier to clear my mind when I'm alone, Father, but if you deem it necessary that I take a companion, I'll do as you say. As your obedient daughter who loves you so dearly, I'll do as you say." She snuck a peek through her lashes, sinking her teeth into the soft flesh inside her bottom lip.

One side of his mouth quirked, and he rubbed both hands over his face. "We're well protected. As long as you stay inside the castle's walls, I see no harm in your having time alone. I imagine you have much to contemplate in these last days here. You may have time each morning to walk in the garden."

Fighting a smile, she stepped from behind her table, sank to her knees and touched her forehead to the floor. "Thank you, Father."

"Come show me your love."

She stood and stepped forward. Before him at the high table, she whispered, "I don't want to leave, but I love you. You say this is best for our country, and so I'll go and do my best to make you proud." Her bottom lip trembled, and she tucked it in to hide her weakness.

"You do make me proud but you're a woman, not a child. Now that Yorifusa has chosen a wife and no longer needs your assistance in Mito, you have a greater duty to see your family and your country succeed."

She nodded. "I just wish it were about love rather than politics. I'll do what I must."

"I know you will." He turned his cheek, and she leaned across the table and kissed it. "Now, when Master Hayashi returns from Kotu, be good to him. He wants to see you shine in Kyōto."

"He does. I know." She returned to her seat and tried to finish her rice, but fluttering in her stomach made her appetite wane. Time in the garden every day. To see the samurai every day. If her father knew about the elite samurai on her bridge, she doubted he would show such generosity.

Despite it, she looked forward to tomorrow in a way she hadn't in a long time.

*   *   *   *

She would come. Takamori paced to the end of the bridge, searched the walkways for a sign of her then paced back. She had invited him. Surely she would come.

"Hello."

He spun on his heel at the sound of her smooth, cultured voice and found her in the middle of the bridge. "You're a quiet one, my lady."

"I suppose I am. I didn't know if you'd be here. I'm glad you are." She smoothed a hand along blue silk with silver cranes shining in the lantern light. Today, she wore combs that bore silver cranes dangling in sparkling dance at the sides of her upswept hair.

Admiring the slender grace of her lovely throat above the pristine gape of her kimono's neckline, he said, "You wore blue yesterday."

A serene smile curved in natural pink upon her fine face and emphasized the slant of her eyes. "You noticed."

"I notice a lot."

"Blue is my favorite color." Delicate lavender veins decorated the pale lids of her downcast eyes.

"You wear it every day?"

"Not every day, but I would if I could." She released a breathy laugh and ran fingertips along the wood framing the bottom of the bridge cover. "What's your favorite color?"

"I don't have one." He took two steps further into the

bridge, delighted when she didn't retreat. "Do you read?"

"Yes. And write. You?"

"Both. I thought... I have to go away for a while. I'd like to write to you while I'm gone."

The slight smile melted from her shapely, unpainted mouth. "I can't. It would dishonor my father."

He advanced closer until he could smell the fragrance of tropical tulip and cinnamon that clung to her clothing. The scent invaded his senses and made him want to taste her skin. "And who's your father?"

"It's better that you don't know."

A mystery. She peaked his interest. "May I have your name?"

"No."

"You may have mine. I'm Hosokawa Takamori. I'm directly descended from Katsumoto, a famous samurai and *kanrei* and guardian of shogun Ashikaga Yoshimasa's successor."

"Hosokawa Katsumoto of the Onin War. He's best known for his loyalty. Yes, I know that name."

She had read of the Onin War? She impressed him. Here was no shallow, simpering miss. "And you'll know mine."

The smile returned. "I already know yours, Hosokawa Takamori. You must be great indeed to serve here. A great man from a great family."

Did she mean that or did she tease? He couldn't tell past her placid expression. "Do you refuse to tell me your name because it lacks honor?"

She chuckled. "My family holds great honor." She traced the outer edge of a pagoda carved into the wood. "I withhold my name to protect you...and for selfish reasons. I want you to keep coming to see me."

"And if I know your family, I'll stop coming?" Did she mean to unnerve him? It wouldn't work.

"Maybe." She cut him a shy glance and continued to trace the engraving. "You're special. I can sense it. Tell me of your battles."

He winced at echoes of death cries and flashes of faces twisted in agony. "A refined lady like you wouldn't want to hear of such things."

"I've read true accountings and heard tell by samurai. Samurai like you."

Had she? An impressive undertaking for such a gentle creature. War? Violence? How did this interest an elegant lady?

She ceased her tracing and faced him, her features serious. Sad. "I understand it's not glorious or always noble."

"Why do you say that?" He found it difficult to believe she spent time on war tales. Refined women read novels and poetry. Did she try to fool him or impress him by claiming she'd read something she hadn't?

The corners of her small, lovely mouth turned downward. "I've read the Tale of the Heike twice, An Account of the Gempei War, and Gikeiki which chronicles Minamoto no Yoshitsune's life. I realize that these works...well, they highlight the honor and glory of the heroes. An intelligent person can sense the ugliness and destructive nature of war that lies underneath."

"I don't think anyone can know war without fighting in one. Without walking the battlefield afterward. No, it's not glorious." He gripped the handle of his *wakizashi* so tightly that his knuckles ached.

"Heroes are born in battle, however. It can test a man's true character."

"In a way nothing else can," he agreed.

Her eyes narrowed a bit, then she stilled like a statue. "I think your character was tested and you were found worthy."

He paused. "Do you?"

"I see your strength."

He leaned a bit closer, catching a whiff of cinnamon in her scent, and said low, "I see your grace."

She tilted her head at a beguiling angle. "Why do you say that?"

He smiled at her use of his earlier wording. "Everything you do looks like a dance."

"Really? You're the first to say so."

He inched fingers along the railing, wanting to learn if the skin of her hand felt as smooth as it appeared. "You haven't told me of your role here."

Her gaze stayed on his sliding fingers, but she kept hers in place. Her voice sounded faint as she said, "I can only tell you I spend most of my days in the princess' chamber."

A lady-in-waiting. Her family must be very honorable indeed. He relaxed, realizing how much he'd feared to learn she was consort to the 'retired' shogun. "I understand."

"You don't. One day you will." Her fine eyebrows drew closer above the dainty bridge of her small nose.

"You speak of deception?" Deception. A serious word. Did she exaggerate? Perhaps she played a game - a more elaborate one than he'd considered. "You underestimate me, my lady. Remember, I'm fearless."

A smile broadened her pretty lips but didn't reach her eyes. "So you've said. You mentioned that you have to leave. You're going with the princess' entourage to Kyōto?"

He nodded. "I'll be protecting her, yes, but I'll return."

"You won't leave for a few more days yet."

He fought a smile. "True."

"I'll see you again before then?"

"If the gods are good to me, yes. If the gods are good to me, I'll see you tomorrow?"

Showing him her back, she took two steps to leave then stopped. Offering her profile over a shoulder, she said, "I hope the gods smile upon you, worthy samurai."

*　　*　　*　　*

Warm. Saiko rolled over, flipped back her bed covers, and inhaled deeply. Warm air filled her nostrils. She opened her eyes and sat. Her ladies hadn't come to her chamber yet. The corner brazier sat unlit, cool. She didn't smell smoke, so the castle hadn't caught on fire.

Grinning, she stood and ran to a window. She slid aside her painted inner window cover then the heavy outer shutter. Bright, warm sunshine spilled in. Delighted, she thrust her bare arms into the morning sun and wiggled her fingers.

Then she wilted. This was the first warm morning in five months. People would visit the garden today, and she'd have difficulty finding privacy with Takamori. Shaking her head, she released a quiet chuckle. She looked forward to visiting that samurai entirely too much. Maybe meeting him wasn't a good idea.

"I simply won't go to the garden today," she said to the empty room. A pang of disappointment jabbed her gut. She hesitated then huffed. She would leave in a matter of days. Why start a friendship now? Except she sensed that what developed between them extended beyond friendship.

The chamber door slid open, and Okiko stood and entered. "Did you say you won't go to the garden? But we ladies talked this morning and hoped you'd let us join you. The weather's so pleasant."

Saiko resisted an urge to give in. Why did she want to see him so much? "How about a shopping trip into town, instead?"

Her friend's face lit. "Shopping! I haven't shopped since my visit home at last year's end. I could use some new socks, and maybe a pretty umbrella."

"Excellent." Her hand shook when she raised it to untie ribbons from her hair. Thinking of Takamori did this.

He unnerved her. Not because of his strength or training. She had her own strength and martial arts training. No, he scared her because she liked him so much more than any man she'd met and after only two brief visits. It didn't bode well, especially since she had set plans.

The crisp silk of her lady's yellow kimono rustled as she stepped near and took over removing the ribbons. "This is a mess. These ribbons only cause tangles rather than preventing them."

After Okiko finished, she brushed Saiko's hip-length hair. Her lady-in-waiting helped her choose robes, kimono, and *obi*, though Saiko made each final decision based on what she'd wear if she intended to see him.

Exhaling sharply, she stood. "Okiko, please make arrangements for our outing. Seek my father's approval. You know how he likes me near right now."

"Yes, I know. You're the prize, and the gods would surely strike us down should any harm come to you before your noble sacrifice to the great and golden Go-Mizunoo." Her friend rolled her eyes then laughed.

"It's not funny. It's true."

"It's funny because it's true." Okiko took her hand. "I don't wish to hurt your feelings, so I'm sorry."

"My feelings aren't hurt." Saiko sagged. "I want to embrace my fate and be a good daughter and a loyal princess. Instead, I resent it. I'm wrong, but I can't help it."

Her friend's gaze saddened, and a shadow of impotence passed behind it.

"I shouldn't have said anything."

"You'll be fine. I'm going with you to Kyōto." Okiko gave her hand a gentle squeeze. She shuffled to the door and folded to her knees then slid it open. She stood, sidestepped into the hall, and knelt once more. As she slid the door closed, she said, "I won't be long. I promise."

She wouldn't be fine. Saiko stared out the window until her pique passed. Behaving like a petulant child didn't befit her position and did no good to anybody.

"I'm better than this," she said aloud.

A maid slid open her chamber door. Head bowed and her body hunched, the young woman slid a tray into the room then bowed until her forehead nearly touched the floor before she slid closed the door. Saiko took a set of chopsticks from the tray along with a bowl of steaming rice. Bits of colorful dried fruit and grilled fish enriched the grains. She returned to the window and ate while enjoying the morning sun on her face.

As she ate breakfast, she wondered if he had favorite foods, and what he had enjoyed eating as a boy. Would it please him if she took him a tasty treat?

What was wrong with her?

Minutes later, the crunch of wheels echoed up the stairs leading to her room. The twittering, laughing sound of her ladies-in-waiting outside let her know their ride had arrived. She smiled, collected her *geta* sandals from her cupboard, and faced the door as it opened.

Okiko's expression told her everything.

"I'm not permitted to go." Saiko tried to summon disappointment. She dug for anger. Only relief settled upon her, however.

"I'm sorry." Her friend held up a small pouch, her lips trembling. "He gave me money to buy you something nice, though. Are you completely crushed?"

Saiko offered a reassuring smile. "I'm fine, as you said I'd be." She glanced at the sandals in her hands, and her stomach did a happy little jump. "I have no lessons this morning, so I'll go to the garden, after all."

"You're not mad?"

"No." She offered her friend a playful shooing gesture. Would Takamori visit the garden this early? "Go. You're keeping my other ladies waiting. Bring me something nice and an interesting story to go along with it. I want an epic tale of your shopping adventure."

Okiko laughed then bowed. "I'll do my best."

Saiko stepped into the hallway and gave her friend a wave. After her lady-in-waiting scurried down the stairs, she followed.

She no longer wanted to analyze why she anticipated seeing him with such eagerness. Her life had become a study in sacrifice, and their visits granted her a secret delight. At any time, her father could rescind his decree that she have these garden walks, so better to enjoy the samurai while she could.

A number of castle workers toiled in the garden, pulling weeds and dead grasses and creating small mounds along the path. Her middle brother strolled with a man in government robes on a path toward the castle's main tower, and she offered him a nod and wave. He offered an acknowledging smile without stopping.

Saiko shuffled slowly, admiring growing buds on the trees that promised to flower. Not a single cloud marred the cobalt sky. The air, light and smelling of disturbed soil and new growth, didn't hold even a hint of a breeze. Normally, she'd soak it in and silently rejoice in the world's awakening. Today, however, her slow feet begged to run to her bridge. Her eyes wanted to ignore the beauties and seek Takamori.

When she reached her goal, he didn't await her. Considering the relatively early hour, it didn't surprise her. The stone arch still retained some cold, so she wandered sunny paths winding toward the castle wall. At a particularly warm opening between trees, she stopped and turned her face to the sky.

"Mm-hm," came a deep clearing of a throat.

Chapter Three

Startled, Saiko spun to find Takamori perched upon a stool, brush suspended above a sheet of rice paper framed in rosewood. Sunlight reflected off of his shiny black hair pulled neatly into a topknot. He wore a plain brown kimono, which blended in a most attractive way with the trees and winter flowers around him. He sent her a curious but unsmiling stare.

"I'm sorry to disturb you," she said, retreating a step. Her stomach fluttered, less by the surprise and more by the mere sight of his handsome, angular features and strong hands.

"Don't go," he said, reaching a hand of welcome in her direction. "I'm glad to see you."

She bit back a smile of delight and ventured two steps closer. "What are you painting?"

The framed paper on his lap remained blank, and he set his brush into a small pot on the ground. "I'm making a folding screen for my room. I conduct business there on occasion, and I want to block my personal belongings from view. Ieyasu-shogun's samurai don't need to see my studies strewn upon my table or my drying paintings."

"I paint, too. I've also begun dabbling in ink drawing." She peered past him to five squares of framed rice paper lying in the yellowed grass. Each depicted an item from the garden, more realistic than anything she could've created. "Those are stunning."

"Thank you."

She went around him and picked up a square. On it he'd

painted a budding three-twigged branch of a flowering maple. Even at close range, it appeared as if she could pluck the branch right off of the paper. "Your precision and detail are masterful. Who did you study under?"

"Nobody. I'm self-taught, though I'm influenced by Hasegawa Tohaku and Kano Eitoku."

"Yes, I see...in the curve of the branch and the shadowing at the twigs' juncture. It's subtle, but I recognize Kano Eitoku in your color choices. My hand isn't as steady as yours. I do better with sweeping strokes, and not as well in the minute details."

He grunted softly. "I'd like to see your paintings."

"You would?" She smiled, unable to prevent it. His genuine interest sent a thrill through her. "Some of my work hangs in the castle. I also decorated a single panel screen and the rice paper window covers in my chamber."

"You must be very good." He picked up his brush and offered it to her. "Perhaps you'd like to paint this final panel?"

"I wouldn't dare." Though she liked that he asked. "I'm not nearly as good as you, and your screen wouldn't maintain its style theme. You should do the last one."

He sighed and set down the brush. "To be completely honest, I've run out of ideas. I hoped you'd paint the last one because I seem to have lost my inspiration."

"I know what you mean. Let me see if I can give you some subjects." She studied his panels, two displaying tree branches and three of winter flowers. A symmetrical screen would require another branch. She scanned nearby sprouts and still-bare boughs, but nothing struck her as properly aesthetic. Then it hit her. "I think I know the perfect subject, but you'll have to move."

"I don't mind." He smiled for the first time, and the day brightened as if his happiness fueled the sun.

He loaded a crude tray, little more than a plank of plain wood, with his pots and brushes. Balancing it on one hand, he collected his stool.

"I'll bring the panels," she said, careful not to smudge any paint in her stacking.

She led the way along a path that ran adjacent to the castle wall, hoping the branch she admired the day before hadn't changed. Takamori followed, and she could almost feel his gaze. It made her both nervous and cheerful. She had spent life in Sumpu with near-constant eyes on her, but something about the way he looked at her gave her the impression he considered her attractive. He stirred womanly sensations in her.

Approaching her bridge from the rear, she searched the area. Nobody was about, and she relaxed. Her name called in recognition would doom her. The moment he realized she was Princess Saiko, he would withdraw, and the idea shot a sharp pain through her center. She paused to prop his paintings against the bridge then pointed to a *beni yutaka* tree with a single white bloom sparkling in delicate perfection against the vibrant sky.

"Oooh," he said in quiet awe. "How did I miss this?"

"It bloomed yesterday. It's so early, maybe because the bridge cover and the black pine tree behind it shelter it from the wind. It gets sun most of the day, too." She smiled and took his tray while he situated his stool. "Anyway, I hope the weather holds. Another cold spell could destroy it."

She set his tray next to his seat and handed him a brush. Their fingers touched briefly, and an electric awareness raced up her arm. Hairs raised across her nape. The brush suspended in his hand, Takamori stared at her with a depth of strength that caused her to tremble. Heat suffused her cheeks, and she ducked before turning, embarrassed.

"Your eyes look for the beauty in the world," he said.

She snuck a peek at him over her shoulder.

Staring at the blossom, he set the final panel on his lap. "I think that's wonderful. I aspire to be that way."

She took three steps and leaned against the smooth wooden cover. Sunlight warmed her cheek and neck. Trying not to let him hear how much he'd rattled her, she cleared her throat and schooled her tone. "If you don't see the beauty, what do you see?"

He chuckled. Touching his brush to the framed paper, he said, "I barely notice the world. I have too much noise in my head. Too many thoughts. Rather than looking around, I stare straight ahead or down at the path I walk, and my thoughts consume me. Half the time, I don't even remember my walk from one place to another. I'm too busy planning my next training session or thinking about what to say to somebody. I've tried to change this, but most of the time I forget to look."

Saiko rested her temple against the cool wood. She liked his firm, deep voice, and he spoke more now than during their other visits combined.

He switched brushes, pulling another color from a different paint pot. "I need to slow down. I live too fast. Always have, really, but our world is changing. I guess I need to change with it."

"Because of Shogun's rule?"

He nodded. "These little skirmishes in the countryside aren't much to samurai who no longer have major battles to wage. Sekigahara, the sieges at Osaka...these are done. The war's over." His brush smoothed color onto the paper with confidence. Fine lines from the tip, fat strokes with the body, he created branch and blossom in steady, sure movements.

"For a man who doesn't seek beauty, you certainly capture it well in your art." She couldn't take her eyes off of his warrior's hand wielding the refined instrument.

"Thank you." He spared her a moment of regard, his dark eyes piercing, though his thin and shapely mouth held gentle humor.

She offered a single nod with a slight smile.

He resumed painting, and they fell into an easy silence for long minutes. Birds flitted in branches overhead and in thickets near the ground, providing a random yet lilting melody through their various songs. It seemed a tribute, almost, of his talk about new peace.

"How do you know?" she asked after a bit.

"How do I know what?"

"That more great battles won't be waged. We still have samurai. We still have daimyo landholders. We still have an emperor with loyal supporters. The Summer Siege at Osaka ended only nine months ago."

"Nine months without major conflict." He dropped his brush into its paint pot and faced her, his expression passive as if he talked of music or books. "Toyotomi Hideyori's intrigues died with him when he committed suicide after the Summer Siege. Ieyasu-shogun has verified shogunate loyalty from every daimyo, unifying Japan once and for all. Any war to fight will be against Korea or China, and we won't start it. Am I certain of peace beyond a doubt? No. But neither do I expect to battle anytime soon."

"You say the skirmishes are nothing, but they worry me." She glanced past the creek, making sure nobody approached this part of the garden. "Reports are increasing. It seems there are more now, not less. I agree that Japan is unified, but there's still unrest."

"I'd like to reassure you, but..."

She straightened and ventured closer, curious as to his progress on the painting. "I can't remember a time when the provinces didn't war."

"Nor I."

"Do you feel the same uneasiness? Forgive me for saying so, but this lack of war almost seems unnatural. As if it won't last. Can't last."

He chuckled. "I feel it, too. We samurai talk of it. Most of us are ready for the fighting to end. Some more than others." A shadow passed across his eyes, but she didn't know how to interpret it.

Her stomach in a twist, she said, "There is fighting. Do you believe the princess going to Kyōto will make a difference? Do you think she can end these small revolts by entering the emperor's household?"

"I don't know. Maybe." He rubbed a finger along a line of paint on his rice paper then turned the frame sideways. "Probably."

She shook her head, unconvinced. She gave his painting a nod. "Are you finished?"

"Yes." He held it up. The image, a section of cherry tree branch with unopened buds and its single, fragile white flower, created a study in nature at its best.

"It's striking. You should teach." She wondered if, had they more time, he would have taught her. He used a simple, unadorned style she admired. Then again, she probably didn't dare ask since she'd only disappoint him. She would never master painting and drawing.

"Your praise means a great deal, but if I teach, it will be in the samurai art of war, not in painting," he said. "I'm glad the gods smiled upon me and let you come this morning."

She laughed at how he tossed her previous day's words back at her. "I almost went shopping."

"Why'd you stay?" He lost his casual tone as he appeared to assess her.

She liked his easy, relaxed way, but she shivered as his intense interest made hairs stand on end along her nape. If she told him she'd been forbidden to go because she was Tokugawa Ieyasu's daughter, would he have such an easy way with her? Would he come to see her again? She suspected not.

Saiko thought fast. "Because it's such a beautiful morning, and we may not have another like it for a while. I didn't wish to spend an hour trapped in a crowded carriage with five ladies-in-waiting. What a waste of sunlight to traipse from shop to shop on busy town streets." She didn't tell the complete truth, but she didn't lie, either.

He studied her for a long, uncomfortable span then said, "Admit it. You didn't go because you wanted to visit with me."

She laughed, though it sounded forced even to her own ears. He had hit too close to the real truth. Aiming for a playful tone, she said, "Maybe I came to the garden so early because I hoped to avoid you."

A glimmer of hurt glinted in his gaze. "Did you?"

Instantly sorry for it, she admitted, "I couldn't wait to see you. I woke thinking of our visit, and I could focus on nothing else this morning. I didn't really want to shop."

A slight smile curved his thin, shapely lips. "I didn't come to the garden so early expecting to see you, but I hoped."

"I came to the bridge first," she whispered. Her stomach clenched.

"Me, too."

They laughed. Relieved she wasn't alone in her fascination of their visits, she relaxed. She opened her mouth to ask him to come again the next day, but a man's shout stopped her.

"I must go," he said, taking a step away.

"But your paintings..."

"I'll have to come back for them." He stood a hesitant second, as though he wanted to say something else. Then he turned on his heel and stalked through the trees.

* * * *

Her father didn't feel well. Nobody knew because his warrior sensibilities wouldn't allow him to complain. He projected a mountain of strength, but Saiko recognized what it meant when he emerged from his room at midmorning. For a man who rose at sunrise, such a late start spoke volumes.

Her brother had asked her to help him placate the emperor's ambassadors who impatiently demanded an audience with their father, so she witnessed his ashen countenance and dull eyes when he stepped into the hallway. He placed a hot hand atop her bent head as he passed but said nothing.

Worry ate at her while she progressed through her routine, while she tried to ignore the irritating twittering of her insipid ladies, and while Master Hayashi droned in his explanation of how knowing the poetry of the great writers would aid her survival in Kyōto high society. Why had he returned early? She had hoped his trip would spare her his lessons for the remainder of her stay in Sumpu.

Within it all, however, the secret delight of her daily escape caused her guilt. How could excitement flit about her stomach when her father appeared ill? She should wish to sit with him and offer him comfort, yet she could only desire time with her samurai.

The compelling need to see Takamori grew overwhelming, and she abandoned the wait. "Hayashi-sensei, please forgive me. I'm weary today and do your instruction no credit. Do you have other duties you could see to this morning?"

In his sitting position, he offered a gracious bow. "I do, Princess Saiko. Perhaps you'd like to enjoy extra time in the garden and practice your poetry? The temperature's still mild."

She sighed with relief. Takamori wouldn't come until later, but she'd sit in the place they shared, and it would bring her peace and anticipation. With a bow of thanks, she collected paper, ink, brush and ink stone into a lacquered writing box decorated with flowers edged in gold.

On her way to the door, she slid her feet onto her sandals and paused under the weight of her stresses. She sought pleasure in the company of a man in her father's service. A man she couldn't have in her life on any permanent basis. A man willing to meet her in secret. Was she a bad daughter? A bad princess?

Swallowing her apprehension, she tucked a cushion under her arm and hurried down steps leading to an exit from her quarters. She stepped into the crisp morning. High above, the lovely tower gleamed white with its elegant curving overhangs and roofline. How she loved this place. Her home. And how she loved her father and brothers.

Though her father had risen from humble origins, he'd secured for his children an education the royals would envy. Ieyasu had ensured that his progeny procured the tools necessary to lead Japan in its new unified state, and she loved him dearly for his care and upbringing of her.

In her blood, she carried his strength and sense of purpose, and in the education he provided, she carried the knowledge and refinement that ensured her success in the royal courts of Kyōto. Her father was the finest of shoguns.

Her feet found the familiar path and took her to the bridge.

As she'd expected, it stood empty. It didn't matter that the sun shone – the servants had still lit the lanterns. She placed her cushion at the highest point of the bridge, right under the middle light and where the air felt warmest.

With a sigh, she withdrew her writing materials and arranged them with great care and ceremony. Although she liked to think she was as a free spirit, she wasn't. She reveled in the formality and tradition intrinsic in poetry writing. Her brush hesitated above a blank page, however. The words swirling in her head didn't allude to an ancient poem or symbolic images. Her thoughts flowed pure and raw and straightforward. Did she dare write of her longing for romantic love or her worries for her father? What of her desire to defy authority by refusing to place her allegiance with the emperor?

Her head cleared the moment her brush touched the paper. Words flowed, each character and each line coming from her spirit, and each representing proof of where her thoughts centered.

Takamori.

In so many ways, he reminded her of her father. Yet he appealed to her on a far more intimate level. Why? Samurai had filled her homes, served her father and brothers, and created a prominent presence everywhere she went. So what made Takamori different? Why did he interest her above all others?

"*Hashi no Kizoku. Konnichiwa.*" Takamori's rich, deep voice filled the bridge.

Before she could smudge the paper, Saiko lifted her brush with a jerk and saved her poem. "Takamori-san. *Konnichiwa.*" She bowed slightly at the waist, holding her breath for a moment. Sitting upright, she quickly took in his handsome face then his family crest done in gold at the end of his sword's hilt. "*Hashi no Kizoku?* Why do you call me Lady of the Bridge?"

He cleared his throat then stepped inside. "Because you refuse to tell me your name. I must call you something."

Hashi no Kizoku. She grinned. "It's perfectly fitting, I suppose. You may call me by this name until you must leave. Are you early today?"

"No. But you clearly are. Time seems to slow when we're busy, and you appear busy. Why do you sit in the cold and write?"

Because she couldn't wait to see him. To be where loneliness fled, if only for the span of each visit. "It's not cold."

"Is that poetry?"

She nodded. "*Waka* poetry."

"So traditional. Are you employing *honkadori*?"

"No." Ashamed, she considered her five lines of writing. "I had a mind to choose an earlier poem and develop its imagery in a new way, but I couldn't get past my own words."

"Your own words?" His voice rose on a current of curiosity. "You've created a work wholly unique?"

"I'd be vain to believe so. Perhaps you could judge it for me. Will you read it?"

"Of course."

Her stomach quivered. His good opinion mattered to her. With a trembling hand, she passed him the paper then wrapped her cool fingers across her suddenly too-warm throat.

As he read, she took advantage of his diverted attention to study him. His feet, bare despite the slight chill, appeared clean and steady atop black lacquered sandals. His gray robe formed impeccable lines. It started at his ankles, cinched at a firm middle by a thin sash of matching gray fabric, widened at broad shoulders, and revealed a single pristine white under-layer of robe at his neckline.

Besides the sheathed samurai sword at his left hip, he wore his shorter *wakizashi* blade tucked into his sash at an angle. His posture held no excessive pride, however. Only members of the warrior class were permitted to wear a second sword, and he wore his with ease as if he'd done so his entire life. While he read, he rested a palm between the two hilts.

His thin lips appeared relaxed, a contradiction to the concentrating slits his eyes formed as they traveled the thirty-one syllables of her poem for the second time. Atop his head, the black knot of his hair shone in the lanterns' yellow glow.

When his gaze shifted to hers, she savored the bold connection and hoped she didn't reveal her hope for his approval.

"This is very fine," he finally said.

"It's not Shunzei or Teika, but I do use traditional language to relate fresh concepts. At lease, I hope they're fresh concepts."

"Yes, fresh and new. Perhaps if I knew your name and your family, I wouldn't experience such an extent of mystery in your writing, but you've certainly attained the aesthetic ideal of depth. You see, I also believe spiritual enlightenment can be achieved in the giving of one's heart." His tone turned playful. "Do you write this from experience, or is this theory?"

An unintentional chortle bubbled past her lips. "Theory, I must admit. I have yet to offer my affection to anyone. My parents loved deeply, and I've never met anyone wiser than my mother was."

"Was?"

"She died a number of years ago. I lived with my brother for a while after she passed. Her words stay with me, though. She taught by example, living every day as a lesson to how I should live. She's really the inspiration behind that poem. I only hope I do her honor." Though Saiko's reluctance to embrace her duty would've saddened her mother. Then again, would she have stood idly by while Shogun traded Saiko to the emperor in exchange for continued solidarity?

His eyes narrowed a bit, but he didn't say anything.

She respected him more for withholding an opinion than offering her a meaningless platitude. "Have you read the eighth imperial anthology, *Shin kokinshu*?"

"I have." His shoulders eased some. "Like you, I'm most influenced by Shunzei and his son, Teika. I also enjoy the poems of Fujiwara no Yoshitsune and Emperor Go-Toba. Which poets do you like from the *Shin kokinshu*? Or do I assume wrongly that you've read the anthology?"

It spoke to his search for spiritual evolution and made Saiko wonder if he read the verses as a form of meditation. The poetry sought to express an ideal of mystery and depth, which she thought definitely reflected Takamori's basic elements.

"You assume correctly. I enjoy the *waka* poems of Princess Shokushi, and I also like Emperor Go-Toba's writings. I think I'm most influenced within that collection by the Buddhist priests, Saigyo and Jien, however."

His lips upturned gently. "I'm not surprised. Those have the most stunning use of nature to symbolize harmony and beauty. I've noticed your love of the outdoors. You impress me more and more each time I meet you."

Heat suffused her cheeks and brought warm moisture to her eyes. Accepting her poem, she tucked it inside her box and began to pack her materials. "And you impress me. I can't claim any in-depth conversations with my father's samurai, but I'm fairly certain none could display such a broad learning in *waka* poetry as you have."

He chuckled. The sound of his amusement invited her to greater intimacy and honesty with him.

She straightened with a jerk, a tingling thrill racing along her spine. Placing her writing box aside, she placed fingertips to the racing pulse at the dip of her throat.

"Perhaps you're right, but I know others like me who seek to expand their minds and spirituality. We haven't had to prepare for war in nearly a year. For six months in Osaka, we only fought small skirmishes instigated by the samurai *ronin* left without a lord after we defeated Toyotomi Hideyori. We had time to read and learn. Are you familiar with *renga*?"

"Yes. It's linked verse. Have you read *Whisperings*?"

He shook his head. "Shinkei wrote it, didn't he? A highly regarded Buddhist priest and poet in his time, I believe."

"Yes. In *Whisperings*, he writes about his experience with *renga* poetry and how it fits many ideals. It made me think and helped me develop my own poetic style."

"I'd like to read it, but I haven't yet encountered a copy."

"I have one. You're very welcome to borrow it, if you like."

He arched his eyebrows. "You wouldn't mind parting with such a valuable book?"

She smiled. "I wouldn't offer if I minded, Takamori-san. I

can't imagine safer or more appreciative hands than yours."

He stood in silence, the weight of his stare bearing upon her yet somehow not making her uncomfortable. "I've never met a woman like you. You contradict everything I know of aristocratic ladies."

"And what do you know?"

"Not much, apparently."

She hid a bigger smile against her shoulder. She liked him so much. His honesty. His curiosity. His open willingness to learn and to enter into intellectual discussions with her. She had to change the subject before she said something that would humiliate them both. "What's the most interesting *renga* you've read?"

"Easily it's the *One Hundred Links by Three Poets at Minase*."

"Yes, I'm familiar. Three *renga* masters - Sogi, Shohaku and Socho."

He nodded. "I believe it's the finest *renga* poem."

"I respect your opinion. It's a fine work. The flow of subject and imagery through word associations is very well done. Truly the work of masters. But, if I may, I'd like to argue. I prefer the *Tsukuba Collection* by Nijo Yoshimoto. It's one of the earliest, and perhaps rougher in its associations, but it makes me feel. With new poems, the flow sweeps me along on obvious connections between symbolic—"

In a movement she'd have missed had she blinked, Takamori dropped into a squat. At her level, an intensity stretched taut the skin over his cheekbones. His gaze ensnared hers, and she couldn't find the will to look away. With a soft gasp, she drowned in his endless depth.

As if he held strings attached to her heart, she felt a tug as surely as the heat flooding her cheeks. Her eyes began to water, but she refused to blink. The moment she did, the magic would extinguish like the flame of a candle at the whim of her puff, and she didn't want this moment to end.

"Who are you?" he asked, his eyes narrowing to slivers.

"I can't say," she whispered. Her fingers made a study of the fine etchings on the writing box at her knee, and she wanted so much to tell him. She despised her inability to introduce a complete honesty between them. It didn't feel right to hold back. Not with him.

He touched her hand where it rested at her thigh, and she reluctantly lowered her gaze. His dark skin contrasted starkly yet harmoniously with the white of hers. Closing her eyes, she savored his touch. His warmth.

"Is your father of the warrior class?" he asked, his voice barely audible yet never wavering.

She drew upon his strength to open her lids and meet his stare. "Yes."

"Then you understand the warrior's code."

She nodded, refusing to lower her gaze in her obstinacy. "Duty and loyalty above all. Death an inevitable end that can come at any time."

"Death." He took her hand, his fingers rough and thick-skinned. "It's always at the forefront of our thoughts, *Hashi no Kizoku*. It drives us. It dictates our thinking and actions. We're resigned to it with no fear. But for two days, something has changed for me. Something has eclipsed death in my mind, and I find my focus has veered."

"What do you mean?" She bit lightly into her bottom lip.

"Yes. I'm dutiful and loyal to my lord, Ieyasu-shogun, above all. Where I should place my attention on perfecting my skills and improving my mind, however, I discover my thoughts wandering to this garden. Where I once devoted myself entirely to a readiness and willingness to die for him at any time, I'm now reluctant."

"Why?" She tensed, hoping and dreading at the same time.

"Because where I once embraced 'the world after death' as a place I welcomed in the name of honor, another place has become the one and only place I want to go."

"Where?"

He released her hand and slid his finger along her jaw from her ear to her chin. "On this bridge. With you."

He stood and stared at her for a long few seconds.

Then he pivoted on his heel and strode from her with the gait of a man secure in his purpose and ability, while she reached for the railing and fought a sudden inability to draw air into her lungs.

Chapter Four

Rubbing his thumb along his fingertips and imagining he still held *Hashi no Kizoku*'s hand, Takamori stood in the corner of the dojo and studied his men's progress. Edo's premier *iaijutsu* master had accepted his invitation and gave his samurai a refresher training in the basics of sword drawing. With the right technique, his warriors could draw a *katana* and cut a death-strike into an opponent in a single, swift strike.

He should sharpen his skill, too. He had lost his balance, though. *Hashi no Kizoku* had knocked him sideways, and his spirit roiled in turmoil. He hadn't misspoken yesterday. His priorities had changed.

Shosan entered the dojo, bowed to the master, and made his way across the vast space while eying the exercises underway. Reaching Takamori, he bowed in respectful greeting then stepped to his side. "Sword should be used for strength and stamina. It's not a practical weapon on the battlefield – not with archery and firearms present."

"Firearms are far from practical. Useful and effective, but not efficient."

"I concede. But why *iaijutsu*?"

"I value the mental and philosophical preparations neces-sary for this martial art as well as the required mastery of fluid motion." He shrugged one shoulder. "It translates to our other skills. We need to steel our minds in whatever we do. Besides, *katana* and *wakizashi* are all we have when fighting becomes close hand-to-hand."

"True. True." Shosan offered a curt nod.

"Have you finished writing for the day?"

His friend barked a laugh. "No. Just taking a break. Before today is through, I have much more to write on Japan's need to return to true Buddhism. I was thinking... Now that we're no longer fighting clan wars, and the shogun's government has a farther-reaching influence on people than the emperor's court ever did, I wonder if political policy could help restore our beliefs to the single, right way of Buddhism."

"You mean Shinto?"

"No," spat his second-in-command, though his eyes held a light of humor. "I mean Buddhism."

"I can't have this conversation with you right now."

"Why not? Is it time to seek that magic elixir you found in the garden?" Shosan chuckled.

Takamori growled quietly. The roiling shifted from his spirit to his gut, tensing him. "I may have tainted the elixir yesterday. The master will have these men working for another three hours, and I have no reason to stay. Maybe it'd do me good to go early today, in case the magic's gone. Better to know as soon as possible."

His friend crossed his arms. "Hmm. I sense deep waters rippling in your soul. You're afraid your elixir may be lost forever?"

"You sound like a priest."

Shosan quirked his mouth to one side then flared his nostrils before asking, "Where will you be in five years?"

"What a question to ask. I'm samurai and so are you. We could be dead tomorrow. What's the use in looking ahead?" Though he said it, he no longer truly subscribed to it. He shook his head while fighting a wry smirk.

"Everything is changing. Yes, we still have earthquakes and fires. A great wave could come and wipe us from our home. But what if the gods smooth our way? What if we're still living in five years? What do you work toward? What do you seek to achieve, Marshal?"

He closed his eyes. A week ago, he would've said without hesitation that he'd continue to serve Tokugawa Ieyasu, the gods willing, until either he or the 'retired' shogun died. If his lord died, Takamori would've immediately switched his allegiance to Ieyasu's son, the current shogun.

But now...

In his mind, *Hashi no Kizoku's* lovely face swam as if on the mirrored surface of a pond. Five years. He knew exactly where he wanted to be. In her arms. Warmed by her smile. He anticipated their time on the bridge with every breath. A future without her seemed bleak. Would she stay in Sumpu after the princess relocated to Kyōto in ten days?

His stomach dropped. Where would *she* be in five years? In a politically arranged marriage with some pompous aristocrat? Serving as a lady-in-waiting at the emperor's court? Married to a rich daimyo in some distant province?

How would he bear it?

"Marshal Hosokawa?" Shosan's voice held a hint of humor. "I think for a second you submerged in those deep waters I mentioned."

"Maybe so. I know one thing for certain." Checking the straightness of his robe's neckline, he headed for the exit.

"What do you know?" called his friend.

"That you have writing to do, and I have magic to seek in the garden."

Outside, the temperature held a mildness in its chill as it had two days before. Would the lady come early? Would she already await him? After he'd left her so abruptly yesterday, would she come at all?

He sighed. He hadn't liked leaving her that way, but she had overwhelmed him. Had he stayed, he'd have said something they both could regret. Or worse, he might've kissed her and sent her running, never to return. Difficult to the point of a painful ache, marching off of that bridge required that he force his feet in their steps.

As he passed each semi-dormant plant, memorizing their

placement along the path as well as changes to heartier plants thriving in the warming air, he couldn't fight a smile. Would she talk to him of poetry? Would she finally relent and tell him her name? If learning her identity would forever alter his view and feelings about her, perhaps he didn't want to know.

Two sleeping cherry trees greeted him at a sharp bend a moment before he caught the gurgle of the creek. Then a flash of pale silk through the trees stopped him. Pebbles settled under his feet with a gentle clicking and rustling shift while the lady glided, slow and smooth, along the path on the other side of the water. He stood in awe of the peaceful grace that surrounded her as she walked.

A light breeze played with her hair where it draped from her temple along her cheek and down to hide her neck before sweeping up the back and into an elaborate knot that resembled a many-petal blossom. Her gaze remained on the bridge while a gentle smile tugged at her blushing lips. As usual, she wore blue. Today, her kimono appeared to undulate with cresting waves.

Such beauty. Did storytellers in her circle fashion their heroines after her? Did painters beg her to sit for them? Takamori considered his time with her a gift. A blessing from the gods, granted as a temporary reward for staying behind in Osaka so many months to defeat the last of the Toyotomi *ronin* and proving his devotion to his lord, Tokugawa Ieyasu.

Was it temporary, or were these daily visits just the beginning? He shook his head and chuckled. Shosan had altered his way of thinking. He was samurai. He shouldn't dare to look into the future. From childhood, he'd been taught never to look beyond the next battle. Yet there formed the crux. Would there be a next battle?

He followed the blue of her kimono until it disappeared behind the bridge's cover. Smiling, he walked the path of shifting pebbles. When he reached earshot of the opening, he used balance and his extensive training to approach silently – no easy feat with the stones under his wooden sandals threatening to announce his arrival.

As he had hoped, she didn't suspect his presence. He didn't pause today, however. "Lovely *Hashi no Kizoku, konnichiwa.*"

Her dark eyes ceased their study of the bridge covering's carvings and found him as her lips parted on a smile of greeting. "Honorable samurai, *konnichiwa.*"

He climbed to the center of the bridge and relaxed in the hint of warmth that lingered there. "No poetry today?"

Her smile didn't falter. "No. Just this." She handed him a book done in red binding with gold print.

"You brought me *Whisperings.*" He accepted it, lost for a moment in the brief brush of her fingers. "You kept your promise."

She nodded sweetly but said in a serious tone, "Your parting words yesterday gave me much to contemplate."

Takamori cringed inwardly. Had he revealed too much? He had taken a chance. Leaning a shoulder against the carvings, he said, "Tell me."

"There's only one place I want to be, too. I spend every morning looking forward to our visit, and the rest of each day wishing it could've been longer."

A thrill arced through his core. Did they stand a chance? Could she be meant for him as he'd hoped and prayed? He ventured a step nearer. He wanted to kiss her so badly his lips tingled.

Her lovely, pale face tilted downward, she said, "I still have difficulty trusting this new peace. You said when you painted that Japan is now unified and there'll be no more organized battles for land or wealth, but..." She ran long, slender fingers along the shiny silk of her sleeve. "There are still uprisings in the countryside. The emperor has supporters."

He leaned his hip against the lip of the bridge covering. "You think it's too early to tell?"

"I want to believe it, but the battle of Osaka Castle was too recent. It doesn't seem long enough to base an opinion."

Takamori chanced another step closer and took encouragement when she remained fixed in her spot. She never demurred or retreated. She had courage and conviction. "Since that final battle, we had nothing more than skirmishes with wayward samurai, my lady. This is monumental. No forces organized for attack because the domain lords have stopped fighting. They now follow the edicts mandated by Shogun's administration. Don't doubt that Ieyasu speaks correctly. He's brought our country together into one nation under one ruler, and I believe it'll stay this way."

"You're samurai, Takamori-san. War is your way, isn't it? If there's no war, what'll become your way?"

He nodded. This very question had consumed him and his men. "Yes, I'm a warrior, but war isn't my way. I'm samurai, more than a soldier. I serve my lord in the highest possible capacity. My *way* is ultimate loyalty and unwavering commitment to my duty, to my lord and to the men I lead and teach. I, and all like me who I know, focus on improvement – of mind and body, of martial skill and conduct."

"Like my father and brothers, you focus on your obligations and on your position within this new system. Now it goes beyond your profession, though, doesn't it?"

She seemed to understand, and he relaxed. "Yes. It's no longer about reward for a battle well fought. We train for inner strength and balance. I bring that strength and balance into every aspect of my life, my dealings, and further honor Shogun in my demeanor, learning, and honed skill."

"So your way used to be about fighting for Tokugawa Ieyasu, but now your way is about striving to become the best possible person. As your best, you reflect favorably and with honor on your lord." She trailed fingertips along the stone edge of the bridge where it met the lacquered cover, her eyes following their progress. "I find you're worthy of the respect afforded you, as samurai and as a leader."

He fought a smile. "Are you impressed?"

"Yes." She cast him a shy glance before returning her gaze to her hand.

She impressed him, too. "And what's your way?" Were she any other lady, he'd guess reading novels and deciding what to wear. With her, however, he had genuine curiosity.

Her lips gently curved into a slight smile. "I wondered that for many years. I was fifteen when my father sent me to my brother's home to help him with the administration of his domain. I didn't understand my purpose beyond doing as I was told. In my brother's home, however, I found a freedom to discover myself."

"Soul searching?" Interesting. And her brother was obviously a daimyo. More interesting yet.

"I like that. Yes, soul searching. I looked inward and found I had a lot to learn and much developing to do. I began to ask what I believed and what I expected from myself. I began to read extensively, and my brother permitted me to train in the early mornings with his chief guard."

Takamori stood straighter. "Train?"

Her smile broadened. "I paid attention. I noticed that every soldier in service to my brother had unfailing confidence. I wanted confidence. I trained with bow and arrows, spear, and in *yawara* – the way of yielding."

Yawara! A breathy chuckle escaped his lips. The art of unarmed combat required an acute level of agility, refinement of mental ability, and preciseness of form. "Did you excel? Can you fight?"

"I can fight, Takamori-san. I can fight." Her eyes twinkled. "I learned how to maneuver through this world without fear or reluctance. I trained hard, and I believe it's the best thing I've ever done."

It explained her assured demeanor. "Would you be willing to practice *yawara* with me?"

She sized him up. "You say you lead and teach. You're distinctly elite samurai - the best of the best. Will you seek to humiliate me?"

Never. "I wish only to determine your level of skill...in case I have to fight by your side one day. I should know your capabilities."

She laughed, a light sound that filled the covered bridge

and lifted his spirits from deep inside. "I doubt I'll ever have to fight for my life, or that you'd find yourself in battle with me. Sparring with you could be fun, though. It won't wound your pride if I put you on the ground?"

His smile graduated to a laugh. It would please him if she *could*. "My pride will survive unscathed, lovely lady of the bridge. Say you will."

Her features lifted playfully for a moment, though her smile faded. "I know a place where we could spar...unseen."

"Tomorrow?"

Her gaze met his for a fleeting second. "Tomorrow. I'll meet you here and show you the path."

* * * *

Saiko's heart hammered against her ribs. She couldn't ask for better weather in which to spar Takamori. She smiled in sweet anticipation.

"Princess, Ono Ozu comes this afternoon to examine your calligraphy. Perhaps you'd forego your visit to the garden and take extra time to practice?" Okiko's mouth formed a thin line as she took in Saiko's plain *hakama* trousers and long jacket of cotton.

"I'd do Ozu-sensei no honor if I came to her with a dull mind. No, I need this time in the garden's fresh air so I can clear my head. Today, I'm exercising but I won't keep her waiting. I promise." Saiko slid bare feet onto *tatami* sandals at the door of her chambers while gathering her hair atop her head and securing it with a thick ribbon.

"Princess, it's cold. Won't you please wear socks?"

"No." Today, she showed Takamori she was a woman of discipline who could handle discomfort without complaint. A thrill ran through her at the idea of touching him. "I'll practice my forms in the beauty of the winter garden, and the exercise will warm me."

"Perhaps I could come with you? I'd like to see your forms."

Saiko gave her lady an indulgent smile. "If you're truly

interested, I'll teach you and we can practice together. But not today."

"I understand," she said in a tone that clearly indicated she didn't. Okiko bowed at the waist then sank to her knees and slid open the chamber door.

Saiko took the stairs as fast as her sandals would allow then rushed outside and gasped as chill air hit her face and bare feet. She could do this. She *would* do this.

Only her brother and his chief guard knew of her skill. If Takamori learned the degree of her ability and approved, he would validate her. She had worked so hard, had spent three years mastering the art, and the samurai's acknowledgement would mean a great deal.

She ran for the bridge and found Takamori. He wore a gray *kosode*, his usual attire. Didn't he take her seriously? His casual air made her more determined to show him what she could do. She turned on her heel. "Come with me."

Through the garden where plants seemed to brace against a cold breeze, she led him to a place at the rear. Work had begun on a large gazebo, and they had cleared the ground of vegetation. She might soil her clothing in the loose dirt, but she didn't care as long as they avoided the curious eyes of guards high on the castle wall-walks. A roof and columns stood secured by a wide, round base frame and support for a floor workers had not yet installed. The bare wood was almost embarrassing in its unfinished state.

Takamori ran an appreciative hand along one column. "I didn't know this was being built."

"It's a good place to spar, I think." She stepped over the base frame into the opening and walked the circumference. Placing her sandals on the frame, she gave her feet a few seconds to adapt to the cold ground. She smiled in anticipation. "Don't be afraid of hurting me."

"I wouldn't hurt you." He stared at her bare feet before a broad grin revealed straight, healthy teeth. He stepped out of his sandals onto the cold earth.

It didn't seem to faze him.

"You're a gentle creature, *Hashi no Kizoku*."

"Perhaps, in some ways, I am. You're about to learn that in some ways, I'm not." She waggled fingers to summon him into an attack. "Come and see, Master Samurai."

He chuckled then burst into a run so fast, he would've taken someone with slower reflexed to the ground in a humiliating assault. She relaxed every muscle in her body and simply shifted right, out of his way. In the flow of her shift, she left her arms to follow and allowed the energy of the movement to course to her hands. He tried to redirect to her new position, but he'd already established his momentum. Her fingers met with his shoulder, sending him off balance and past her.

"Very good!" He recovered without contacting the rear of the enclosure. "You're fast. Let me see what you do with this."

In two steps, he leaped into a mid-air spinning front snap kick with arms outstretched and hands open. He held back. She could tell.

Stifling a giggle, she dropped into a crouch and poked him hard in the back of his thigh as he passed overhead.

He grunted but landed on his feet. Rubbing his leg, he laughed. "You got me. I see I can't go easy on you."

"I'm insulted that you thought you should."

He squinted with a teasing intensity. "What else do you know? Why do I suspect you hide a skill?"

Should she tell him? She trusted him, though she couldn't understand why. She'd only known him a week. "Fine. I've trained in secret with the short *wakizashi* sword. I'm no master, but I do well."

"Ah." He stamped his foot then gave his leg a healthy shake. "I might've guessed. In that case, definitely no more going easy." He ran toward her.

Leaning into a loose back stance that would allow her to adjust in any direction, she thrust her palms toward him. He aimed a fist at her left shoulder. She swung her torso right and blocked with her arm. His fist missed, but he pivoted into a sexy knife-hand strike toward her ribs.

Saiko slid a foot over the chilly soil, finishing a complete rotation at her waist, and down-blocked while arcing a chop to his shoulder. Not wanting to cause true injury, she allowed only enough force to inflict pain.

His face grew hard with concentration as he spun and directed a sweeping kick toward her feet.

She leapt slightly, letting his foot meet with air, and landed on the balls of her feet. Exhaling hard, she touched the tip of her finger to his forehead before settling once again in her ready stance.

His eyes widened a fraction. When he pulled loose the front of his *kosode* and under-robe and shrugged out, baring himself from the waist up and letting the top portion drape from his sash, she wanted to sing. She was working him, and that, more than words, presented a worthy compliment to her ability.

"Okay. You've done well. Now let me see you take what I would give any of my samurai." As his eyes narrowed and his eyebrows angled into a fierce frown, he released a loud, slow breath and formed his arms and hands into rigid weapons. Striations formed across his chest as every muscle flexed and hardened.

Saiko melted a bit. The man was beautiful. She smiled. This was going to be seriously fun.

Rather than tensing in preparation of his attack, she relaxed. *Yawara* was the art of yielding. She wouldn't engage him. Instead, she'd avoid his attempted strikes and do her best to manipulate him into a submissive posture by sending him off balance.

Growling low, he lunged. She released the last of the air in her lungs and waited. She wouldn't move until she could calculate where he'd aim his first punch or kick. When he reached her, his arms and legs worked like lightening. She drew her focus to pinpoint precision at the center of his chest, using her senses to dictate how she should shift her weight.

The world went still. Silent.

She deflected each strike, but he didn't relent. Unable to keep her feet grounded and her balance centered amidst his offense, she began to work her way around him. She worked her arms with speed and her torso with agility to block and evade hits, but she grew tired. His stamina far overshadowed hers.

He lunged, his face mere inches from hers.

She open-palm blocked his attempt at a strike to her thorax, but she blinked. In that moment of hesitation, he inserted a foot between hers and twisted. Before she could anticipate him, he slid behind her while his toes insinuated into her arch.

She lost her balance. He poked the tips of his thumbs into the small of her back, making it impossible for her to recover. With a cry, she began to collapse. In a final effort to save the battle, she reached around and managed to hook fingers into his collarbone.

Her shoulder blades hit the ground before her hips. She exhaled so the impact wouldn't knock the air from her. He landed, his arm catching his fall and preventing him from crushing her. By instinct, she lifted a hand in alarm. It found his bare, hot chest.

His eyes locked with hers. Alarm turned to need. Surprising, passionate, trembling need. Takamori's knee had landed between her legs, his pelvis pressed to hers, and his free hand rested at her waist.

"My lovely lady of the bridge," he whispered, his gaze dropping to her lips as he stirred and hardened where their hips met.

Saiko wanted him to kiss her. She'd never wanted anything so much. Between her thighs, a tingling wetness formed within her folds. Heat blossomed at her center and radiated outward, suffusing her limbs and making her welcome the chill of the ground at her back.

She adored his open mind, his curious nature, and the mastery he held over himself and his surroundings. But this... His subtle dominance created an awareness of him she'd never experienced. Though she'd found him interesting and had looked forward to each visit they shared, this moment formed a bond she hadn't expected. A bond that threatened everything.

My lovely lady of the bridge, he'd said. He thought of her as *his*. Her stomach somersaulted at the same time dread settled into the pit of her belly.

If her father learned of this, she'd suffer the kind of punishment only a father could deliver – both physical and full of emotional anguish. If the emperor found out, it would ruin her, and the shogunate would suffer.

Yet none of that mattered. How, she didn't know. Everything in her life to this point had focused on duty to her family and to Japan. Now, Takamori filled her world and became the only part of the universe that held any real meaning. Skimming her fingers along his weather-roughened skin, she followed his chest to his neck then his cheek.

"Honorable samurai." As the words fell from her lips, she winced. Yes, he had honor. If he knew her identity, he'd comprehend how this position alone was an insult to his lord. How just being alone with her betrayed her father in a way. Her deception would devastate him.

"Are you hurt?"

"No," she whispered, lowering her lashes.

"Tell me your name."

"I won't. I can't."

"Why?" He put fingers to her chin and urged her to look at him.

"Because you've become important to me, and I refuse to let you go. Not yet. Not before I have to."

Tracing her lush bottom lip with his thumb, he said, "If I have any say, you'll never have to let me go. Let me come to you. Tonight."

She wished she could say yes. Denying him shot a stab of disappointment through her. "I don't have the freedom to grant you such liberty, Takamori-san. This time in the garden every day is a gift, but the rest of my time is not my own."

"Who are you?" His thumb did not cease its caress of her lower lip.

"Not yet. You'll learn in time." And he'd hate her. "I want your friendship for as long as I can have it, so not yet."

"I'll never be just your friend." He hesitated a long moment, scanning her features as if he tried to memorize them. Slowly, he lowered his lips to hers.

The instant he made contact, an intensity so sweet and yearning overwhelmed her. She inhaled sharply as full awareness of her womanhood washed over her. Of Takamori as a man. Of *them*.

Closing her eyes, she pressed her lips to his and welcomed the embrace of his scent – a mixture of outdoors, sweet incense, and a hint of wood smoke. It filled her senses.

His hand caressed her face then skimmed into her hair. Sliding the ribbon free, he swept her loose hair over her shoulder and combed his fingers through it. The gesture both soothed and excited her.

Slanting his face, he worked his firm lips atop hers. The tingling between her thighs increased to an insistent throbbing. Unable to resist, she placed both hands on his chest and began to explore.

Everything about his body felt hard. His muscles. His firm skin. At his shoulders and ribs, her fingers brushed over raised scars. He'd endured a great deal of pain, and she hated how she'd inflict unseen wounds when he discovered that Shogun was her brother. That his lord was her father. That her destiny placed her life in Kyōto with another man.

She needed to tell him, but if she did, he'd stop kissing her. Stop touching her. Their visits would cease. He made her happier than she could remember, and she clung to him. Just a few more days. A few more days of this fleeting joy wouldn't make a difference one way or the other, would it?

When the tip of his tongue met with the crease of her mouth, all thought evaporated like the morning mists off of the garden creek. Takamori enveloped her, invaded her, filled a piece in her she had not realized was missing until he supplied it. Everything in her cried out to him. Reached for him from her depths.

He stirred a desire in her unlike anything she'd ever felt. She sensed they only tapped into the surface of some ultimate connection, and she wanted more.

So much more.

"Stop," she whispered against his mouth. *Please don't stop.* "I..." She wanted him in a way she couldn't put into words.

He released her mouth only to place two softer, lingering kisses upon her lips. Then he lifted enough to stare down upon her. "You have to return?"

"Yes." She tried to squirm from under his weight, but he didn't let her loose. "The calligraphy instructor comes today. I have to return in time to meet her."

"*Hashi no Kizoku,* you make me feel. You make me want in ways I haven't wanted since I joined Tokugawa Ieyasu's service four years ago. Let me come to you tonight. Let us share pleasures in each other's arms."

Shoving him hard, Saiko managed to free her hips. She struggled to her feet and stumbled to where she'd left her sandals. "Takamori-san, I can't. Please understand that I'm not rejecting you. I simply don't have the ability or right to invite you. I must go." She shoved her dirty feet onto the *tatami.*

He rolled to a sitting position and propped an elbow onto a knee while removing his hair from its topknot. The thick, dark length fell to his shoulders in smooth waves. "You impressed me with your skill. If I thought you could, I'd ask you to come teach my men."

"But I can't." She grew weary of the words 'I can't.' Did he share her frustration? Would he want to see her after she refused him? "Will you meet me at the bridge tomorrow?"

He studied her an awkward second. "I'll try, lovely lady." He stood and brushed dirt from his clothes.

With a heavy tread and the sense that *I'll try* really meant he'd now seek to avoid her, Saiko jogged to her quarters. She'd been gone too long.

Chapter Five

In the dark of his room, with the press of a cotton-filled futon under him, Takamori stared into unrelenting blackness. The lady's lips beckoned him. Her slender throat, her intelligent eyes, her gentle touch. Could he find her, and would she turn him away if he did?

Her poem repeated in his mind, memorized easily upon his second reading at the bridge. Had she written it about him? Did she think of him that way? Her kiss said she did.

She had such a fine mind. It amazed him how extensive her education reached. That she'd learned so much, and clearly exercised her knowledge, told him she'd taken her learning seriously.

For her to have developed such a level of ability with *yawara* proved her determination and dedication. He looked forward to observing her skill at archery and spear. Would she consider meeting him hand-to-hand with the *wakizashi* sword? Had she been born male, she would surely enjoy a high rank in the samurai hierarchy as his equal.

Takamori frowned. Who was her father? What kind of man arranged for his daughter to receive the kind of education any man would covet? She obviously held a position in the aristocracy, so why did she serve the shogun's family rather than living in luxury and refinement in Edo? Sumpu had its charms, but it couldn't compare with the capitol.

Still, she seemed content. Happy, even. Surely she served a role of great honor within the household to have the time and freedom to walk the garden every day. Though she did admit to great restriction within the castle. His curiosity grew. If only he could convince her to confide her identity to him. Who was she that knowledge of her name would make him lose interest?

More importantly, did he waste his time? If she spoke the truth, did he misplace his growing devotion by seeking her out day after day? Because she intrigued him in more ways than simply by withholding her name.

Sitting, he rubbed a hand down his face. He'd find no rest if he didn't expel her from his thoughts. As Shosan had taught him, he recited the *nembutsu*, chanting the name of Amida Buddha. It didn't work.

On a growl of frustration, he threw aside his covers and rose. He welcomed the winter chill through the thin fabric of his sleep shirt, his charcoal brazier left unused in the corner. Sliding aside the window screen then protective outer wooden cover, he inhaled clear night air. The garden lay in dark shadow. In the faint light of a half moon, he discerned outlines of trees and bushes.

Closing his eyes, he pictured their bridge. He imagined her meeting him there, her arms outstretched in welcome and a smile of greeting upon her lips. A kiss. A whisper. A promise of forever.

"I'm a fool."

He closed the window then dressed. In the quiet, he made his way to the dojo. He lit a lantern, settled into a ready stance then worked on perfecting the precision of his form until the sun brought morning light through the high windows. The lady had challenged him in their sparring session – something he hadn't anticipated. It did him no good to grow complacent. He had to constantly work on his technique, as he urged his warriors to do.

As the castle stirred to life, Takamori melted into the shadows. He took his morning meal in the privacy of his room and ignored knocks that sounded on his door. "My lord comes first. Duty and honor. I am here to serve Tokugawa Ieyasu, not myself. Duty and honor."

Upon his new folding screen, the branch with the single white cherry blossom brought her beguiling conversation and beautiful features into vivid clarity. He groaned. She was everywhere. Around him. Inside him.

When the time approached for him to meet her, he strode with determination to the bridge. After yesterday, would she come? She'd refused him her bed, despite their kiss. Was there a circumstance he hadn't considered? The woman was remarkable in every way – her appearance, her knowledge, her artistic sensibilities, and her physical prowess. She wouldn't escape the notice of powerful men. She certainly hadn't escaped his.

She didn't await him when he arrived. Blowing a loud puff through his nostrils, he crossed his arms and turned his back on the way she always arrived. In the white light of late morning, he studied the bare branches of his two favorite cherry blossom trees. Somehow, the single bloom survived the cold. It glistened on its branch.

These trees had become his favorites because he saw them on his way to see her. She'd introduced them to him, and they now represented his approach to the lady who was changing his priorities. Changing his view of himself and his place in the world.

Changing his life.

*   *   *   *

The click of Saiko's wooden *geta* on the stairs matched the pounding of her heart. For once, she looked forward to a rush of cold air on her face. She needed it to revive her. She'd spent most of the night pacing her chamber between restless, exhausting dreams of Takamori.

Was she foolhardy to hope he'd meet her after denying him her bed? Probably, but she couldn't help it.

She hurried through the garden, paying the landscape no attention. She kept her focus on the bridge and the possibility of seeing her handsome samurai once more. She shouldn't go, but she had to. If only to let him know she wouldn't meet him the next day.

As the pale stone of her bridge appeared between dormant trees, a dark cloud wafted against a gray sky. Rain began to fall. With a shriek at the icy bite of drops, she bowed her head and hurried. The shower increased to a downpour seconds before she reached the creek, and she entered the haven of the cover with a gasp.

At the other end, Takamori offered his profile over one shoulder.

He waited. Joy surged over her, and she smoothed a hand on her wet hair. She surely looked a mess. She swiped a drop of water from the tip of her nose and gave her kimono's hem-length sleeves a shake. "*Konnichiwa.*"

"*Konnichiwa.*" He approached but stopped at the center.

She combed wet hair off of her forehead and shivered.

"You should go inside. Dry off and get warm."

Her spirit wanted to sink, but she wouldn't let it. He had come. After yesterday, it meant something. "I wanted to see you."

"Why?" His thumb worked back and forth along a ridge on his *wakizashi's* hilt.

"Ask me an easier question."

"No."

Unyielding samurai. She pressed her lips together, shivering harder, then said, "I'm sorry about yesterday. Having to refuse you, I mean."

"Does that mean you change your mind?"

She ventured a step closer to the warmth at the center, fighting a chill that seeped bone-deep. "I would if I could. My life isn't my own." She took another step. "I wish I could make you understand."

"Tell me your name. Then I'll understand."

She wilted a bit, the cold making her shake violently. Refusing to retreat, however, she lifted her chin and looked him in the eye. "True. But I won't. You may be angry with me or disappointed. I don't know what you feel. I only know that every day you meet me on this bridge is a day worth living. This time with you is the only thing I have to look forward to."

She closed her eyes and let his confidence surround her like a shield. The world couldn't reach her in the safety of his presence.

If only she could be his. In his arms. In his bed. In his future.

He said nothing. He didn't move.

Frustration settled like a heavy rock in her stomach. "I'll go then. I won't come tomorrow." She wrapped her arms across her middle and headed for the exit. Before she stepped into the rain, she stopped. "I don't know what you think of me, but I want you to know that you've earned my respect and admiration. I won't give up until it's too late."

Saiko bowed her head and ran into the downpour. Their meeting didn't go as she'd hoped, but at least he came. At least he gave her a chance to speak, and he didn't rebuke her.

She had gone ten steps when a hand took her by the shoulder.

Takamori turned her, his eyes desperately scanning her face and his brow wrinkled.

"I'm sorry," she said, meaning it more than she ever had. "I wish..."

Water ran in rivulets down his forehead and cheeks, dripping from his eyelashes, nose and chin. "Me, too. I begin to despise this princess who's so demanding of you." Grasping her by the shoulders, he put his mouth to hers.

The cold and rain disappeared, and only this man existed. His arms encircled her, and she welcomed his hard strength and heat. Hugging him close, she pressed into his kiss.

With an insistence against her bottom lip, he urged her to open. She did, letting him inside and drowning in the sensations he aroused. His clean scent filled her nostrils as his taste of sweet boiled rice and ginger laced her tongue where he caressed it in an eager but leisurely manner. Weakening, her knees gave a little, and she sagged against him. She wanted to lose herself in him. She wanted to escape her obligations and become a different woman – a woman whose life had a place for him.

Fire flowed through her as dragonflies flitted within her stomach. Takamori created a need in her she couldn't ignore. He also created a longing she suspected would haunt her the rest of her days in Kyōto.

Cupping her cheek, he ended the kiss and gazed at her with a sleepy hunger. "Go. Warm up."

The drenching winter day rushed in, invasive and unwellcome. "I'll see you again? The day after tomorrow?"

"I'll try." He skimmed warm fingers into her sopping hair and traced the outer edge of her ear.

She smiled. He never promised to meet her, implying that he might not, yet he always did. "I'll come to the bridge. I'll wait for you."

He offered a single nod then stepped away.

She stood a moment, wishing she could know his thoughts. Wishing she could read his passive expression and have a certainty he'd meet her. When a blast of wind sent cold water through to the layer closest to her skin, she abandoned the attempt. If she didn't go inside and change into dry clothes, she'd suffer.

As she left him standing on the path, pain of departure cinched a band of tightness around her ribs. If it hurt like this after only six days, how would she do it when she left Sumpu for good? And what would happen when he learned she was the princess he claimed to resent?

*　　*　　*　　*

He had to secure the lady's affections before he left to take Ieyasu's daughter to Kyōto, but how if he couldn't convince her to confess her name? Takamori engaged Shosan with verve, perhaps too aggressive in his offense with the *katana*.

"Show no mercy," his friend ground through clenched teeth as he held his own against the onslaught. His bare feet slapped the hardwood dojo floor.

The clang of steel rang throughout as other sparring pairs tested one another. They'd practiced the morning through but would accompany Tokugawa Ieyasu to the village for the afternoon's festival procession.

Takamori sent his frustration and anger into a final effort to defeat his friend. "You're done."

"Not if I have anything to do with it, Marshal." Shosan bent deep at the knees and brought his sword up in a bracing block. Letting out a battle cry, he lunged.

Takamori had prepared and now deflected the blow that would've felled a lesser warrior. Baring his teeth, he growled and gripped his *katana* with all his might. He struck Shosan's sword with everything he had left, but Shosan's grip held. Takamori used brute force to bring his blade's tip to his friend's neck, and as it touched, he also felt the touch of cold, sharp steel on his own neck.

Shosan laughed. "We're both dead!"

"You're a worthy opponent. You always have been." Takamori accepted his friend's bow a moment before he offered his own. "We should bathe and dress for the festival."

He sheathed his weapon then took a step toward the center of the dojo and stood at attention. Immediately, the sparring sessions ended and the samurai faced him and bowed.

The men hurried into action to ready for the afternoon's procession, and Takamori gave Shosan a small wave before heading to the baths. At the rear of the barracks, men already soaked in heated bathing pools. He stripped, rinsed away sweat with cool water from a basin, and waded into the nearest.

Would his lady accompany the princess to the festival? He hadn't expected to miss her so much after one day. She was, by far, the most intriguing, engrossing woman he'd ever met. Did the fact that she denied him her bed create a curiosity of the unknown and hold his interest? Somehow, he suspected it went deeper.

Much deeper.

Unfastening his topknot, he submerged and scrubbed until his scalp ached. He surfaced and took a rough stone from the poolside and scoured his skin. When he finished, his red skin stung. He could only think, however, how much he would enjoy a pleasure bath with his lady of the bridge.

Steam rose from him as he left the hot water for a cool pool. Chill water soothed his skin and refreshed him. He sat for a minute, letting the water soothe the redness from his body while he pictured his lady in the village.

He imagined her with her hair elaborately arranged into a flower design like she wore two days earlier. He had liked it a great deal. She'd wear blue. He smiled. He would too. Would she appreciate the gesture? He suspected she would.

How she could distract him without being in the room amazed him. Thanks to intensive training and immense self-discipline, he steeled his mind against images of her. He had preparations to make.

In his chamber, he dressed in pale blue and donned his weapons with practiced ceremony. He drew his damp hair into a tight topknot and secured it with a strip of black cloth. Shosan arrived and helped him into his armor. It bore his family crest as well as the symbols of his status and lineage, and he switched out the thick yellow sash for a blue one. He didn't need to see his reflection to know he'd achieved as close to perfection in his appearance as humanly possible. He'd do his lord proud.

With his helmet tucked under an arm, he strode with purpose to the spacious staging area just inside the main castle gates, hoping to arrive in time to see the princess' party leave. He didn't make it, however. The soldiers bringing up the rear of her party turned the first curve in the castle road and marched out of sight as Takamori approached the gates.

From the stables, workers and lesser guards led horses and positioned them in rows for the samurai. Ieyasu emerged, larger than life in full armor, from an inner gateway positioned in the outermost circle of castle outbuildings.

"My lord, *konnichiwa*," said Takamori loudly, alerting everyone to the arrival of their master. He bowed low and stayed so until Ieyasu spoke.

"Hosokawa, *konnichiwa*. I'll ride today." The elderly ruler assessed the horseflesh on display.

"Yes, my lord. All will be ready shortly." Takamori waved a retainer to outfit the retired shogun's horse with the finest regalia.

The stable hand bowed and headed for the stable at a run. Ieyasu inspected the forming lines as arriving samurai quickly retrieved bows, quivers, and spears from weapons storage built into one of the small towers before mounting awaiting horses. Foot soldiers filed at the rear. In no time, the stable hand-led Ieyasu's horse to the staging area.

Vapor spurted from the beast's nostrils, and its eyes flashed as if it understood its superior role in the procession. Its elaborate, red lacquered saddle stood out amidst the plain black ones of the other samurai. An artist had painted golden dragon scales along the thick cantle and burr plate, and braided cord with threads of shimmering gold strapped the saddle to the horse.

Despite his advanced age, the ruler didn't need assistance to mount. Takamori donned his helmet then took his seat at the head. Beyond the fore guard of mounted samurai, Ieyasu gathered braided red silk reins then gave a nearly imperceptible nod to indicate his readiness to proceed. Dragonflies on his armor appeared to flick their wings, and Takamori blinked. This wasn't the time for his eyes to play tricks.

He couldn't remember the last time he looked forward to attending a festival so much. He led the warrior's parade down the castle road into the village streets lined with commoners as well as up-and-coming merchants and artisans. Children squealed in delight as a slender white hand waved from the window of the princess' slow-moving palanquin. The unusually large conveyance accommodated as many as four ladies and required twelve men to bear the weight of the poles that protruded from front and back. Surely his lady of the bridge rode inside.

Moving at a pace comfortable for the foot soldiers at the rear, he took long minutes to close the distance. By the time he reached the back end of her party, the palanquin turned off the roadway to a cleared space where musicians and dancers in masks and brightly colored costumes prepared to perform.

In the distance, priests at the shrine made joyous music by beating upon chimes and bells. Smiles greeted all around. The Tokugawa shoguns had wrought a new beginning that already provided an increase in prosperity and security these people hadn't seen before. Takamori couldn't serve a better family.

Laughter and cheers met Ieyasu who sat upon his saddle in stoic pride. Within his helmet, a glint of moisture reflected light from the weak winter sun. The old man had changed Japan for the better, and the people showed their appreciation.

With a brief nod, Takamori led the retired shogun's procession into a cleared space at the village's center. A servant placed a fancy chair next to the palanquin.

Takamori made sure a small contingent surrounded the old man and his daughter's conveyance before he reined his horse to and circle the clearing. Drummers began a complex beat that reverberated off of buildings. People ran to join a crowd forming around dancers who took positions for their exhibition.

Wanting a glimpse of his lady, he craned his neck and rode at a sedate pace until the window on the palanquin slid open. Three women's faces crowded the gap, but not the one he sought. Had she remained at the castle? He studied the tower above. Would his lord understand if he left the festival in search of her? No, he wouldn't. Takamori's obligation required that he oversee the safety of the event, and especially that of the Tokugawa family and those in their direct service. He couldn't go.

Dancers began a traditional performance to the accompaniment of a small but talented group of musicians. The lilting yet happy sound of bamboo wind instruments filled the air while a man worked the strings of a *biwa* to create a strong melody over the insistent beat of drums.

The scents of barbequed meat and tangy sauces added to the spirit of celebration. Takamori dismounted and handed his horse's reins to a nearby foot soldier then dropped a coin into the hand of a food vendor at a street stall and accepted a skewer of chicken. Not taking his eyes from the palanquin in the hopes that he'd merely overlooked his lady, he ate the meat in two bites.

The dancers finished, and still he didn't see her. The figure of a woman hung back in the shadows, but he couldn't discern any features. Was she the princess or his lady? Her head appeared bowed, as if she sat in prayer or sleep.

A group of rowdy boys ran past. They wielded sticks as swords and used noisemakers to create a racket without a mind to the horses. As credit to their battle training, the animals didn't shy. Still, his men shooed the boys beyond the danger of hooves and teeth, just in case. Soldiers and samurai not on guard duty shopped, ate, and took in the amusements.

In the cleared area, a troupe of lute priests began the performance of a war story. They started into the telling of the Gempei War, opening with a chanted narrative while playing a complex, energetic melody on three *biwa hoshi* lutes. Takamori enjoyed their performance along with flashy and funny entertainments by various street performers who employed puppets, trained animals, and song.

The afternoon could only be better if *Hashi no Kizoku* walked at his side and joined her laughter with his. He gave the palanquin his periodic attention. Despite comings and goings of servants and the three ladies who laughed and tittered, he never managed a look at the mysterious lady in the shadows with her head perpetually bowed.

That evening, he oversaw the return of the palanquin and his lord to the safety of the castle walls. Inside the gates, he eyed the palanquin while waving Shosan near. "Return to the village and make sure the soldiers and samurai who live on

castle grounds finish their business and make it back before
dark."

As his friend rode out, Takamori dismounted and thrust his
horse's reins into the hands of a stable worker. He spun,
wanting to catch sight of the ladies exiting the boxy conveyance. He fought the urge to shout as four men carried the now
empty palanquin toward storage while a lady entered the
gateway that led to the castle's inner citadel, the pink of her
kimono glowing in the dusk light. Did his lady precede her?

Untying the chord of his helmet, he dug his feet into the
dirt of the staging area and took off at a run. He sprinted for the
gateway while lifting off his headgear. Rounding the corner, he
caught sight of the pink kimono disappearing around a curved
way toward the second circle where the family and their closest
retainers resided.

He had to learn where she stayed. He had to. Surely if he
sought her in the night, she wouldn't turn him away. Had her
kiss not told him she shared his desire? Her acceptance of his
affection implied she wanted him.

Putting his effort into his run, he pumped his legs and
traveled the curve. When he reached a long line of two-story
buildings similar in design to the main tower and subsequent
smaller towers, he found he stood alone in the walkway. He
studied every doorway, waiting for a motion or sign as to which
they entered, but nothing revealed their direction.

Fisting his hands, he squeezed his helmet between his forearm and armored torso. With a terrible disappointment eating
at his insides, he strode to the back corner of the walled castle
where the barracks awaited.

Tomorrow. Tomorrow he would learn what he wanted.

*   *   *   *

Two days. Saiko pressed her forehead against the smooth
carvings of the bridge cover and ran her palms over the uneven
surface. Two days remaining before she left for Kyōto. She had

not wanted to go in the first place, but now that Takamori had come into her life, the idea tortured her. She had spent the entire time at the festival in meditation, trying somehow to determine if she could change this.

"Two days." His voice caressed her ears.

She closed her eyes, trying to memorize the tenor of his tone. "You know?" Had he seen her at the festival yesterday? Did he discover her true identity? She braced for the worst – his rejection.

"Yes. I leave in two days," he whispered in her ear, his warm breath brushing her cheek. His heat translated through the layers of her clothing from behind as he aligned his body to hers. His palms covered the backs of her hands.

He left. So he didn't know that he would accompany her on the journey to Kyōto. She sighed. Testing him, she asked, "For Tokugawa Ieyasu-shogun?"

"His daughter, the princess."

"So you go to the emperor's court." She opened her eyes, staring at rich woodcarvings reflecting warm, orange lantern light. Her body trembled at his nearness. At the intimacy of his whisper.

His cheek pressed softly to hers as his hand met her waist. "Yes. Do you?"

Saiko held her breath.

He touched lips to her cheekbones then her temple. "Will you accompany her? Will I see you and spend time with you on the journey? I hope not."

"Why not?" His kisses caused a thrilled shiver, and she closed her eyes, savoring his touch.

"Because if you travel to Kyōto as lady-in-waiting to the princess, you might stay in the old capital while I have to come back to Sumpu. I can stand the idea of parting with you for a month, but not forever. Tell me you're staying here. Tell me we have a future beyond the next two days."

Her soul groaned with anguish. "I can only tell you that I don't travel to Kyōto as lady-in waiting."

"Thank the gods." He turned her to face him.

She opened her eyes and drank in his features. While she ached at the thought of hurting him, deceiving him, her body strained toward him.

"You look at me with desperation in your eyes. I'll return. I promise. With you to come back to, I'll make it happen no matter what."

His countenance revealed genuine affection. Genuine admiration. Without his prompting, she leaned close and touched her mouth to his.

"Two days," he said against her lips. "Two nights. Tell me where to find your chamber."

"No." She wrapped her fingers around his nape, enjoying the texture of his hair. His skin. The rub of his *kosode's* collar. She thrilled at the press of his sword against her belly.

Pulling away a bit, he asked, "You'll let me leave without the promise of what awaits when I return?" He kissed her forehead then placed a lingering kiss to her mouth.

She inhaled sharply, wishing she could make it all go away. If only she could convince her father not to send her. Moisture built in her eyes, threatening to spill. Tightly squeezing her lids shut, she sighed.

It wouldn't matter. All the talk in the world would change nothing because her connection with Emperor Go-Mizunoo had nothing to do with need or want. It had to do with associating the Tokugawa shogunate with the ancient line of ruling royals. Never mind that Go-Mizunoo no longer ruled Japan. No argument existed against her going. Any attempt would meet with failure.

"*Hashi no Kizoku*, you'll be here when I return. Tell me you'll be here when I get back." He scowled.

"I can't." Emotion clogged her throat, making the last sound strangled.

"My lady..." He took a step away, his hands dropping to his sides. "What's this game you play with me?"

"Honorable samurai. Takamori-san, I've played no game. I've treasured our time." She swallowed against a lump as a tear escaped from the corner of her eye and slid along the side of her nose. "I don't want to leave you."

"Please." His voice hardened, but he cupped her face with the gentleness he would use if he held a baby bird. "Don't say goodbye."

Unable to say more, she choked on a sob and sank until her forehead met her knees. She simply shook her head.

For a long minute, he stood unmoving. Did he hate her? Did he suffer the way she did? How had she arrived at this place?

"Will you come tomorrow?" he asked.

"Yes," she barely managed.

"And you'll tell me everything? Who you are? Where you'll go when you leave my lord's castle?"

"Yes." The gods help her, the words would rip her heart from her chest, but she'd confess everything.

Chapter Six

Anger. Takamori had experienced anger in many forms and situations throughout his life, but nothing like this.

She'd promised to tell him everything, yet she'd taken too long. Perhaps they had no chance from the start, but he couldn't believe it. In eight days, she'd shown him a glimpse of her soul – a beautiful soul within a gorgeous woman. He'd begun to fall in love with her.

In his room, he stood and shook with rage. He wanted her here with him. In his bed. Under him, on him, surrounding him. He wished he had a way to change this. As a man of honor, position, and means, he'd make a worthy husband, but he'd read a hopelessness in her demeanor. Looking back over the past week, he realized she'd had it the entire time. Whatever fate those in authority had chosen for her, it was bigger than them both.

As a samurai and a leader of samurai, he'd grown used to control. He'd become accustomed to making decisions that affected lives. Accustomed to standing strong in the face of adversity. War had hardened him and leadership had honed him. This helplessness to change what threatened to break him, however, made him tremble with impotence.

In an attempt to calm his burning mind, he lowered to the floor and meditated. He prayed for enlightenment. Whether he received enlightenment in the form of an answer about how he could make her his own or come to terms with losing her, he didn't care. He needed an answer. A path to walk. And for the moment, he could only see how losing her would crush him.

When had he become so connected with her? When had she come to mean so much? She was lovely, yes. She was intelligent, yes. She was skilled in martial arts, to be sure. But she was a woman.

He attained enlightenment suddenly in the acknowledgement of yin and yang. He had never met a woman like her because no woman embodied his essence in female form like she did. She was his female counterpart. His other half. The one and only woman who could complete him.

Crumpling, he put his head to the floor. He would never recover from losing her. When she left, he'd lose his ability to ever find completeness.

Sitting bolt upright, he fisted his hands on his knees. No. He wouldn't surrender. He'd never simply accepted that which he could change. Many had called him rebellious in his earlier years, but now it served him well. He had yet to learn her identity, so perhaps with more information, he could develop a plan. Perhaps he'd see a course she couldn't.

*   *   *   *

Saiko used to love nighttime. The quiet, the solitude and peace in stark contrast to noise and bustling of the day. Since meeting Takamori, however, she had come to disdain it, especially since their sparring session when he had asked to visit her bed.

While lying in the dark, she fought against her constant longing for such a visit from him. Night's sanctuary no longer offered peace. It served to magnify her loneliness, the futility of her desire, and the desperation in her irreversible situation.

She wanted to hate her father, but she loved him too dearly. It didn't help that she admired him to no end. In his leadership, he had brought a broken and warring Japan into peaceful unity. Again and again, he had ridden into battle and risked his life for this.

Now he asked her to help. Who was she to deny him? Compared to all he had done, her contribution couldn't compare. He'd killed men he once called friends, and he suffered the atrocities of war time and again. Her sacrifice called for her to live a life of luxury surrounded by beauty. Complaining was not an option. She had a clear duty, and to defy it would paint her as an ungrateful and selfish daughter. She was neither.

Abandoning sleep, she left her futon and crept to a window. She opened it, and chill air poured in, cooling the front of her thin silk robe and settling about her feet.

No clouds blocked the moon, and its meager light shined upon the deeply shadowed garden. She could not see her bridge from here, but she could barely discern the unique roofline of the distant samurai barracks.

Did Takamori sleep soundly, or did he toss and turn? Did he also stand at his window and stare out, thinking of her? Would she appear the worst of harlots to seek him in the night?

No, she wouldn't go to the barracks. Sleep eluded her, however, and a walk might do her good. She closed the shutter and pane then glanced through the open doorway that led to Okiko's bedchamber. Her first lady-in-waiting slept like a corpse. Okiko had a calm...well, usually calm demeanor. Surely if she woke and found Saiko missing, she'd understand. Nobody knew better than her friend how much appeal the south garden held for Saiko, even if she didn't comprehend why.

Saiko put on a lined under-robe and the plain gray-blue kimono she'd worn that afternoon. Doing her best to keep from making her *tatami* floor crackle under her feet, she made her way to the door. Her white quilted coat and warm boots sat in a pile in the corner thanks to packing her ladies had begun. She quickly donned them.

Not a soul stirred as she felt her way down the dark steps and out into the bracing air. Her feet seemed to know the way to her bridge, and she arrived before she realized she headed there. She hadn't visited it at night in years – before she left to live at Mito Castle.

The lanterns didn't glow, and she hesitated to enter. A cold breeze pained her cheek and nose and drove her into the pitch darkness. Grimacing, she took tiny steps until she didn't feel the bite of the wind. Because the bridge sat in utter darkness, the garden seemed to glow in moonlight at each end. It reassured her, offering an unexpected security, and she settled onto her boots on the hard stone.

Maybe alone on this dark bridge, she would find an answer. An alternative to Kyōto her father might deem acceptable. She laughed, a quiet, hopeless sound, aware more than ever how unlikely that was.

A flash of metal caught her attention, and she froze. Takamori approached, and a thrill shook her.

"*Hashi no Kizoku?*" he asked.

"Yes." How had he known?

"I can almost make you out. Are you wearing white?" His shoulders lost their stiffness, and he approached a step.

She touched shaking fingertips to the quilting of her coat. "Yes."

"I don't believe I've seen you in anything but blue." He left the path to enter the bridge, eliminating all detail and becoming a black shape against the moonlit garden behind him. "You didn't expect me to come."

"No, though until you arrived, I didn't realize I hoped you would." She stared, wishing she could see his face and wondering if he could discern hers. "This morning between us was..."

"Tense." He ventured near and sat.

"Yes. Good word."

He chuckled. "I don't want tension between us tonight."

"Nor do I." Though where she was concerned, she'd always feel tension around him. Sensual tension, certainly. And always the tension of knowing they had no future together.

She wanted to reach out to him. Touch him. After their meeting that afternoon and the way she wanted him so badly now, she wouldn't be able to stop and walk away as she'd done after their sparring session. She barely had the strength necessary to resist him. Were he to kiss her, she'd become his, give herself over fully, and go so far that there'd be no turning back. No way to undo the bond they formed.

"I understand," he said.

"What do you understand?" The gods help her if he had any inkling of her thoughts.

"The princess is about to leave Sumpu. Upheaval in her life means upheaval in yours, and change is never easy."

She sagged with a sigh. "You're right. Change is never easy."

He said nothing. He sat unmoving, their soft breathing the only sound inside the bridge.

"You have something you want to say?" she asked.

"I can't escape a sense that I'm about to lose you."

The truth in his statement fractured her. Perhaps now was the time to reveal her identity instead of tomorrow. She opened her lips to confess, but she couldn't summon the words.

"Either you go with Princess Saiko to Kyōto and live there as her lady-in-waiting, or you return to your family. Am I right?"

She didn't answer, though he had it correct. Her ladies-in-waiting except Okiko planned to leave her service when she departed. She was the last princess in Sumpu. When she left, they had no reason to stay.

"How will I see you?"

He wouldn't see her or talk with her or touch her. They couldn't even correspond because she'd have to do it secretly, which meant dishonoring her family and her position. Her world crumbled further.

"Your silence says a lot." He shifted then stood. "This bridge is sending cold into my bones."

"Mine, too." Not really. She sat atop her thick boots, but moving would help dispel a sadness that hung in the air around her. She stood and gripped the smooth wooden lip of the bridge cover. "I don't want to go," she said, horrified when her voice caught on a half sob.

"My lady," he said, his voice low and gentle. "I have feelings for you that I shouldn't."

She did, too.

"I wonder how I've connected so strongly with you when it seems I hardly know you."

She did, too.

"Yet, I know you. Maybe I don't know who your family is or where you grew up. I don't know how you've lived or what you've suffered. But I know your spirit. I know your thinking and your determination. Maybe I'm wrong, but somehow I know we're meant for each other."

She turned away, her mouth open on a silent wail of pain as the dagger of his words entered her limping heart and rent her in two. She clung to the wooden lip, afraid if she let go she'd collapse. This was her fault. She'd encouraged him. She'd let this happen.

She loved him.

*   *   *   *

Takamori squeezed his hands into fists. How could he convince her to stay? To give him a chance?

He stared at the black cascade of loose hair that rested against the paleness of her clothing. Despite the shadows, he saw her shoulders shaking. If only he could see her face and gauge her reaction to his declaration. Even if she turned, however, the darkness would leave her features unclear.

He stood straighter and stepped to her side, careful not to touch her for fear of making her flee. "I've trained in the legacy of *bushido* my entire life. I can't remember a time, including my very earliest memories, when I didn't train. My father and uncles would go to battle, and still my brothers, cousins and I trained. Samurai is who we are. War. Honor. Duty. This has been my reason to exist."

She bowed her head and stopped shaking.

He let his fingers find curves and grooves in the cover's carvings. At the same time, his stomach shuddered on a nervous twist. He needed her to know him. Truly know him. "I entered battle for the first time when I was fourteen. I was scared. Less for my life and more for the violence I was capable of committing. I survived with a wound to my shoulder and was stronger and even more capable." He touched fingertips to the place where his scar constantly reminded him of that day.

"I never really had a childhood, but that day ended any possibility of one. I killed on that battlefield. Part of me resented my father for making this my life. I'm not violent by nature. Now and then, I wonder what I missed because I'm samurai. I learned to embrace the way of *bushido*, though. I realized later that this life, this training and discipline, is what made me strong. Made me who I am." He hesitated, studying the faint shape of the profile she offered. "Made me worthy of you."

She made a small sound, but he didn't understand what it meant.

"There are no great battles left to fight. The last siege at Osaka Castle finished it. We who are samurai are in a confusing place. We trained to fight, to live hard. There are few fights, and living has grown easier. We continue to train, but we find there's time for other things, too. I study. My best friend seeks enlightenment. We each have a chance to be something more than a warrior."

"And...?" she asked quietly.

"And that's how you found me – serving the most powerful man in Japan, training for a battle that'll never happen, and trying to figure out what to do with my life."

"Have you reached a conclusion?"

He relaxed. "I've learned that I enjoy training and teaching, but I'm ready to leave my violent past behind. I want a quiet life with more freedom. How I'll make that happen, I don't know yet."

"I think Ieyasu-shogun will be reluctant to release a samurai from his service who'd rode into so many battles with him." She pivoted to face him, her clothing rustling in the quiet.

"I'm hesitant to leave him. He's been a demanding but fair

master. I've served him on campaign for many years and known him a long time. I've grown as close to him as I ever was to my own father. Though I've visited Sumpu since my promotion two years ago, this is my first time residing here. I must admit to a sort of restlessness." Would she think him weak for his confession?

"I'm restless, too," she said, surely unaware how she put him at ease. Her voice vibrated. "I only wish I had some control in my life. Some choice."

"Is there no way you can remain in Sumpu? At least until my return?"

She didn't answer, and he wanted to rail at the gods for dangling this delight in front of him then yanking her away before he could grasp the happiness.

He refused to say that he'd also learned how much he wanted her. He wanted to love her and be loved by her. He wanted her for his wife. His partner. His completion. If he spoke it and she pushed him away, as she'd warned him repeatedly that she'd have to do, she'd split the ground from under him.

"Please promise you'll try," he said, desperately attempting not to sound like he begged.

She sniffed and brought a hand to her eye. Did she cry? "I'm in no position to make promises, Takamori-san."

She hadn't said no. He dared hope.

His lady retreated a step. "I'm suddenly exhausted. I must bid you goodnight."

He fought the urge to take her hand and keep her near. "I'll see you tomorrow?"

"If the gods allow, yes."

If the gods allow...

*   *   *   *

"I need to change." Saiko headed for her chamber, glad the promise ceremony that began her transition to imperial consort hadn't taken as long as anticipated. As the weight from yesterday lessened, she quickened her pace. She had to take this chance to see her samurai.

Fast on her heels, Okiko's socked feet swished over lush carpeting centered along the stone corridor. "But Princess, you've already changed twice today. Your kimono's fine for the banquet."

"I want to wear blue." Saiko didn't mean to cause her first lady vexation, but this was important. She had reached her last day. One more day with Takamori. When he learned the truth, he would despise her.

"Your clothes are in chests, Princess. Do you know which you wish to wear?"

Saiko slid open the door to her chamber. It hardly resembled her room with so much packed away. "Yes. The sky blue with pink butterflies." She began untying the wide red *date-jime* belt at her waist.

Okiko snapped her fingers. "I know where it is. One moment, Princess." She sidled between two rows of trunks and opened one that sat against the wall. "Here it is."

Saiko held her arms out wide. Eyeing a mountain scene painted upon the cloth screen covering her window as her friend switched the kimonos, she reflected how the whine and howl of wind along the eaves mirrored the howling despair within her. Was she too late? Had she missed him? She silently begged her friend to hurry.

With a white *date-jime* belt complimenting the pink and blue of the kimono, Saiko kissed Okiko's fingers. "Thank you. I need only a brief time in the garden then I'll return." She didn't miss her first lady's suspicious scowl, but to her friend's credit, she said nothing.

Saiko headed for the door, but Okiko stopped her. "You must wear a coat. It's too cold, even for fifteen minutes. Here, wear the red one I made for your journey." She bent over a trunk. "I think I put it in here."

With a quiet groan at the added delay, Saiko shook her head. She picked up her white down coat from atop her boots and shrugged into it, hoping against hope that Takamori awaited her. "I'll just wear this one."

She rushed to the garden and wished her restrictive under-robes allowed for wider steps so she could run outright. As she neared the bridge, snowflakes whisked past and stuck to her coat, but she didn't sense Takamori. Didn't detect any disturbance beyond the rush of frigid wind.

She feared he had come and gone when she didn't meet him.

Now was her last chance to pretend a normal...anything. Her wooden sandals clopped along the stone path and onto the bridge. As she feared, it was empty. She proceeded to the other opening.

Acute disappointment took her to her knees. He had become so important to her.

Last night, he'd spoken of his family. Of his past. He'd given her a piece of himself. He didn't bow and scrape, fake a smile, and maintain a distance like everyone else. He spoke honestly, with depth in his gaze and a fierceness in his countenance. He touched her deeply. He'd seeped into her soul where she carried him everywhere.

Gripping the railing, she tipped her head backward and found their single white cherry blossom. It had shriveled and turned brown in the cold. A sharp pang twisted in her gut. That blossom had represented her happiness, and now it showed her what to expect – her joy's shriveled, empty death. She bent her forehead to the cold stone and let her tears fall. Tears of disappointment. Of worry for an unsure future with a man she'd never met. Of anger for having no say in her own destiny. But mostly, tears for a love lost before it was found.

Her face tightened in the agony of loss and pulled her hair at her temples. It pinched painfully. She yanked silver sticks from her braided bun and let the heavy length fall over one shoulder. It still pulled, however, so she sank her hip to the bridge and released the plaits as tears coursed unchecked down her cheeks. Her loosened hair gave her immediate relief, and she buried her face in her hands.

"My lady?"

With a gasp, she straightened. "Takamori-san."

"I'm sorry to be late. Are you weeping because of me?" His eyebrows lowered as he puckered his lips. Coming to her side, he squatted and brushed the tears from her cheek.

She shook her head but said, "Yes. I was late, too. I thought you didn't wait for me."

The lines of his face gentled as tension left his mouth and his forehead smoothed, the first softening she'd seen in him. He eyed the hair down her back then boldly took a handful and draped it across his palm. "I'd wait all day for you, my lady."

"You would?"

"If I could. There's a lot to do to prepare for tomorrow." He pressed her hair to his nose and inhaled. "Sweet Lady of the Bridge, you've brought light into my dark life. Something to look forward to each day."

"But it has to end."

"Yes." He settled her hair over her shoulder, trading it for her hand. His calloused thumb drew an invisible, tingling circle on her skin. "I can't stay. I'm duty-bound to accompany the princess to Kyōto."

She closed her eyes. He'd mentioned leading and teaching, but at what level? Last night, he'd talked of his promotion. Would he lead a contingent within her caravan? The gods help her if he'd lead the personal guard her father had chosen. How awful to contemplate him riding next to her palanquin for the three-day journey, the whole while reminding her of what she couldn't have. "The time has come for my confession."

His expression tightened, and he closed his eyes. "Not yet."

She sighed with relief. Another moment to bask in his admiration and affection. Another moment to know, for now, that he wanted to be here with her.

"Is there any hope?" he asked. "I'll return. I'll come for you."

She ached with longing. If only he could. "You know nothing of me."

"I know you're lovely and kind and sweet yet fierce in your

way. I know you're loyal and dependable. I know you feel deeply about me." He wiped a tear from her other cheek. "You're my motivation. I see your gorgeous face in my mind all day. No matter where I go or what I do, you're with me. Is it the same for you?"

"Yes," she managed past a throat gone thick with bridled grief. "How can this be? We hardly know each other."

A sad smile transformed his face, removing the hard edge and replacing it with hope. "I know. Yesterday, I had such anger and hopelessness at the thought of our parting. Last night, I was sad but hopeful. Today, I'm determined. This isn't the end, *Hashi no Kizoku*. My father once told me that the heart wants what the heart wants. We're meant for each other. If not, it wouldn't be so clear to us after such a short time. We are one. Meant to unite."

Speechless, Saiko stared at his thumb rubbing circles on her hand. He spoke the truth, and it hurt beyond measure. Now the future didn't simply bear a series of unknowns. It bore the possibility of endless despair. To serve as consort to one man when she loved another would eat away at her. How could she bear it?

A man's shout barked through the garden.

"I must go. Tell me who you are. What's your name? If you're not in Sumpu when I return, I'll find you."

Would he hate her? Would he punish her for letting him fall in love with her before she entered the bed of the emperor? She opened her mouth to speak her name, but Okiko's whistle stopped her. Alarmed, she sprang to her feet. "Something's happened. I have to go."

"Your name. I need your name." He refused to release her hand.

"Yes." She braced. "My name is—"

"Your father wants you. Now!" Okiko ran onto the bridge and grasped Saiko's arm while shooting Takamori a scathing frown. Behind her first lady, three of her father's guard stood ready, their shoulders squared and their jaws flexed.

He let go and backed for the end of the bridge as the man,

sounding desperate, called for him again. "Tell me."

She opened her mouth, but Okiko jerked her toward the bridge opening. Her name tangled on a forced exhale.

"What?" Takamori called, his face darkening into a fierce scowl. He took a step toward her.

"Now," shrieked her lady-in-waiting as five more guards sprinted toward them from the castle. "Your father sends an escort. Hurry."

Two samurai ran along the path on the other side of the creek and joined Takamori on the bridge. Saiko tried to run and look over her shoulder at the same time. "Tokugawa Saiko," she shouted, afraid the wind snatched her shaking voice rather than carrying it to his ears.

When he didn't respond, she knew he hadn't heard. To Okiko, she said, "He'll never forgive me."

Her friend's grim frown didn't relent. "It doesn't matter. You're meant for another. Now hurry. The emperor has sent escort emissaries who just arrived, and your father wants you there when he allows them admittance into the reception room."

Her life as she'd known it had ended. With the arrival of the emissaries, her world would now take on the meaningless and purposeless existence of a Kyōto aristocratic lady. Inside, the light of hope sputtered then blinked out.

*　　*　　*　　*

Organized chaos reigned as Takamori oversaw the forming of the princess' entourage along the castle road. Dawn brought snow. He didn't care. Nothing mattered but getting back. The lady-in-waiting had said her father wanted her. That meant he was in Sumpu, and so would she when he returned. He grinned, but it soon slipped to a frown. He was missing a clue. It seemed like it should be obvious, but he couldn't see it.

Riding on horseback toward the castle's main gates, he made sure samurai worked to direct the loading of travel packs and the princess' possessions. Between the horses and a number of palanquin, workers scurried to secure provisions into carts sufficient to support the battle-sized contingent of foot soldiers and mounted samurai. He searched the bustle for her, hoping to catch another glimpse of her beauty before he left. She didn't come, however.

Before long, flurries began to whiten the ground and stick to horses' manes. Takamori waved his men into position while Shosan inspected to make sure each man had a full complement of weapons and armor. When the princess arrived in a figure-engulfing red coat with a large hood concealing her face and headed for the eight-man palanquin at the middle of the train, Takamori accepted a wool cape from one of the samurai who would remain behind.

He couldn't leave, however. His lady had tried to tell him her name, but he hadn't heard. He couldn't go until he had it and, with it, a way to find her when he returned. His horse's hooves thundered as he rode through the gateway leading to the inner citadel and galloped to the row of two-story buildings where he'd lost sight of the ladies the day of the festival.

With his courage in his throat, he reined his horse to a halt and hurried through the first of three doors. The first floor clearly included rooms belonging to male retainers. This was not her residence.

He climbed to the second door and found the rooms on the first floor barren. He took the stairs two at a time and found a scholar's room lined with books and scrolls. Next door, he recognized the second he stepped through the door that he'd found the princess' residence. Everything appeared pristine. The rooms, however, were empty. Had his lady already gone to her father's rooms? Where was she? More importantly, who was her father that he had authority enough to engage Tokugawa guards to fetch his daughter? Again, he had the impression he failed to recognize something that should be obvious.

He grasped a newel post at the base of the stairs and fought an overwhelming sense of loss.

"Marshal," said a soft voice from the main entrance. Shosan

held the reins to his horse and gave him a questioning look from the doorway.

"I'm coming. I'd hoped to find something here that I lost."

"Did you find it?"

"No. It's gone." A fist twisted in his gut. Accepting the reins, he stepped outside and mounted. He put on his helmet. "Let's move. This snow doesn't appear like it'll stop, and I want to reach Kanagawa before night."

Chapter Seven

Nine days into travel, fear of a confrontation with Takamori had Saiko cranky. If she'd properly let him know her name in the garden that last day, she wouldn't be so uptight. But she couldn't let him learn of her identity on the Tokaido Road in front of his men. It'd humiliate him, and he deserved better.

Now, however, she couldn't take it anymore. Why didn't the pain lessen? Why couldn't she detach him from her affections? She had hoped she'd lose the desire to seek his face, but the idea consumed every minute of every day.

Adjusting a quilted cover over her aching legs, she glanced at Okiko. "The light fades but we continue. When will we stop?"

"I don't know, Princess. I'm weary, too. And hungry."

"We stay in Kugatsu tonight?"

"Yes. I understand it's a post station, but I'm told there's a good-quality inn and a couple excellent restaurants. It's the last stop before Kyōto."

Kugatsu. She would reach the imperial court by noon the next day. Could she live with not at least trying to see Takamori one more time? She stared at her fingers on the palanquin's window slider. Did he ride next to her this moment? Could she open the window and seek his dark eyes? Drink in his hard beauty?

"Princess?" Okiko's gentle voice held concern.

"I'm fine." She wasn't.

"You haven't been yourself."

"Who have I been?" Saiko caressed the slider bar, fighting the temptation to open the window. Just a little. Just a crack. Was he out there right now?

"That's not what I mean." Okiko inched the quilt higher then sighed. "Days before we left, you grew quiet but seemed happy. Maybe happier than I've seen you. Now, you seem so sad."

"I'm to become a consort tomorrow. I do this because my father tells me my family and Japan require it to help insure the success of our unification. But I didn't live my life until now with a mind to becoming some man's plaything."

"Go-Mizunoo isn't 'some man.' He's the emperor. And you'll be more than his plaything. You'll have time with him and, therefore, the chance to earn his trust and the ability to influence him."

"To what purpose?" Saiko spat. "My father and brother rule. Go-Mizunoo does nothing more than preside over ceremonies."

"He represents all that's refined and noble."

"Nonsense." Saiko had never wanted anything so much as she wanted to see Takamori's face right now. Unable to exert another ounce of willpower, she slid the window enough to peer outside. The light had faded too much, however. Men marching beside her palanquin appeared as no more than shadows. Two samurai passed on horseback, their dark outlines silhouetting their intimidating bearing against the graying landscape. Neither were Takamori, though. She sensed it.

As she closed the window, the energy in the air changed.

"Something's different," said Okiko.

"Yes. I think we near Kugatsu."

A shout sounded a moment before the palanquin halted.

Her lady-in-waiting took her hand and whispered, "I know about the samurai on the bridge. I'll do anything you ask. Anything."

Saiko's heart stumbled over a beat. "How much do you know?" The palanquin met the ground, jolting her, and she placed a steadying hand on the wall.

"Only that you met him every day, and that you had a light in your eyes whenever you returned. You deserve happiness."

The door slid open, preventing further conversation. Saiko lifted her hood and followed her friend out. Surrounding them, armored samurai escorted them to an inn. For the first time since beginning this journey, she searched the entourage for Takamori. It did no good. The lack of light made it impossible to make out anything but brisk activity as warriors set about forming their camp for the night.

She moved through the evening in a daze, barely aware of bathing, dressing, dining, and settling in for bed. Takamori haunted her. He'd asked to share pleasure with her, and now that she faced her last night outside the emperor's authority, she regretted refusing him.

She couldn't seek him, however. Without knowing his exact rank and precise location, she'd have to involve others. A scandal was out of the question. Though Okiko had offered to do anything she asked, she couldn't send her lady-in-waiting. He wasn't a man to be fetched.

It hurt that she hadn't kept her promise to tell him her true identity, but perhaps it was for the best. He'd remember her as a lady with a kind disposition and a natural curiosity, not the deceptive princess. So why couldn't she reconcile to the idea?

Because he was nothing but honest with her. Because he touched her soul and made her realize that she could love. Because he deserved the truth.

Rolling on her futon to put her back to Okiko, she rubbed stinging eyes. Her mind raced. Without the prospect of sleep, morning would be long in coming. She didn't care that she would meet Go-Mizunoo with bloodshot eyes and an exhaustion-induced pallor. She wanted to make it right with Takamori.

* * * *

Tapping an impatient foot, Takamori crossed his arms and stared into the flames of a campfire.

"The men are grumbling," said Shosan, coming to his side. "You've driven them hard for nine days. Now that we're within hours of Kyōto and the rest they'd hoped for, you announce we'll leave immediately after delivering the princess?"

"I must go back." He had to find his lady of the bridge.

"To pursue this magic elixir you've discovered? How can a woman be worth this trouble?"

"She is. Simple as that. So here's my question to you. How is it that a noblewoman in service to the old shogun's daughter isn't known by sight and name? Since our last day in Sumpu, I've made inquiries. Nobody knows of a lady who wore blue and visited the garden every day." Tucked into the crooks of his elbows, his fists tightened.

"Easy. Princess Saiko and her ladies arrived in Sumpu only a week after we did. Other than a few Tokugawa castle guard, nobody saw the women. I personally couldn't tell you which of the two women inside is the princess." His friend chuckled.

Takamori sniffed. "That's because you're a sad excuse for a samurai."

Shosan elbowed him hard. "Is that so? Which one's the princess?"

"I have no idea." He barked a laugh. "Whichever one wears a fancier kimono, I guess."

His second-in-command rolled his eyes. "Great. We're both sad excuses for samurai. There's no hope for this mission."

"There was no time. I'm sure Ieyasu-shogun assumed we knew her, and I was distracted with my lady of the bridge. I didn't think to ask." He couldn't remember ever being so lax in preparing for a mission. *Hashi no Kizoku* had really stolen his focus. He didn't regret a moment, however.

"You're not alone. This book I'm writing is all I think about. Maybe it's time for us to become monks."

"Monks? You've lost your senses. I'm samurai. I'll live as a warrior until I die as one." Though as he had told his lady, he wouldn't complain if he never saw another battle.

"So this cruel pace is about this lady who visited you on the garden bridge?" Shosan's features danced in the fire's light but held no censure.

"Yes. Am I pathetic?" Takamori couldn't fake a desperation to return and begin his search for the woman who completed him.

"Maybe." His friend chuckled. "I don't know, but I won't argue. The sooner we reach Sumpu, the sooner I can write more of my book."

I'll find you, Hashi no Kizoku. I will have a chance at the promise of love.

*   *   *   *

Pounding woke Saiko from dreaming about Takamori's kiss, and she sat with a groan. Beside her, Okiko stirred slightly. A ray of light seeped in around the window's wooden sliding cover. Night had passed despite the gloom in the room.

"Princess," a man shouted through the door. He rapped incessantly. "It's time to leave. The marshal needs you outside."

Her lady-in-waiting yanked her quilted coat to her throat, leaving her feet uncovered and exposed to the room's chill. "What is it?"

Saiko slouched under the warmth of her own coat and wished they had the luxury of a down-filled comforter rather than having to sleep under their clothing. "He says the entourage is waiting for us. I think he exaggerates. We just woke."

Okiko groaned then shrugged into her coat and stood. As she padded barefoot to the window, she said with every step, "Cold. Cold. Cold." She slid the cloth-covered window aside then the outer wood shutter and gasped. "Oh, no. They must've risen before the sun."

"What?" Saiko stood and traipsed in a high-stepping dance across the cold floorboards to her lady's side. Why had she thought a room on the second floor would offer more warmth? It seemed no heat seeped up from the common rooms below.

Outside, the soldiers had already dismantled their camp.

The jingle of horses' tack around the corner of the inn announced the formation of the train.

"We haven't eaten." Okiko rushed to her futon and bent to retrieve her gray and black kimono. "We'll come out shortly."

"Hurry. The marshal wants to reach Kyōto by midmorning." The man's footsteps clomped down the hallway before fading.

"Midmorning? When did the schedule change? And why didn't they tell us last night? We should make them wait," said her friend with a frown.

Saiko closed the window and shivered, her breath white and wispy before her face. "Why's he so impatient? Does he expect me to appear before the emperor with unkempt hair and a wrinkled kimono? And we're into April. When will the weather turn warm?"

At her trunk, instead of choosing her prettiest kimono, she decided on a lavender one that complimented the plum and pink under-layers she had worn the day before and through the night. It irritated her that she had no time to select layers in colors that best complimented her loveliest kimono. She'd hoped for an opportunity to seek Takamori before they left. To explain and apologize.

Her lady-in-waiting dressed simply in tan and yellow then assisted Saiko with the details of her clothing. "We'll fashion your hair in the palanquin. This isn't right. You should have at least an hour to purify and prepare your appearance by the warmth of a brazier."

"It's fine. I doubt the emperor will receive me, anyway. He'll likely meet with Father's marshal and second-in-command then welcome me in a more casual setting." Like in his bed. She shuddered.

Okiko finished tucking the kimono's excess silk under the wide *obi* sash and took a step back with an approving nod. "I don't know how you can be so calm."

"I'm not calm. More like resigned. Complaining would do no good and be undignified. But there's something I must do before we go. Someone I must speak with." He had said he would try to find her when he returned to Sumpu, and she didn't want him embarking on a futile journey guaranteed to fail. Or worse, learn that she was the princess from someone else and think she'd chosen to let the lie live.

No, she needed to find him and tell him herself. Now. Before they reached Kyōto. Before the court absorbed her, and her new position robbed her of any final chance to speak with him.

The insistent knock returned. "Please, Princess. The marshal threatens to come fetch you himself. That would be unpleasant."

Her lady-in-waiting harrumphed daintily with disgust. She thrust their loose items into the chest then stomped to the door while Saiko gathered a brush, combs, and hairpins.

Okiko slid open the door and stepped aside so the man could go to the trunk. "Are we to travel to Kyōto the morning through with empty bellies?"

The man bowed with great respect. "I do apologize. Please understand that I'm following orders."

Saiko shrugged into her coat and lifted the hood. "I understand, but the marshal will also need to understand that I have important business to see to this morning."

The man snatched the trunk off of the floor with a grunt and made it to the door before she could go five steps. He blocked her way but bowed. "I'm sorry, Princess, but the marshal assigned me to see you to your palanquin without delay, and I won't fail him."

Saiko set her jaw. "Step aside, Soldier."

He backed out of the doorway on a second bow but didn't clear a path for her. Instead, he used the width of the trunk to control her progress.

She had to talk with Takamori. She simply had to. She tried to hurry past him when he maneuvered too far toward one wall, but he quickly adjusted to block her.

"I'm sorry, Princess."

She planted a fist on her hip. "So you say, but if you were truly sorry, you'd show it by letting me pass."

"Okay, then. I'm not sorry."

Insufferable pig's behind! Saiko pressed her lips together.

Okiko hurried to her side and whispered, "We're nine days gone from home. What business can you have in Kugatsu? Who do you need to speak with?"

Saiko shot the unyielding soldier a glare. "The man from the bridge."

"He's here?" her friend squeaked. "I'll help you."

Rushing along the hall, Okiko shrieked at him to step aside. People opened doors and peered out, but the soldier appeared unfazed. He kept apologizing, which only made it worse.

*   *   *   *

A cacophony erupted from the inn as Takamori's soldier backed through the exit with the sound of women's shrieks in his wake. The soldier talked at the top of his voice, adding to the racket.

Shosan covered his ears. "It's too early for such shrieking."

"You say that as if there's actually a good time for it." Takamori sat with his back to the inn. He shifted to rein his horse around and quiet the three then order the women into the waiting palanquin.

"I'll go," said his friend, holding out a staying arm. "We don't want the princess arriving at court in tears."

"Tears? I'm not so cruel."

"Maybe not to your lady of the bridge. The princess delays your return, however, and the gods help her." Shosan laughed.

Takamori couldn't deny the truth. He would deal impatiently with the women, and it wouldn't go well. "They're all yours, but be quick. I want to leave in a few minutes." He stared at the ladies, disappointed. For the first time, he saw the princess' attendant without her hood and realized he'd spent the trip hoping she was his *Hashi no Kizoku* – if only for the chance to see her again. If only for the chance to convince her to return to Sumpu with him.

He nudged his horse and galloped to the head of the entourage.

Chapter Eight

"That hurts." Saiko gripped her knees to keep from yelling as Okiko twisted her hair into an elaborate coiffure. Adding to her discomfort, her empty stomach grumbled and her left knee still smarted after bumping it on the doorway of the palanquin when the marshal's second-in-command had literally herded her inside.

"You're just mad because you weren't given time to search for your samurai."

She closed her eyes as a tear coated her lashes. Not sure if the tear resulted from her stinging scalp or her disappointment, she said in a tight voice, "He's not *my* samurai."

"Maybe not, but I think he would be if you had a choice in the matter." Her lady-in-waiting smoothed a hand over the top of Saiko's head then cranked her hair one more twist.

"Do you want me to arrive at the imperial court with a headache?"

"No. I want you to arrive flawless. All eyes will be on you, and you can't appear weak or imperfect in any way."

"One thing's certain. Even the strongest wind couldn't unwind this helmet you've created out of my hair." Saiko touched fingertips to a smooth, unyielding curve of a twist behind one ear. When her friend wiggled a hairpin into the resistant coif, she winced at the scrape against her scalp and the pull of individual strands.

"There," said Okiko with a satisfied thump on Saiko's

shoulder. "It's perfect."

"Perfectly torturous. My face feels tight." Her forehead ached under the strain, and she waggled her eyebrows to relieve it. At least the morning had warmed. Spring had come. Finally.

"When word spreads through Kyōto of your beauty, you'll thank me." Her lady-in-waiting slid a tortoise shell comb into her hair at the temple. "Now let me powder your face and throat white. I put some *oshiroi* in this satchel this morning."

"Must I?" Saiko pivoted on the seat to face her friend. "It makes me itch. Do you want me to meet the emperor with streaks scratched into my ghostly pallor?"

"Nonsense." Okiko waved a dismissive hand. "You'll simply resist the urge to scratch. You join the aristocrats in their world today. You have to fit in." She released a small squeal of delight. "I found it."

Before Okiko could withdraw the powder from the satchel, however, a man shouted. The palanquin tilted at an alarming angle. Saiko caught her friend, preventing her from pitching onto the narrow floor space. Okiko screamed as the conveyance tipped backward, slamming them against the backrest.

Gasping, Saiko reached to open the window. The palanquin hit the ground with a jarring thump. Her teeth hurting from the jolt, she reached again to slide aside the window's wooden cover.

Horses' hooves pounded past as men yelled and officers barked orders.

"Attack!"

She stiffened. In the distance ahead, gunfire echoed. She slammed the window shut, not wanting to give her enemies the knowledge as to which of the three palanquins she occupied.

"Princess?" Okiko's wide eyes sought hers. "What's happening?"

Saiko wanted to say she didn't know, but she did. Or at least she suspected. "Supporters of imperial rule."

"I don't understand." Her lady's voice rose on a panicked note.

She took her friend's hand, trying to will her racing pulse to slow. "Some don't approve of Shogun's rule. My imminent association, a most *intimate* association, will further cement my family's power as Shogun and leader of the new samurai government."

Something large bumped into the palanquin, sending it sliding over the roadway's gravel. Okiko screamed.

"We have to remain calm. I'm sure the marshal has us surrounded by armed soldiers. We're safe." No gravel rustled around them, however, the battle sounded far but grew nearer.

Then a bullet splintered through the wall with a loud crack.

The ball missed her head by inches and created another hole as it exited through the back wall. Her stomach dropped. On a gasp, she sank to the floor. The confined space sent her knees to her chest. She yanked her lady-in-waiting down beside her.

She could die. The next shot would strike her, and she'd die with regrets because of Takamori.

"I have to find him." An urgency clutched her in a grip that robbed her of sense. She lifted a hip to the seat then reached for the door. "I have to tell him. I have to explain."

Okiko grabbed her wrist. "Princess! No!"

"I have to. You don't understand." For that matter, Saiko didn't, either.

"You're not in love," insisted her friend. "A week of meeting some man on a bridge isn't enough to build the kind of love that would have you risking your life."

She shook her head. Was she an idiot? Yet the idea of dying, or worse, living a meaningless life with the knowledge that she'd never made her situation with Takamori right would break her heart beyond bearing. It would break her mind, as well.

Hoof beats drumming on hard ground scared her. Did the enemy come for her? She had to do this. Now.

"I don't have a choice." Saiko shook off her lady-in-waiting's hand and leaned for the exit.

Before she could reach it, the handle lowered. The door

flung open. Takamori filled the entryway, his expression fierce and his armor intimidating.

"*Hashi no Kizoku!*" His gaze dropped to Okiko on the floor, and his scowl deepened. "We have no time. Where's the princess?"

*   *   *   *

Everything in Takamori demanded he take his lady. Escort her somewhere safe. Escape to a place where nobody would find them. But he couldn't ignore his obligation to the Tokugawa family. To the Tokugawa princess.

"I am Princess Saiko," she said. "I'm so sorry."

Her? The princess? He tried to wrap his brain around the very idea. Then it made sense, and he mentally kicked himself for not putting the clues together sooner.

"Not now," he growled, grasping her wrist and dragging her practically over top of her cowering lady-in-waiting. "You need to leave. Now."

He had to somehow pretend she hadn't played him for a fool. Never had he suffered such conflict – utter joy to find his lady, and misery in the sure knowledge that he could in no way have her.

"Abandon Okiko-san? If something happens to her—"

"Go, Princess," said her friend. "Your safety is most important."

Saiko resisted his pull, but Takamori didn't relent. "She'll follow us. One of my men will bring her." He admired her loyalty and selflessness. Questions raced through his mind, but he had no time to contemplate them.

"Stay low," she said to her lady-in-waiting then stepped from the palanquin.

The moment her feet hit the gravel, she became a blur of motion. She shoved him hard and leaned backward. An arrow passed through the space between their separating torsos. He stood upright as the arrow sliced into the grassy roadside, but she shoved him again.

He turned in time to flinch as her slender arm thrust inches from his face. Her lightning reflex allowed her to palm-slap another oncoming arrow. It deflected and clattered benignly to the road. She had greater speed than he thought possible.

"Hurry," he said, mounting his waiting horse. He was used to fear and exhilaration in battle, but this acute awareness of her danger opened the possibility for mistakes, and he couldn't permit that. He leaned down and offered her a surprisingly steady hand.

She didn't accept it. Her features appeared calm. Beautiful. Her eyes belied her anxiety, however, as they darted left then right. "I need a bow. We won't escape without a defensive."

"Look around. We're surrounded by my defensive. Let's go." They'd escape faster if they rode alone and left his men to prevent enemy pursuit. When she stood her ground, her chin firm, he searched for danger over his shoulder. The enemy hadn't made much progress. "Very well, Warrior Princess. Take his." He pointed to a bowman crouched behind the palanquin.

As the soldier handed over bow and quiver, Takamori signaled to a mounted samurai then pointed into the conveyance. He held up two fingers – the unspoken symbol they used to refer to the Summer Siege at Osaka Castle. His man nodded before shifting in his saddle to reload his gun. It would be a push, but they could reach the castle by nightfall if they rode hard.

Takamori handed his own rifle to the unarmed bowman. Three arrows arced from a rocky outcropping forming a wall along the road, indicating that the enemy crept close on the other side. Damn it. They grew closer than he realized.

His horse issued a complaining nicker, stepping out of the path of the oncoming threat. Takamori shouted, "Move!"

Princess Saiko glanced up, but a fraction too late. One arrow planted its point in the conveyance's roof. The second caught her sleeve and ripped cleanly through. The third, however, hit the back of her head.

"No!" His heart shuddered to a halt for a painful second. He reined his horse in her direction, desperate to catch her before she collapsed. Attackers began to climb over the outcropping and drop to the roadway. Their armor bore the crests and markings of defeated daimyo, confirming his suspicion.

Ronin.

Rogue samurai had formed a bandit band, but how large? None wore the symbol of Toyotomi Hideyori, which told him they hadn't served his lord's enemy at Osaka Castle before the sieges. He didn't have time to ponder where they originated, however. Saiko remained standing on the roadway. If he had to dismount, he may not get her to safety.

As his horse attempted to find a rhythm into a run, Takamori leaned as far as he dared and thrust a forearm into her armpit. She grabbed the top edge of his armor. With a fierce growl of sheer determination, he hauled her, facing him, onto his lap. The horse found its gait and took off across the swaying grass.

He silently pleaded with her not to die. She provided the only light in his world. She couldn't die.

Wrapping one arm around her slender waist, he leaned forward and urged his horse faster. A bullet whistled past. *Too close.*

"Let go." The princess squirmed. "I can't breathe."

He grunted assent, relieved, and loosened his arm. "You're injured."

"I don't think so." She reached up, her arm bouncing slightly in time to the horses' pace. A mild smile touched her mouth. Bending her head to the side, she wiggled the arrow then produced it with triumph in her long fingers. "We'll thank my lady-in-waiting later for her way with hair."

Hair? Her hair had stopped an arrow? If he hadn't seen it with his own eyes, and the fact that the tip bore not a single drop of blood, he would never have believed it. She lived, and he thanked the gods.

Another bullet tore through the air with a shriek. He tried to check behind, but his helmet hit the shoulder guard on his armor.

Princess Saiko adjusted her bow then leaned a bit to the right. "We're being followed. Three samurai on horses. Two with guns and one with a bow. Shall we return this arrow to them? It seems the polite thing to do."

She joked? How could she joke? In all the battles he'd fought, he'd never been so afraid. Never had so much to lose. He cleared his throat. "Can you hit a target from a moving horse?"

"I haven't tried. We're about to find out." She peeled the layers of her kimono enough to free her creamy, pale legs and straddle him.

Despite their danger, his body acknowledged with enthusiasm her exposed proximity. When she hooked her feet behind his knees, he braced in the stirrups to give her a firm foundation. Never had he found a woman as sexy as he did his *Hashi no Kizoku.*

Could she do this? Would it make a difference? She had mastered *yawara*, but archery held a completely different skill set. Further, to hit a moving target from a moving base... Perhaps she took on too much.

"You're fearless," he said, struggling with the idea of her as Princess Saiko rather than his elegant lady of the bridge.

She leaned right, past his shoulder, and loaded the arrow in the bow. "I've never been more scared."

"You seem calm."

"I don't want to die." A stillness settled over her as she cocked the weapon, regardless of the rocking of the horse's run. Her eyes narrowed. Her lips thinned. Then she released the arrow.

When her face relaxed, Takamori bowed his head to adjust the angle of his helmet where it protected his nape. He glanced over his shoulder as the first of the three *ronin* tipped off his saddle with the arrow protruding from his throat.

"You amaze me," he said. She truly was a warrior princess.

"I really hit him. I've never killed someone," she said quietly, no hint of joy in her tone. She reached back and took an arrow from her quiver.

"It's kill or be killed."

She nodded grimly. "I don't take this lightly."

A gunshot ripped like thunder along the tips of straw grass rippling over the field. Whistling, a bullet whipped past Takamori's right ear. "His aim is good. Another shot like that will hit one of us. We have time. He needs to reload."

The horse's hooves pounded into a dip in the landscape. Over the beat, the princess shouted, "Turn left. I can't target him from this angle."

Hoping the terrain held no surprises for his horse's straining legs, he reined left with an eye on the ground.

She released her arrow.

He followed its trajectory straight into the Samurai's eye.

The man screamed then slumped over his mount's neck.

Saiko gasped, her face twisted into an awed horror as she shuddered violently against him.

"Stay strong," he encouraged, redirecting his horse west toward Osaka.

He urged the animal faster, but encroaching hoofbeats told him the final pursuer closed in, his horse faster under the weight of only a single rider.

"Can you do this?" Takamori asked, concerned by her trembling distress.

Her features hardened. "I have to. He won't retreat, will he?"

"No."

"He has a bow. Turn!"

An arrow struck the armor covering Takamori's back. The lacquered leather did its job, and the arrow snapped on impact then fell away. She had to hurry, though. Ahead, the Yodo River glistened in the morning light. They'd be vulnerable and off course in minutes. Saiko loaded her bow and fired.

"I missed," she cried with dismay.

Without hesitation, she reloaded and shot. Her knuckles whitened on the bow's grip.

"Yes," she shouted. Throwing her arms around him, she laid

her cheek on his shoulder armor. "He's down. Ride, Samurai."

Taking the reins in one hand, he wrapped an arm around her. She shook, though he didn't know if it had to do with a breeze or the stress of battle. Hugging her, he hated that her true identity changed everything.

Why had she kept the truth from him? Why had she led him to believe she wouldn't come on this trip? Did she think of him as her father's retainer, or as someone dearer? When he thought of their kisses then considered she may have only used him to alleviate her boredom, he shook with rage.

He raced toward the river and guided his horse to a shallow section of riverbed to cross. Had he learned her identity in Sumpu, he would've kept up his guard. Tempered his words. Never kissed her. Now, it was too late. Now, she existed in his deepest affection. Now he had to take her to Osaka Castle.

Safe.

Alone.

Chapter Nine

Escape. Saiko needed to retreat. From enemies of Shogun. From the images of samurai she'd killed. From herself.

"Are you taking me to Kyōto?" She leaned into him, absorbing his strength and clutching her bow behind his back. Her quiver of arrows bounced in a reassuring rhythm against her ribs.

"No. It's not safe. There's only one place I can take you while we wait for instruction from your father." His face held determination and nothing more.

"One place? Where?"

"Osaka."

Osaka was further than Kyōto. "Can we make it there today?"

Holding her tighter, he leaned forward and nudged the horse faster. "Without your retinue slowing us, yes."

Her lungs expanded in time with the animal's labored breaths. "You'll run the horse to its death."

"I have a friend, a comrade from the Osaka Sieges, in the Yamashiro province halfway to the castle. We can trust him. He'll trade my tired horse for a fresh one." He dropped a hand to the firm curve of her bare thigh where it straddled his.

A breeze and their pace made the air feel cold, but his palm warmed her leg.

"Would he be willing to share some food?" This sprint to Osaka would take an entire day, and she wouldn't make it on an empty stomach.

Her fingers ached in their grip on the bow. She peeked over his shoulder, afraid of more pursuers. Nobody followed.

"I'm sure he'd be pleased to offer us rice."

Her stomach rumbled in anticipation.

"Be alert," he said. As they approached the road that led south from Kyōto to Nara, Takamori urged the horse even faster. He put his chin against Saiko's forehead.

She sat straighter, sorry to leave the protective gesture, and searched the area behind them. Other than a man chopping wood and a boy stacking the pieces next to a long, rough woodcutter's house, nothing stirred.

The horse's hooves hit the road's gravel, the sound reverberating off of the gray-brown boards of the long house. The man appeared unimpressed, as if he watched a samurai and princess gallop at top speed across the shipping road every day. Regardless of the sense of the ridiculous, she couldn't summon a smile. This day had proven a powerful reminder of life's uncertainty.

She had no promise of tomorrow. Nothing ensured they'd reach Osaka Castle safely. Nothing to promise a modicum of security in anything. Yet she couldn't deny the sense of sanctuary she found with his arm around her, and she refused to ignore the happiness generated merely by his company.

Not wanting to disrupt his concentration, she settled against his shoulder while he left the road for the Yodo River valley. From time to time, she searched behind them, partly for any sign of a threat and partly in hope of catching sight of Okiko.

With the sun approaching its zenith, Takamori encouraged his lathering, exhausted horse up a hill toward a cluster of buildings half shrouded in low clouds. Moisture hung in the air, making the midday feel heavy and, with it, a bite of cold more acute than the chill of the windy lowlands.

"Why'd you refuse to tell me your true identity?"

"I tried the day before we left. I didn't expect to be summoned."

"You kept it from me. For days, we met and talked. You never told me who you are. Why?"

She sighed, sorry the truth weighed so heavily between them. "Would you have talked with me the way you did? Sparred with me as an equal?" Kissed her?

He said nothing as their mount struggled up the hill, its hooves sliding on occasion and making for a jostling ride. When they neared the crest, he said, "No."

Her back hurt, and when he drew the animal to a halt outside an A-framed, two-story house at the center of the quiet compound, her stiff legs protested with pain as she shifted to dismount.

"Are you okay?" he asked, helping her to the ground.

"I'm not used to riding so hard for so long." Her feet hit the damp earth, making her glad for her thick boots. The loamy scent of rich soil reminded her of peaceful days spent inventorying on farms in Mito. Still, she couldn't rid her mouth of the foul taste left from the morning's harrowing events.

His booted feet hit damp dirt with a thud.

Across a grassy yard, a boy emerged from a long building. Hesitating, he called, "Master!" then ran back in.

Takamori slowly lifted Saiko's hood to cover her head. "Your nephews are training here. They can't know you visit."

She wouldn't compromise the boys' safety. If they knew she had come, and her enemies questioned them, such knowledge could cost them their lives. Nodding, she clutched her bow and checked the way they'd come. It remained clear. What delayed Okiko?

She should accept that Takamori's men subdued the *ronin* attackers before they could send more than the three she had downed, yet she couldn't shake the sensation of being hunted. Takamori lent her courage, but she worried for her friend. "You're my father's marshal."

He nodded.

She should've guessed. Only the most skilled of her father's men held such a position. She stood taller. Together, she and this warrior who'd come to mean so much could outrun a *ronin* threat. "How long before your samurai catches up to us with my lady-in-waiting?"

"They won't." He sent her a look she couldn't decipher. "He's one of my best. If he escaped from the fighting with her, he'd have taken her into hiding. They'll ride a half day or better behind us."

If... She sent a small prayer for Okiko's safety to the gods, wishing she had access to a temple.

A samurai with a smattering of silver in his topknot emerged from the long building. Behind him, a few boys peeked through the doorway then disappeared inside. The middle-aged war instructor adjusted a curved *katana* across the small of his back and headed toward the house. He wore no armor, yet his authority and confidence proclaimed him a master samurai as plainly as his weapons and apparel.

When Takamori removed his helmet, the man grinned and increased his pace across the wet grass. "Most honorable friend, *konnichiwa*. Welcome to my school, Takamori-san."

"Yagyu Munenori, *konnichiwa*. It's good to see you."

"And you. Please, come inside." Master Yagyu entered the house and waved them to follow. "Would you like one of my students to take your horse to the stable?"

"Yes, please." Takamori ushered Saiko inside.

Away from the dreary clouds and threat of rain, the abode gave her a sense of comfort. A glowing brazier at the center of the open space radiated fortifying heat. She set her bow and quiver against the wall right inside the doorway and pushed her hood off of her head.

The inside of the farmhouse-style dwelling surprised her. Rather than a packed dirt area for cooking with a rough wooden floor for living spaces, the entire first level employed smooth, lacquered floorboards that shone with cleanliness. A sitting room sported a pristine *tatami* mat over the floorboards along with screen partitions where mountain scenes painted onto the translucent white paper sections inspired tranquility and a respect for nature.

A built-in desk next to a set of two staggered shelves displaying various weapons and artwork used four sliding paper screens as windows. At the back wall, a section of floor stood raised to form an alcove where a full set of stately, brightly colored samurai armor stood on a stand. The interior reminded her more of a lord's townhouse in Edo than a rural home along the Yodo River.

Yagyu Munenori waved them toward a large stone slab where a cooking station offered warmth. Saiko had never seen anything like it.

"We can't stay long," said Takamori, pulling off his boots and joining the instructor at the slab.

Saiko pulled her feet from her own muddy boots and left them next to her bow.

"I noticed you pushed your horse," said Master Yagyu. "Do you go far?"

"To Osaka Castle," said Takamori, sinking cross-legged across from the older man.

"Accept my hospitality. Stay the night here and let's talk. I haven't seen you since the end of the Osaka Summer Siege."

As she padded in socks toward the men, Saiko hoped he'd accept. They'd traveled hours without a sign of pursuers, and every step had her thighs and lower back muscles objecting.

"Thank you for the offer. Were circumstances different, I'd gladly accept, but we can't. We must reach Osaka Castle tonight."

Saiko stifled a moan and tried not to appear stiff as she sat. She made a sighing hum at how good it felt to stretch her stiff thighs.

Munenori's brows arched. Feeding fuel to the fire, he asked, "Do you need assistance? I haven't seen excitement since the siege. I can come along and leave my school in the care of my sons for a while."

His wife, an attractive middle-aged woman, scurried in wearing quality green silk with watered brown branches creating an elegant pattern. She offered a bow and shy smile then lowered gracefully next to the instructor, tucking her legs under so she sat upon her feet. Her generous expression placid, she took over the feeding of the fire then put a pot of water on to heat.

Saiko offered a nod of acceptance to the woman's unspoken offer of tea.

"I couldn't ask it." Takamori shook his head. "I have an army at my back, but I travel ahead. You can assist, however, by taking my horse in exchange for a fresh one. And this fine lady's in need of food, but we have to hurry."

Saiko kept her face fixed and calm, though the idea of mounting another horse made her internally cringe. Kneeling, on the other hand, stretched stiff muscles and felt good. Perhaps she'd survive this desperate escape with the ability to walk.

Master Yagyu inclined his head. "It would be my pleasure. I hope you know I'd be honored to help you – the one man I could always rely on to fight bravely by my side. I'd help you in any way you ask."

"I'm of the same mind." Takamori bent forward with respect.

The instructor eyed the longbow then asked Saiko, "This samurai bow is yours?"

"No, *Sensei*. I borrowed it to carry us safely away."

"You were attacked." It was not a question.

"Yes," said Takamori.

"I see." Yagyu Munenori shared a glance with his wife. Wistfully, he said, "If only I could come with you. My lady, you clearly travel with my dear friend as a warrior and, I suspect, a target."

Saiko held her tongue. She didn't know these people and had to trust that Takamori wouldn't appreciate her revealing more than he'd tell. He hadn't told them her true identity. To protect them or to protect her? Either way, she wouldn't compromise his precautions.

She questioned in a cursory look, and he gave a nearly imperceptible nod. As her legs began to throb, she shifted her hips sideways off of her feet, settling into a more casual and comfortable position on the polished wood floor. "I've learned *kyudo* - the way of the bow. Yes, I used it to eliminate our enemy from the chase this morning. I'm no warrior, however."

Takamori shook his head. "Though my lady's main training hasn't focused on martial arts, she *is* a warrior." He faced her, his dark eyes full of meaning she couldn't comprehend. "You fought with skill and integrity. I'm honored to have you battle at my side."

Saiko's empty stomach somersaulted. Perhaps if he didn't have such handsome features, he wouldn't thrill her so. Perhaps if he didn't conduct his matters with such distinction or have such a fine mind. But he did. Regardless of how she understood the impossibility of a personal relationship with him, she wanted him. He touched a longing deep inside, and only with him did she experience true, engulfing happiness.

"Then you should have your own horse." Master Yagyu slapped his knees then stood. "Takamori-san, you'll have my own horse. I'll have it no other way. My lady, you'll ride my second warhorse. Both are fast and strong in stamina. They'll see you to Osaka by sundown." He placed a hand on his wife's shoulder then headed for the door.

"I'll come with you," said Takamori. Before standing, he leaned near Saiko and whispered, "Rest and eat. Stay inside. I'll return for you when it's time to leave."

She nodded. Her hunger growled. She wouldn't make it another hour without sustenance. So far, she'd managed thanks to a nearly constant infusion of adrenaline. It wouldn't see her to the end, however.

* * * *

Leading Munenori's horse to the house, Takamori said, "I expect one of my samurai to arrive soon with another lady. You'll remember him from the Summer Siege, too. He'll need a horse to carry them to Osaka. It's acceptable, however, if the lady's exhausted and needs to stay the night. They don't face the same level of danger."

"I'll be happy to have them here. You can count on me," said his old friend. "I heard Suzuki Shosan served Ieyasu-shogun with you. Is he the one who follows?"

"No. Shosan-san is my second-in-command. I left him in charge of my men."

"Of course. Call on me if you need extra help. I don't expect you will, since you're Ieyasu's marshal with an army at your disposal, but keep me in mind. I haven't gone weak."

Takamori secured the horse's reins then stepped to the door. "I can't think of anyone else I'd rather have at my back in the frenzy of battle than you. We've both done well, I think. You've earned fame thanks to your bravery and skill at the Battle of Sekigahara and the Winter and Summer Sieges at Osaka. Tokugawa Ieyasu was most fortunate to have you fighting on his side. Now you have this school and serve Shogun as sword instructor to his family. There's none better than you."

"You've won fame alongside me, Takamori-san." Master Yagyu opened the door. "There are few who could serve as Ieyasu-shogun's marshal, and none better than you. Have you considered moving to Edo to serve Shogun Hidetada?"

"I'm undecided." Inside, he found the princess still sitting at the cooking area. Collecting her bow and quiver, he said, "I'll serve the Tokugawa Family in whatever capacity Ieyasu-shogun wishes."

"You're an ideal samurai." Yagyu Munenori left his *tatami* sandals at the door as he joined his wife at the stone slab. "You need only send a messenger and I'll come immediately."

"I will." Takamori had no doubt his friend's word was true. His waning dedication to his lord, thanks to his shift of loyalty to Saiko, however, made him far less an ideal samurai than he wished. He noted an empty teacup and rice bowl in front of the princess. "We need to leave. Thank you for your generous kindness."

Munenori and his wife bowed.

Saiko offered him a sweet smile that stirred his loins. Then her lips pulled thin as she stood stiffly and bowed low to the sword instructor. "I won't forget your kindness, Yagyu Munenori."

The couple bowed in unison then followed her to the door. Takamori offered his shoulder while she put on her boots. She managed well and covered her head with her hood. Outside, he helped her into her saddle and handed her the bow and quiver. Being outside with her had him on edge. He needed her in the Osaka fortress as soon as possible.

He donned his helmet before adjusting his *katana* and mounting Master Yagyu's horse. Experiencing a sense of familiarity, as if he'd done this a hundred times with her, he had to concentrate on not staring at her.

"I wish you both speed and safety," said his friend.

Takamori acknowledged the wish with a wave. He signaled Princess Saiko and rode from the compound at her side.

They raced for safety. Their horses' hooves devoured the miles. On his guard for danger, Takamori searched the river valley ahead. He kept her lovely profile in his peripheral vision, glancing from time to time to make sure she didn't advance from stiff discomfort into outright pain. The further they rode, however, the more relaxed and natural she appeared in the saddle.

Behind her, the earth rose in gentle, verdant contrast to a smooth, clear gentian sky. If not for his intense awareness and urgency to reach Osaka safely, perhaps he could pretend they enjoyed a ride in the countryside to pass the afternoon.

She offered him a weak smile from within the shadows of her hood. Her way of letting him know she withstood the ride and could keep going, he suspected.

As the sky went awash in shades of blush and mandarin with the setting sun, a haze of smoke on the horizon announced their approach to Osaka. Huts and workshops met them at the outskirts. Slowing, Takamori took the lead through streets he had memorized.

Signs of the Summer Siege that had won his lord the

demise of the resident warlord still clung to buildings and showed in the wall surrounding the looming castle. Osaka Castle had suffered near destruction of its fortifications between Tokugawa Ieyasu's two campaigns, but the last six months had seen much rebuilding under the care of Shogun's appointed castle keeper, Osaka Jodai.

He hadn't realized he'd missed the place; but the massive fortification, cast into shades of dun and damson by the sunset, brought back memories both fond and horrific. War and the skirmishes that followed had allowed him the honor of fighting beside great warriors and heroes. Quiet times between had afforded him a chance to forge lifelong friendships like the ones he had with Shosan and Munenori.

He proceeded slowly, as much to offer their horses a needed rest before they climbed the castle road as to search darkening streets and doorways for threats. Alert, he made sure Saiko's mount stayed by his horse's side. He couldn't let her slip behind. Not here. Not now. He didn't begin to relax until they reached the base of the fortress road and began to ride along the outermost fortification.

Over the wall, a swarm of dragonflies formed a cloud ahead. He stopped and held out a hand for the princess to halt. Glittering onyx, absinthe, aquamarine and amethyst, they reflected the last of the day's light as they flitted and hovered. Then they swarmed toward the wall but didn't go over. Instead, they lined the outer edge, each facing the road as if forming a defensive line.

"This is a sign." Takamori tapped a finger on a green and ebony dragonfly painted onto the crimson lacquer of his *waidate* shoulder armor. "Dragonflies mean a hope for no retreat."

"My father bears the dragonfly." Saiko urged her horse forward a couple steps while removing the bow from her shoulder and scanning the crowded street ahead.

A few people gawked at her and shied off of the roadway. Placing a ready hand on the hilt of his sword, he used the other to steer his mount. He needed to lead and maintain a protective position. Despite conversations among the townspeople, he honed his hearing on the hum of dragonfly wings as the insects undulated their formation. They held their line on the wall.

Many noticed the phenomenon. An old man, while easing backward through a doorway, glanced between the dragonflies and Takamori's hand on the *katana's* hilt.

Takamori's senses heightened. His blood thundered in his ears. His insides tightened in anticipation of combat.

The sky darkened, purple now a mere halo against flint gray as glowing coral melted beyond the rooftops. Between two buildings at a curve a short distance along, two figures emerged from pronounced shadows. They wore the plain russet capes of monks. The cross of short sword and long sword at their sashes proclaimed them samurai, however.

"Imperialists," spat Takamori, drawing his *katana*.

Women screamed. Children squealed and cried. Along the street, men rushed to usher the vulnerable out of the way.

The two imperialists drew their swords. Behind him, the princess' bow creaked as she loaded and primed it. Takamori would eliminate this threat without her help, however.

"Tokugawa rule will end soon, and control will belong in the hands of the emperor where it belongs," said the first samurai.

"Not while I have any command. Who's your lord?" Takamori demanded.

The two samurai swung into motion at once, clearly well-trained, seasoned partners. He had the advantage atop his steed, though. Taking his sword to the ready, he widened his eyes and viewed the attack as a single entity rather than focusing on one opponent or the other.

He used a combination of instinct, skill, and experience to send his *katana* down a fraction of a second after the first warrior's blade arced upward. This put his sharp edge behind his attacker's and into the man's neck. The samurai's sword glanced off of a metal portion of Takamori's thigh plating.

The second samurai didn't pause in his charge. He ran,

issuing a battle cry with his *katana* held high. Takamori almost shook his head with disappointment. The man wore minimal armor.

He couldn't lower his guard for an instant, though. If the imperialist bluffed and struck with another stance at the last second, Takamori or his horse could suffer a crippling blow. He had to think of his *Hashi no Kizoku*. If he took a hit, he would leave her vulnerable.

He considered sending her ahead, but if they had anticipated such a decision and positioned men to ambush her, he could lose her. No, he did better to keep her near. Though she fought as well as many men in his ranks, she'd last only so long as a single fighter against battle-hardened samurai such as these.

The attacker didn't shift position in mid-stride, so Takamori bent low. Arcing his arm in a maneuver taught to novice samurai as a basic technique, he sliced the man's abdomen. His sword carried such momentum that it sent the imperialist's *wakizashi* flying from his sash and completed a full disembowelment. Immediately, a stench filled the air and sent the few remaining bystanders inside. Slapping soles on packed dirt echoed through encroaching gloom.

"Ride!" he shouted.

The princess released an arrow into a lantern-lit alleyway. A man's scream rewarded her shot. She grabbed her reins and snapped the stirrups against her mount's sides.

They galloped to the top of the winding road toward the gate of Osaka Castle while shouts echoed through side streets. Takamori didn't slow, however. He loved this woman. He'd see her safe, even if it meant his death.

Chapter Ten

Saiko sent a final frantic glance toward the village then preceded Takamori inside. Relief consumed her when the castle's immense main gate closed without incident.

Dusk shadows cut across a flurry of activity. The people's screams must've alerted them to the imperialists' attack because soldiers and castle workers scrambled about in seeming chaos, their feet stirring dirt into the air from the packed soil of the main staging area.

Men shouted. Pike bearers and archers ran along high wall-walks. Servants lit torches and tall standing lanterns, which rendered a sienna cast against white walls of every tower and building while sending the shadows in retreat.

She halted her horse at the center of the activity. Struggling to maintain some semblance of dignity despite a trembling that began in her limbs, she counted sentries atop the wall and tried to assess how many men-at-arms served here as she contemplated her next move.

There had been more *ronin*, but how many? Would they try to gain entry to the castle? Did they dare? Takamori reined his mount alongside.

"What should I do?" she asked.

Before he could answer, a middle-aged man wearing the distinguished wing-like *kamishimo* over-robe of Shogun's administrative branch of government approached. He held his mouth tight, and the muscles of his neck flexed. He bowed then said, "Marshal Hosokawa. I hadn't expected you."

Takamori offered a bow from atop his horse. "Osaka Jodai, I apologize. There was no time to send word. As you see, we brought trouble."

The man relaxed a bit and chuckled. "Trouble we can handle. You'll notice we're readying for attack. Are you here on business, or is there something I can do for you?"

Takamori lifted a reassuring hand and smiled. "Both. I suspect there'll be no attack. At least not tonight."

Saiko didn't like the way the jodai's nostrils flared. He hid something. Whether it had to do with the attack, she couldn't guess.

Takamori dismounted and adjusted his swords then strode to her horse. "Jodai, please meet Tokugawa no Saiko, Ieyasu-shogun's daughter. I'm protecting her on her journey to Kyōto."

Her stomach twisted painfully at the reminder of her destination. Then a dragonfly descended and alighted on the back of her hand where she gripped her saddle. Its wings became motionless, and a calm washed over her.

"Princess Saiko," said the jodai on a deep bow. He waved at a servant, spoke in a hushed tone, and sent the man on his way. "*Dozo yoroshiku*. I'm honored to provide safe and comfortable accommodations, Your Highness."

"*Dozo yoroshiku. Hajimemashite*," she replied, not yet sure how pleased she should be to meet him.

Slowly, the day's shock waned in the face of her safe haven, and reality asserted its dominance. Lives had been lost, some at her own hand. The violence that day had happened because of this journey she despised.

The dragonfly gave its wings a couple quick flicks.

"You're a little out of the way to come to Osaka on your way to Kyōto."

Remaining silent, she shifted in the saddle, shaking and hating that her chattering teeth might reveal her agitation. The dragonfly left her hand. It hovered briefly between her horse's ears before disappearing into the dusk.

She needed to dismount and placed a trembling hand upon

Takamori's shoulder.

As if reading her mind, he pursed his lips then assisted her down. His steady hands eased her nerves, and the shaking lessened. She resisted the urge to rest her head against his shoulder. Amidst the curse of attack and lives lost nestled a precious gift in the form of more time with her samurai. She didn't know whether the gods' demented manipulations appalled her or made her begrudgingly grateful.

"Yes, a little out of our way," agreed Takamori with a scowl. "A band of *ronin* ambushed our retinue early this morning. We've ridden hard all day."

"You came to the right place." The jodai bowed then indicated a young woman in a plain cotton commoner's kimono done in vertical gray and black stripes. "Katsumi-san will show you to a fine chamber, Your Highness. She's at your disposal for the duration of your stay."

"Thank you," said Saiko, gaining strength by the second but hesitant to leave the comforting feel of Takamori's hands on her arms. "My lady-in-waiting follows. She may arrive tonight, but more likely tomorrow."

"Of course, Princess. I look forward to receiving your entire retinue. It's an honor to serve you."

Saiko took a step toward Katsumi then stopped. "Speaking of my retinue, I think it only fair that I warn you. Two of Emperor Go-Mizunoo's emissaries are in attendance. I expect they'll come here rather than continuing on, in order to fulfill their purpose in arriving with me in Kyōto." The name of her prison stuck in her throat, and she swallowed.

Osaka Jodai offered a nod, but not before she detected a mild grimace. No samurai enjoyed dealing with elitist noblemen, especially the samurai in service to Shogun.

Saiko sighed. She sent Takamori a small wave and accompanied the maid into the castle's innermost rings of defense. When she'd first rode in, she'd thought of needing rest. Now, she could only think how much she hoped Takamori would find her. Soon.

*   *   *   *

Takamori surveyed rebuilt sections of battlement. With the jodai's permission, he added reinforcements to the number of men protecting the walls. He hadn't expected a *ronin* attack in Osaka of all places. He couldn't lower his guard, despite his assurances to the jodai when he'd arrived.

As he assembled a team to search the streets outside for *ronin* threats and secure the city, he fought an urgency to go to Saiko. He didn't like having her out of his sight, partly because her protection and well-being were his sole purpose, but mainly because after spending an entire day with her, he couldn't shake the sense that she had become part of him. Connected to him. Without her near, a vital part of him was missing.

While the team assembled their horses, Takamori climbed to a wall-walk overlooking Osaka. The thought of Saiko had his stomach in knots. He'd never felt for anyone what he did for her. Today, his respect and affection for her had grown. Each passing second increased it. He'd entered foreign ground and didn't know where to turn.

If he went to her, he wouldn't want to leave. If he stayed away, he'd slowly lose his mind.

He was a man. A leader. A samurai. What was this weakness she stirred in him? She stole his focus. His determination. His entire reason for being.

No, that was unfair.

He sank to his haunches, studying shadowed people moving below. She'd changed him. He wouldn't deny that truth. He had to believe the change an improvement.

She made him want more – from himself and from life in general. He began to view the world differently. As he'd wanted before he met her, he began witnessing beauty in places previously lacking.

He'd become more of a man when standing next to her undeniable, emanating femininity. She had no weakness or frailty, and yet she aroused his strength and protectiveness.

With her, he was complete. Whole. No longer the shell of a man he hadn't realized he had become until now.

In the vast lower court just inside the main gate, samurai mounted horses. Takamori descended from the wall-walk on stairs still bearing damage from the Summer Siege. A shout from the jodai had the gate opening.

He'd done what he could for tonight. He had one remaining responsibility – learn where Saiko rested.

* * * *

"I'm her protector and I need to know where Princess Saiko is at all times." Takamori's authoritative tone grew nearer.

Saiko gently waved Katsumi from the rare luxury of a fireplace and shooed her out of the chamber. Taking over feeding fuel to the fire, she bid her hands to stop trembling.

She moved to a low table near the hearth. She feigned casual nonchalance and focused on her private tea ceremony. Her back to the door, she felt his presence before he slid aside the rice paper paneled frame.

"Has my lady-in-waiting arrived?" she asked without turning. "I heard horses below."

Straw matting rustled as he stepped inside and slid the door closed.

"They won't come tonight." His calm voice worried her.

"They didn't survive?"

"May I sit?"

Giving him her profile and feigning a calm she couldn't summon, she bowed in consent. She shifted to the hearth and positioned a kettle over burgeoning flames. Did she appear as unaffected as she hoped? In his presence, her mouth lost its moisture and her stomach fluttered.

His feet rasped across the *tatami*. As he passed, smudges inadvertently scraped onto the pale matting. She returned to the table, quietly glad when her fingers didn't shake while she purified a finely wrought bamboo tea scoop by wiping it with a silken cloth.

Settling onto a crimson cushion, he presented her with a slight bow then adjusted his *wakizashi* short blade in his sash and the curved sword across the small of his back. "I haven't received word that any harm has come to them. It's late, simple as that. They'll likely stay the night with Master Yagyu. I expect them to reach here tomorrow, and the rest of my men the day after."

"Are you sure?" How could she sleep knowing her friend hadn't yet reached the safety of Osaka's castle fortress?

"No." A minute smirk quirked one corner of his mouth. "The samurai I assigned to escort her is one of my most skilled. Since she's unimportant in relations between Shogun and the emperor, she's not a target for attack. If anything, she may be followed, but nothing more. It's very likely your lady-in-waiting will come to you tomorrow."

Saiko set a perfectly crafted ceramic bowl on the table. It tottered a bit thanks to her nervous fingers. What was it about Takamori that made her so self-aware? "And the horses?"

"Warriors sent into the city to find the imperialist samurai. We don't know how many there are or where they hide. If they stay in Osaka, they have to be routed." He eyed the ceramic *chawan* then the kettle over the flames.

"I imagine you're anxious."

Takamori's expression hardened. "Anxious that we'll be attacked?"

"No. Anxious because you wish you had gone into the city with the warriors. Anxious because you wish you looked for the imperialists." She pressed her lips together. Did she go too far? Did she insult him?

The lines of his face relaxed. His eyes sparkled in the firelight, and he chuckled. "You know me. I like that. Yes, Princess, I'd like to hunt those imperialist rats and rid us of that threat."

"But...?"

He held his silence for the length of two breaths. "But protecting you is my only purpose, so I'm here with you. I'm pleased to sit with you."

With her hands folded in the clean gray silk of her borrowed kimono, she asked, "Am I their target?"

"I'm certain."

How did he sit so still when she wanted to come out of her skin?

Unable to remain serene, she abandoned her attempt then stood and wandered to a window. She could open a shutter and let in chilly air, unlike in Sumpu. Unfortunately, the night streets, though dotted with lantern light, refused her a clear view of anything worth seeing. "They knew I'd come to Osaka? But I was headed for Kyōto."

She caught his stare from the corner of her eye and closed the shutter with a nervous hand. She plucked at a white embroidered snowflake against the pale gray background of her sleeve.

"Maybe I made a mistake bringing you here," he said.

She swayed a moment before she caught the window ledge. A mistake? Did he wish he'd delivered her to Go-Mizunoo? She straightened her spine and returned to her cushion. Without a word, she lifted her eyes to his.

"They know I'm your father's marshal. It makes sense that I led your retinue."

It seemed many people knew of his position with her family. She was so blind. No. She hadn't wanted to know.

"Of course I'd bring you here. I know this city and stronghold better than Sumpu or Edo. If I'd taken a second to consider their strategies, I would've taken you somewhere else." His gaze never wavered as he added, "If you hadn't fought, they would've succeeded."

Saiko nodded. "The element they had not known - that I would fight. That I have skills."

"Yes, Warrior Princess. You have skills." A small smile tugged at his lips. "I'm glad to see you're not stiff. I worried so much hard riding would leave you sore."

She had, too. "Thank you. I'm well."

"Why do you make tea? After our troubles and efforts, I

thought I'd find you resting."

"I killed today." Her voice wavered. She swallowed. Fighting the pressure of tears behind her eyes, she forced words past a closing throat. "My life changed in a way I hadn't prepared for, so I need this tea ceremony...to refresh my spirit."

She went to the crackling fire and added a large piece of wood. The respite gave her a chance to regain her composure, and she sighed. A wisp of steam rose from the kettle's spout and formed lovely tendrils in the air before dissipating.

"So you excel at *kujutsu, yawara,* and *chado.* Impressive."

"Archery and unarmed combat...maybe. The way of tea? Not so much, but I'm learning. It brings me a connection to my world – something I lost a bit today." She eyed his feet under his folded knees. "You haven't washed."

He flipped his palms and stared at his fingers then shot her a sheepish grin. "I hadn't expected to walk into a tea ceremony."

"But you expected to walk into my chamber?"

"No."

"I have water." Saiko fought a smile. She indicated a low stool behind a lovely porcelain basin decorated with ocean waves and flying gulls.

"I'll retire to my room."

She lifted a staying hand and shifted from her formal kneel before the hearth. "Join me for tea?"

He paused, his eyes narrowing. Tired lines showed across his forehead and around his mouth for the first time since she'd met him.

"I think perhaps you could use a renewal too?" She wanted to rise but waited for his response.

"Yes. Tea would refresh me."

She stood and pushed her sleeves to her elbows. "As your hostess, may I please be allowed the honor of bathing your feet?"

"You should call a servant to do it. A princess is above bathing a samurai's feet." He released a sharp huff through his nostrils.

"Please let me do this. Not as a princess but as a friend. As a woman for a man."

He offered a polite nod, but the slant of his eyes increased as he compressed his lips. He rose with grace and strength in a single, smooth lift off of the floor. In silence, he slid the *wakizashi* from his sash and set it on the straw matting next to his cushion. He left his *katana* slung at his back.

He sat on the stool, parting the bottom of his robe, and placed his feet in the water. His intense eyes challenged her as the soft sound of disturbed water replaced the fire's crackle.

She didn't interpret his stare as confrontational. It held too many unsaid words, too much turbulence for her to mistake it for anything but curious and perhaps a sign of the same excitement that caused her own body to shiver. Lowering softly to her knees, she took a ball of chunky soap and dipped it into the basin. When her fingers brushed his cool ankle, a thrill tripped along her nerves. She inhaled a quick breath.

Saiko soaped a linen cloth. Trying to control a tremor in her hands, she slipped fingertips behind his heel and urged him to lift his foot. The soap held a wholesome scent. It made her want to hum in memory of cold winter mornings in a warm bath. The feel of clean hair, dried by a brazier, upon her shoulders. The sound of laughter from floors below.

Slowly, with a deliberate tenderness that belied a growing restlessness, she washed his foot. She took special care between his toes and let her fingers trail his arch in the wake of the washcloth's path.

He grunted quietly. His eyebrows lowered and his mouth relaxed. He followed her hands as they roamed his foot, more exploring than cleaning now. The whitewashed room appeared orange in the firelight, and he created a perfect shadow on the smooth wall behind him.

Repeating her efforts with his second foot, she tried to ignore the grip his hands had on the gray fabric covering his knees. His knuckles turned pale with pressure. She also tried to ignore an urgent need forming between her thighs as the delicate folds there began to swell around a building moisture.

Most of all, she tried to ignore the fact that a world existed outside of her temporary chamber – a world that had plans for her which didn't include this vital, intoxicating, handsome man who consumed her every waking thought.

The soft rustle of hot coals leaving their burning logs invaded her intense focus on his nearness. For a second, she resented the tea, but she needed the peace the ceremony invoked. The upheaval and desire in her withheld her far from peace.

She took a clean, folded cloth from the floor next to the basin. Draping it across her lap, she motioned him to place his feet upon it.

He lifted from the water, drops landing into the basin with plops and plinks that made her want to smile. Such a happy sound soothed her, and she sighed. She employed more care than she needed as she patted every bit of moisture from his skin.

Takamori cleared his throat then slowly withdrew his feet from her lap. She sagged at his departure. Reluctantly, she slid her fingers from his thick calf and set the cloth aside. She didn't trust her voice, so she bowed low, touching her forehead to the mat.

"Don't..." He touched a hand to her shoulder but didn't let it linger. Standing, he cleared his throat louder and took a step from the basin. "I consider you an equal, Princess. A fellow warrior."

Her stomach fluttered. What kind of samurai considered a woman an equal? Memories of their talks on her bridge had her realizing that before he knew of her true identity, he'd treated her with respect. He'd spoken to her as a fellow scholar and artist. In battle, he had fought as a partner rather than a protector.

But now she missed his affection. Did he experience a thrill at her touch? Did he want her like he used to? Like she wanted him now, more than ever?

* * * *

Nothing in any of his training had prepared Takamori for the level of control he had to exercise this moment. Everything in him demanded her. Demanded her lips. Her intimate touch. If he relaxed, he'd shake with the need to bury himself in her heat. He was a fool to visit with her in her chamber.

"Thank you," she said, her rich voice warm silk washing over him. She leaned forward and rose in an undulating shift upward that made him jerk.

He stiffened to semi-hardness in an instant.

"I don't know if I deserve such praise. I'm just me. Just Saiko."

"I don't say this merely as praise, Princess."

"Please call me Saiko." She glided to the hearth and, by demurely inclining her head, indicated he should take his place on the red cushion.

Relieved to have a table between them, he settled to the large pillow and pressed his lips together. She was no longer his *Hashi no Kizoku*. He could meet her halfway. "I don't seek to flatter you, Princess *Saiko*, though you deserve it. I think if people knew of your skill, they'd compare you with the woman samurai, Tomoe Gozen. I do consider you an equal."

Lowering to her cushion, she poured hot water into a large ceramic tea bowl he recognized from the Osaka Castle collection of fine Mino Province pottery. In the bowl, a bamboo tea whisk also received a cleaning.

While discarding the water from the bowl into a waste water basin on the mat, she asked, "If Yagyu Munenori-sensei is such a trusted friend, why didn't you tell him who I am, and why didn't we stay the night?"

"We, you and I, have many enemies right now. I don't know who or where they are, which makes us vulnerable to attack any time we leave the protected walls of a fortress. Munenori-sensei has his wife and many students who are untried in the war arts. We couldn't stay and risk an assault on the school. The less he knows, the safer we keep them." Takamori swallowed, glad for his ability to maintain a reasonable conversation and steady voice when her beauty threatened to rob him of thought. The idea of peeling off her layers of silk and releasing her long hair from its simple knot at the back of her head had him hot and ready.

She resumed her place at the other side of the table. With a tilt of her head, she used a bamboo scoop to measure powdered green tea from a ceramic caddy into the bowl. Her grace and deliberate movements lent her a dancer's quality.

Takamori said nothing, admiring her exact care in using a single tap on the rim to rid the scoop of clinging powder. She poured water from the kettle into the bowl. Her grip appeared dainty, almost inconsequential. Steam sent wisps of loose hair swaying over her small ears and along the sweet curve of her cheeks.

Tilting her head a bit more, she set the kettle onto a small bamboo mat then whisked the tea to a frothy brew. An ethereal smile curved her pretty mouth as she ladled tea into a small cup and handed it to him.

A thrill shivered through him as their fingers brushed. Presenting her a bow of thanks, he waited for her to serve her own tea before using both hands at the rim to bring his cup to his lips. Hot tea, crisp and fragrant with a touch of earthy sweetness, infused warmth into him and increased his alertness.

"I apologize. There's no hanging scroll or flower container for an arrangement," she said. "In this season, I would've chosen well-shaped bare branches and perhaps some long grasses—"

"I can't have this conversation." Takamori closed his eyes for a second, sorry to speak so bluntly and hoping she'd forgive his rudeness.

She blinked then took a sip of tea. "There's a fleeting beauty in winter. Too soon, spring will arrive, but it'll pass—"

"Princess. Saiko. I can't talk of nature with you. Not right now."

"Why not? This is traditional tea conversation."

He set his exceptionally delicious tea onto the table. Should he tell her the truth? Did he dare? Squaring his shoulders, he said, "I can't talk to you of nature's beauty when yours puts all seasons to shame. When yours steals my ability to reason and makes me want you and only you."

"Takamori-san—"

He held up a hand and released a pent breath. "Please. If I don't say this now, I may lack the courage later. Since the moment I saw you that first day on the bridge, I can't stop thinking about you. The more I learn about you, the more you haunt me. I thought I left you in Sumpu, and a part of me stayed there, longing to be with you always." He shook his head. "I can't figure out if you weaken me because a samurai should only have a mind to his lord and his personal improvement, or if you strengthen me because you make me work hard to be worthy of you."

"May I speak?" Her lovely eyes held no censure, though the skin above the slender, sloping bridge of her nose crinkled some.

His stomach churned, but he nodded assent and took up his cup of tea. Would she chastise him? Tell him he was a fool for growing attached to a stranger on a bridge?

"Takamori-san, I didn't want you on my bridge that first day. I'd wanted to be alone. But every day after, I didn't want my bridge *without* you on it. I knew I had to leave. I had to fulfill a duty to shogun, my family, and our nation by moving to Kyōto and serving as consort to the emperor. The last thing I wanted was to meet a samurai who shared my interests. Meet a man who stirred my interest...and more. Meet *you*." She slid her gaze from his chest to the table before her. "But I did, and you made me regret."

His heart skipped a horrified beat. "Regret?"

She put her emptied cup on the table then reached high to free her hair. "Yes. I regret being born into such a powerful family. I regret what I have to do – this political role I'm forced to play."

Her hair fell heavy and straight over her shoulders and spilled down her front, covering the gray clouds and white snowflakes of her kimono's design. She placed two combs and a black lacquered stick next to her cup, and slowly raised her shining eyes to his.

She said, "Because from our first conversation on that bridge, all I wanted to do was to spend as much time with you as the gods would grant me. It occurred to me to defy my father, which I'd never done. The idea of moving to Kyōto, disappearing into the emperor's household, and never seeing you again..." She swallowed then whispered, "Tortures me."

He stilled, afraid to break the magic her words had woven. In a voice rough with need, he asked, "It tortures you?"

Did he dream? Was it a nightmare in the guise of heaven?

Taking as much care as she had in the preparation of tea, she began a lithe cleansing of the tea bowl and bamboo utensils. Her bottom lip trembled.

He realized how much she attempted to hide.

"I can't know how you feel, Takamori-san. As for me, you've claimed my devotion. Whether you meant to or not, you have it. No matter where I am or with whom, for the rest of my days it'll be you who holds my affection. You who has my love."

Love. His mind spun.

Love. Yes.

"I've never met a woman like you. I know I've said it before, but it's never been truer than now." He reached across the table and gently took hold of her wrist.

She stopped cleaning. Her eyes went soft and liquid then she whispered, "Stay. Stay the night with me."

Chapter Eleven

Tomorrow made no promise, and since she couldn't predict what the next day would hold or how long she had with Takamori, Saiko had to cherish every moment. She didn't regret asking him to stay.

The light in his eyes changed from questioning curiosity to tender hunger. He wanted her as much as she wanted him – that much she couldn't mistake.

Taking encouragement from his steady gaze, she withdrew her wrist from his hand and set the cleaning cloth onto the table. Any peace she'd gained from the tea ceremony vanished. Her stomach tumbled and her pulse increased. She gathered her hair behind her neck then brought it over one shoulder to pool in her lap.

When she reached both hands around to untie her wide silver sash, Takamori's eyebrows lifted a fraction. He leaned forward. "My *Hashi no Kizoku*, please give me the pleasure?"

As the image of his hand upon her, undressing her, flashed at the forefront of her mind, a shiver sent goose bumps along her arms. She put her hands on her knees and nodded permission. With a resonance that vibrated throughout, her heartbeat hammered a rhythm reflected in the tremble of her fingers and the throb between her thighs.

His eyes darkened to intense black as he stood. A slight, almost bemused smile softened the lines around his mouth. Then he squatted behind her, and while he untied the bow the maid had fashioned, Saiko fought nerves rent from desire.

He worked the material far more efficiently than she could have with her unsteady hands. Heat from his fingers transferred through the layers of material, making her eager to shed the silk and have his hands upon her skin.

When the sash slackened, she filled her senses with him. He intoxicated her. The scents of rich wood smoke and balmy green tea mingled with the musky, male fragrance of Takamori. As the room began a lazy twirl, cool lips settled into the bared curve where her neck met her shoulder. She closed her eyes and melted.

Their kisses on the bridge had spoken of wishes for a forbidden tomorrow. His caresses upon her thigh as they'd raced for Yagyu Munenori's sword-fighting school had comforted and titillated but reminded her of what she couldn't have. His kiss now, however, promised her desire would be met. If not for a lifetime, at least for tonight.

Joy to meld with him mixed with sorrow over their too-brief time, forming a bittersweet longing so strong she couldn't restrain herself. She twisted into his arms and whispered, "Takamori, my love."

"Saiko." His voice, deep and rough, charged along the skin of her throat like wonderful sparks of electricity. "My lovely Lady of the Bridge. My fearless warrior princess. I'm yours."

He ran warm fingertips from her nape, along the collar of her kimono, to the V in front. Anticipation skittered across her skin, and she shivered with delight. She closed her eyes as he parted the outer silk kimono and slid it over her shoulders then down her arms. The soft, smooth fabric flowed past her fingers like water.

By feel, she found his shoulders while he untied a thin cloth belt holding her under-robes closed. She followed sinewy muscle chorded up the sides of his neck. Tracing the curve of his ears, she smiled a bit at his husky hum of approval.

Tenderly, he skimmed his lips along the sensitive skin just behind her earlobe. A wave of pleasure surged through her, starting where he scattered tiny kisses and rushing to light a fire deep in her belly before returning upward to force an empyrean gasp.

"If only..." she barely managed on a quavering voice, sending hands to his hair.

"Don't," he said against her throat. "Tonight is forever. There's nothing beyond."

Nothing beyond tonight. Endlessly in his arms, in his eyes, lost in his kiss... She traced the tie securing his hair into a topknot and undid it. At the same time, he finished peeling open the front of her multiple *kosode* robes. She combed fingers into his hair, from the hairline at his square forehead to the ends past his shoulders and followed his firm lines downward. She found his *katana* and unfastened its straps.

Takamori took the weapon and laid it upon the *tatami* matting with reverence. Then he bared Saiko to the fire-heated air. Grasping his shoulder, she squeezed her lids tighter, waiting for him to touch her.

He didn't.

His muscles bunched under her fingers as his hands combed into her hair and cupped the sides of her head. He covered her mouth with his. Desire sent a shot of molten need through her veins. Pressing her body against him, she hugged him close. All thought, all worry fled as he tilted his lips over hers – first one way then the other.

More. She needed more of him.

As if reading her mind, he added pressure, urging her to open. She welcomed his tongue inside with a quick inhale. Its tip met hers before entering into a sensual assault that had her surrendering.

Without a mind to it, she instinctively unfastened the sash at his waist. His *kosode* gaped. She splayed her hands on his hard, hot chest. Her exploring fingers told her a story of this warrior's body – the lines speaking of long hours in training, thick muscles attesting to his tremendous strength, and stiff scars telling of injuries won in battle. For a samurai, he'd experienced and accomplished as much as a warrior twice his age.

As soon as the thought occurred to her, it escaped on a sigh as his mouth atop hers conveyed his intent to have her. He groaned low, drawing her bared breasts against his chest. Skin to skin, Saiko sent her hands inside his robe to his broad back and hugged him close. Her head dropped back as he rose slightly higher, the taste of green tea lacing his tongue as she engaged him in the dueling kiss.

She'd dreamt of this since their first meeting. The idea of such intimacy with him had plagued her since their second. And she'd stopped denying how much she wanted him the moment he'd landed atop her during their sparring match. Now, she'd have him. Her dream, her desire met reality, and the reality of him far surpassed her imaginings.

He took her wrists and slowly brought them from around his back. He eased her inner robes down her arms, divesting her of the last of her clothing. Breaking the kiss, she inhaled his rich, male scent.

The fire's heat touched her bared body. It intensified her awareness. It made her want his eyes on her. Want his approval. Want his need to match hers.

"You complete me," she said, touching one hand to the place over the center of her greatest affection while placing the other at his muscled side. Passion's juices dripped along her inner thigh, proof of how much she needed to connect with Takamori.

His eyes narrowed and his lips parted, as if she'd said something deeply profound. He settled his rough, thick palm over the hand covering her heart. He whispered, "How will I let you go?"

She shook her head. "Don't think of that. Remember, tonight is forever."

"Right." Not taking his eyes from hers, he combed fingers through her hair. He leaned away, shrugging off his robe to reveal his brown, samurai's physique. His gaze caressed her body. "You're so lovely."

Under his languid perusal, Saiko trembled. The pucker of

his bottom lip and the slight lift of his eyebrows let her know he liked what he saw. In response, her nipples tightened and a weight settled low in her belly.

His eyes narrowed a moment before he took her under the arms and drew her onto his lap. Her sensitive breasts pressed against him. She straddled his thighs, thrilling as his hard length jutted into the juncture of her legs. She wanted him in her, but she didn't want to rush. One night had to be everything, and she savored each moment. Each look. Each touch.

She grasped his shoulders and arched as he ran both hands first over her breasts then around back to skim fingertips up her spine. He smoothed them down, cupped her rear end, and stood. She gasped. Saiko hugged him around the neck. Wrapping her legs around his hips, she placed kisses along the side of his neck.

At the other end of the room, he stopped. He brushed his lips across hers until she whimpered, wanting more. With a hand in the hair at the back of his head, she held him while deepening the kiss. He parted for her, devouring her.

Lost in him, she didn't realize he unrolled her mattress with his feet until he lowered her to it. This end of the chamber didn't enjoy as much warmth from the fireplace, but the cooler temperature felt good in contrast to his heat as he stretched over her. His lips never left hers while his hands began a sensual exploration. Adoring the freedom such intimacy afforded, she let her fingers learn his every line and plane.

His caresses and occasional grazes over her nipples shot bolts of excitement through her. She squirmed with need. She wrapped her arms and legs around him, unable to get enough of touching him. Being touched by him. Loving him.

"Takamori," she said on two broken breaths. "Please."

He dipped his face into the curve of her neck and planted a gently sucking kiss on her tender skin. Sliding down her body, he lowered his mouth to one nipple and gave it a tender bite.

Her excitement thrummed electric. Charges of need zapped awareness over the skin of her arms and legs, sending the fine hairs on end. Quivering, she cried, "I need you!"

"Patience, Saiko," he said, his lips on her breast and the vibration of his voice creating an uncomfortable hardness to her nipple.

He took it between his teeth then drew it into his mouth. He worked it against the roof of his mouth with his tongue, turning discomfort into an intensifying sensation tied directly to the tugging, growing weight in her womb.

Gasping, she tangled her fingers into his hair and arched. Her need bordered on painful. The throbbing between her thighs demanded relief.

"I need you. Now." Saiko slipped the heels of her feet behind his knees.

Releasing her nipple, he licked his way to the other and slid a finger into her slick, waiting folds. She cried out, but his intimate caress didn't give her what she sought.

"Please," she begged, near to tears in her need. Reaching between them, she stroked his rigid length.

Takamori lifted, his dark eyes meeting hers. A section of hair fell forward to rest on his cheek. "I need you too, Saiko."

He devoured her lips in a slow, sensuous kiss as he tilted his hips and fitted his tip to her wet opening. When he met with her barrier, he froze. Gradually, he lifted his face and gave her a penetrating stare. "You're untouched."

"Touched only by you," she whispered, her voice thick.

"Does the emperor know?"

"I don't know. I don't care." Tightening her hold on his shoulders, she urged him further. A slight burning began.

He didn't move. "Saiko. Princess, you—"

"Takamori, I love you. Don't let me suffer. Make me yours."

He squeezed his lids closed, his features developing an edge, as if in pain.

A dagger pierced her desire and rent it into a shred of sadness. Unable to bear his rejection, she lowered her lashes.

"Look at me," he said, inching backward.

"No." Her voice broke on a sob.

"Shh." He tipped her chin until her eyes met his. His stare softened but didn't waver. "I'm sorry."

He pushed past her barrier. Pain burned like fire. Saiko sucked air between her teeth and dug fingertips into his shoulders.

As he eased inside, she inhaled sharply. The pain didn't increase. Her stomach tensed while the woodsy scent of his skin filled her senses. Her need overrode her nerves, and he captured her mouth once again. Moving her hands from his hair to his shoulders, she tilted her hips further.

He moaned against her lips, and she answered in kind. Touching her tongue to his top lip, she opened for his invasion. Her body shuddered with need as he slid deeper while accepting her invitation, his tongue sweeping inside to dance with hers.

Her womb grew heavier with need. The burning decreased. The repetitive grip and release of her walls around his hard length sent waves of pleasure pulsating through her. Muscles in her stomach, arms and legs tightened. Her lungs labored.

He seated his length fully inside her and broke the kiss. He rose above her, his elbows locking.

His gaze, black and steady, connected her to him in a deeper way than their joining. As though he cradled her love in his hands. As though their souls mingled and became one.

The pain subsided altogether, and her passage began to pulse around his unmoving member. Changing her hold on his shoulders from a grip to a caress, she offered what she hoped passed for a smile.

Takamori didn't smile in return. His forehead wrinkled, and he withdrew then met the unrelenting entrance to her womb with his tip.

Saiko groaned, partly with renewed pain but mostly from pleasure. Her walls grasped his length then released. Her moan mingled with his.

Her lungs labored for air, and perspiration formed a cooling layer of moisture along her hairline and upper lip. In her, he began a rhythm that had her tensing with anticipation.

She couldn't guess at what, but instinct had her straining for it. Straining for him.

She met each of his thrusts with a tilt of her pelvis. Faster and faster. Harder and harder until whimpers of pleasure escaped her lips to join his panting breaths.

As pressure built, she sensed she approached an enigmatic goal. She reached for it with everything in her. When she thought it would elude her, it hit her so hard it knocked the air from her lungs.

Release. Pure, jolting release slammed into her with the force of a tsunami. It ripped her essence from her body, suspending her in midair where ecstasy shook her soul until she melded with Takamori. Heart to soul, her body joined to his, Saiko became part of him. Accepted him as part of her.

He was hers. She was his. For that moment, all was right in her world.

The intensity grew to more than she could bear, wetting her eyes. Not wanting to cry, she closed her lids and tried to will the moisture away. Tears slipped from the outer corners anyway, and she turned her face, hoping he didn't witness her weakness.

"I'm sorry for hurting you," he said, freeing his length from her body and lowering to the futon beside her. He attempted to gather her into his arms, and she resisted a moment before curling into his warm embrace.

Shifting with a wince as her newly used passage pulled painfully, she pressed her cheek to his chest.

She envied him. He controlled his own destiny, while others had predetermined hers. While hers, apparently, had doomed her to a life spent servicing a man, an emperor, whose ideals and lifestyle she despised.

"Saiko-san—"

"I think I just experienced heaven. I don't want this life in Kyōto I'm told I must accept and embrace. That if I refuse, I dishonor my family. My country. The very gods." Her voice cracked, and she rolled over. She slowly shook her head then combed hair off of her face. As she stared into wavering flames in the fireplace, he pulled her against him and held her close. She whispered, "You brought me such joy tonight, and I don't want to give you up."

She tucked angry fists under her chin. Her hated future warred with the sheer pleasure of what they'd shared and of being at his side this night. It warred with the rare freedom to speak her mind. She wiped moisture from her lashes with her knuckles.

He took her wrist and drew it across his chest, bringing her around so her cheek rested on his shoulder. "Honor is important. It separates us from the animals and acts as the foundation of our humanity. Without it, people would do as they please and chaos would rule."

"So you'll say goodbye to me then, with no hesitation?" she asked. His arms around her somehow eased the sting of fear for an impending separation...for the moment.

His hold tightened a bit, but he didn't answer.

"Takamori-san?"

"I can't say what I feel."

Saiko sank an elbow into the futon, resting her cheek on her palm and studying the sharp angles of his face. "Because you don't know what you feel?"

"Because what I want to say – what I want to do – goes against everything I stand for. It goes against everything I've been taught to value and everything I've fought for." Confusion and suffering eddied in his black depths.

She smoothed fingertips along his forehead where the skin buckled above his eyebrows. "I love you."

He released an anguished sigh and turned his eyes to the ceiling. "Disgrace is a samurai's greatest fear, yet I lie here trying to deny that I'm prepared to bring it on us both."

"You are?" She placed her cheek upon his firm shoulder and hugged him, eager for the words she longed to hear.

* * * *

Don't say it. Did he dare admit he couldn't let her go? That the idea of saying farewell threatened to destroy him? *Don't say it.*

"I love you," he said instead. He kissed the top of her head. "We have this night."

"Yes." Her voice had softened, the edge of remorse now gone. "Can we live only in the moment?"

"I can. For now." He wished he knew how long *now* would last. Closing his eyes, he soaked in the feel of her silken, warm skin against him. "It's not good to guess what'll happen."

"There's no need to guess. We know what'll happen. Heartache." She hugged him closer.

"Maybe. Maybe not." The love he had for her overpowered every lesson and value instilled in him since childhood. Takamori had never experienced anything like it. Never suspected such a human connection could exist.

Legendary love stories spoke of it, but to him, they were simply stories made up because people needed to believe in something greater than what real life had to offer. She made him realize it could really happen.

Saiko was no goddess nor did she have superhuman abilities. The woman in his arms, however, was a warrior princess. She held a position that allowed her to influence Japan's political environment. After such an attack, he imagined all eyes faced Osaka.

What would be said of him? He'd practically announced his love for her on the street below the castle. Did the people call him a fool? What kind of samurai let a woman sway his purpose?

Yet Saiko wasn't any woman. She had courage and fierceness. She had honor and a tremendous sense of duty. Guilt pierced his gut at the knowledge that her love for him caused her to consider jeopardizing that honor and duty. Because of him, she might face *hara-kiri* by demand of her father or the emperor.

Yet she loved him. Despite the forces in their lives making a love between them impossible, they had become one will. One desire.

No longer did he consider it weakened or hindered him. Not now. In fact, he experienced the opposite. In battle, in conversation, in bed, she partnered him to perfection, and made him a better man, a better samurai than before.

"My *Hashi no Kizoku*, you've changed me. I don't know what'll happen, but you're mine."

"I'm yours," she whispered then pressed her soft lips to his.

How long before this heaven on earth faced its trial when her father rightfully accused them of betrayal? Disloyalty? Maybe even treason?

Chapter Twelve

Saiko chanced a peek at Takamori's mouth, wishing they could secret away so he could use it on her. Passing through a stone and iron gateway, she took an opportunity to brush fingers against his. They continued into another area of maze-like walkway where soldiers atop castle walls observed their progress.

"This was an easy fortress to defend," said Takamori. "The only reason we overtook it was because we had so many. No castle could've withstood an assault by two hundred thousand samurai." He pointed to a square opening high in the wall on the right where a soldier offered a slight nod. "Its design is excellent, well thought-out. We could use arrows against attackers who made it past the first gate. There are gates barring the way to each of the five inner circles, stopping invaders and allowing us to prevent them from reaching the center where everyone and everything important is kept."

"Isn't it the point of defense to keep the enemies *out*?"

"Of course. After I took possession, sometimes I had fewer men than we needed. Those inner defenses were essential. When I had sufficient resources, we met the enemy outside and used the castle at our backs."

"So if an army arrived today..."

"We'd have no choice but to use the inner defenses." His lips pulled into a hard line.

"It's possible? If the army that attacked yesterday morning

follows us..."

"My contingent follows, too. So yes, it's possible they could trace the steps of my men to find you. At least we'll have my soldiers and samurai to add to the numbers already here serving Osaka Jodai."

"Will it be enough?"

"It'll have to be. We have the advantage of you, my warrior princess. We can't lose." He took her hand in both of his and gently squeezed.

She didn't want him to let go, and she sighed when he did. Men watched from above, so he shouldn't have shown such affection in the first place. Inside, she yearned for the freedom to openly love this man who had become her world. With a gentle ache in her chest, she fell into step beside him and shoved her hands into the down-filled sleeves of her coat.

As the sun slowly made its way from its midmorning position to a place overhead, Takamori walked her through the castle's winding, walled corridors. He pointed to landmarks, helping her identify each location. He showed her how to work the inner gates. Finally, when midday brought more warmth than chill, he led Saiko to a guard tower.

"This is where the weapons are kept," he said, opening a door at the base. Inside, he lit a lantern while she closed the door.

A thrill shimmied through her at the realization that her wish had come true. They were alone. In two steps, she reached him while unfastening her quilted wrap. When he turned from the lantern, she took his cold face between her warm hands and kissed him.

A low moan rumbled from his throat as he slipped his arms inside her gaping coat. Holding her close, he assumed control and mastered her into delightful submission. He used his height to bend her slightly backward. His strong hands supported her when her knees softened. He urged her to open, inhaling sharply through his nostrils and touching his tongue to hers.

She didn't mind his cold nose nor the hardness of his

armor. She could only think of how much she liked the taste of tea in his kiss. How much she wanted to give him her heat. How much she wanted to run to her chamber, strip naked, and crawl into bed with him. She adored time alone with him.

He released her mouth and rested his forehead against hers. "I've been wanting to do that since I left your bed last night."

Saiko smiled, the warmth of connection blossoming in her stomach. "I didn't like waking this morning to find you gone. It helps to know you've wanted the same as I have."

"You and I are the same."

"Two halves of a whole." She stared into the endless depths of his dark eyes.

His hot exhale caressed her cheek, and he lifted his forehead from hers. "Back to our task. It's important that you know the layout of the armory."

"Then you do expect an attack." She shivered. Her tremble had nothing to do with the temperature. Nevertheless, she closed her coat and secured its tie.

"I have to." The lines around his mouth grew hard. "Even if one doesn't come, it's better to be prepared."

A dark dread squeezed her hope. She nodded and paid close attention while he explained how weapons were placed and how to detach them from their racks. He showed her a cabinet at the rear where stored quivers containing fifty arrows each lined its shelves. Against the tall wooden repository leaned bows in a neat row. They made her want to choose one and have an afternoon target practice.

She suspected she'd have no time, if the sound of hooves passing on packed earth was any indication. Her stomach fluttered. She shared a quick look with Takamori then hurried to hold the door while he extinguished the lantern.

*   *   *   *

"You're alive," screamed Okiko, nearly falling off of the

horse she shared with a dark, scowling samurai. "I saw an arrow in your head, then the marshal scooped you off the road, and I didn't know if you were hurt or dead or—"

The fierce samurai eased Okiko to the ground, his hands under her arms while he said, "As you see, Princess Saiko is well."

"No thanks to you!"

Saiko chuckled. She had never seen her friend in such a fit. "I survived thanks to your extraordinary way with hair."

Her lady-in-waiting spun and wrapped arms about her shoulders.

The samurai rolled his eyes then dismounted. He approached Takamori but didn't say a word. Instead, he crossed his arms over his chest and glared at Okiko.

"What an ordeal," said Okiko. She regained her composure with a comical wiggle, and offered a perfect bow. Then her posture sagged like a half-cooked noodle. "I'm so glad to be here and see you're safe."

Takamori's man crossed muscular arms over his thick chest and scowled.

Saiko stifled a smile. "Yes. I'm sure you had a difficult journey."

"You can't know." Her friend lifted a bag with wooden handles from the saddle as though it weighed fifty pounds. Placing a dramatic hand on her forehead, she shuffled toward an inner gate like an old woman. "Please tell me we don't have a long walk to our quarters."

"It isn't too long," promised Saiko.

Takamori leaned near and whispered, "Take her to your chamber so she can rest. I'll find you after I receive Hoshihiro-san's report."

She nodded. She hurried to her lady and put an arm around her narrow shoulders. Accompanying her up a winding walkway, she asked, "Did you stop at Yagyu Munenori-sensei's school?"

"Yes. It was the only tolerable part of our trip. I wanted to stay longer, but that hardheaded samurai insisted we leave the moment the sun rose. He rode us relentlessly and refused to let me rest more than three times." Okiko's voice quavered in agitation.

"Three times? How'd you manage?"

"Well, I'm stronger than I look." She straightened, lifting her chin. "I didn't let that stubborn samurai see me cry, and I never complained that he didn't feed me."

With a solemn nod, despite a desire to laugh, Saiko gave her lady-in-waiting a pat between the shoulder blades. "You're the finest of ladies, and I commend you for suffering with such grace. I'm glad you're here."

"How'd you ever get along without me?" Her friend fingered a strand of Saiko's hair and pursed her lips. "You had no one to dress your hair?"

"I had help. There are maids here, but nobody can do what you do so well. Thank the gods I only had to do without you for one night." They reached the jodai's main residence at the center, and she held out an arm to indicate they should go inside.

Okiko raked the five-story structure in an assessing glance. "It's not as well-appointed as Sumpu, but I suppose it'll serve."

Saiko chuckled. Bright sunlight shone on green rooftops and eaves that curved and arched in delightful style, giving the tower an almost flower-like appearance. "Any fortress would have difficulty comparing to Sumpu. Considering the violence this place has seen, the reconstruction has been impressive." She slid her feet from her sandals and left the pretty platforms near the door. A servant opened the entrance with a bow too deep and enthusiastic, and she passed inside. She didn't miss her friend's raised eyebrows, however. "Come with me, Okiko-san. I'm well pleased by the elegance and offerings of the interior."

Her lady left her boots outside then gave the place a once-over. She eyed painted paper screens, ran a fingertip along the edges of fine lacquer boxes on display, and offered an approving nod toward a number of pristine suits of samurai armor on stands at various points along the walls. "It's clean. It'll do."

"My chamber's on the third level. Can you make it that far, or should I summon a servant to carry you?" Saiko led the way up a wooden staircase. A small spurt of laughter escaped, and she disguised it in a fake cough.

Her lady-in-waiting huffed an indignant burst of air through her nostrils. "Carry me, indeed. You don't know my strength, Your Highness."

Glad her friend had missed her mirth, Saiko said, "I've always suspected you hid great strength of will."

Okiko said nothing as they reached the second floor and traveled a white hallway lit by open windows on each end. At a stairway halfway along, she said, "Your father's soldiers follow. I never observed them, but that impossible samurai said so."

"You trust what he says?"

"Of course." Okiko waved an impatient hand.

A maid wearing a simple smoke-gray cotton kimono, bare feet, and a solemn expression descended above them. Three steps from the base, she offered a formal bow.

Saiko and her lady bowed in return, taking a step back. The servant bowed repeatedly while passing. Okiko cleared her throat, but Saiko cleared her throat too and tried to appear as if nothing happened out of the norm.

When the maid moved out of earshot, Saiko climbed to the next level. "You seem so upset by him."

"Well, maybe not *so* upset."

"What's his name?"

"Hoshihiro-san."

"It's good to know you came to friendly terms with the marshal's man."

"*Friendly* terms? With that stubborn samurai?" Her friend snorted, though her tone held a quality that spoke more of familiarity than irritation.

At the door to her chamber, Saiko paused. "You have his name, so you must've talked."

"What else did we have to do? Two days, Princess. Two days with that obstinate man." Her lady-in-waiting tilted her head to an indignant angle and planted a hand on her hip. A twinkle glistened in the lady's dark eyes.

"Two days without talking? No. I can understand how you wouldn't survive that." She suspected her lady had affection for the samurai, which could work in Saiko's favor when Okiko learned of Takamori's attentions.

"I could...okay, maybe not. There were times..." Her friend's cheeks pinked. She said in a conspiratorial whisper, eyes wide, "When we had to be silent and still for our safety. It was a dangerous ride."

Saiko clamped her lips to prevent a smile. Her solemnity in place, she indicated the door. "Come in and rest."

Her maid slid dark wood aside, and *tatami* matting created a comforting shushing sound against the bottom panel. Heat from her fireplace met them, rushing past their faces into the chill hallway. As she stepped inside, the straw issued a shifting crackle both familiar and comforting.

"Princess, Osaka Jodai honors you with this chamber."

Saiko followed and closed the door. She avoided looking toward the far corner where her bedding waited along with memories of Takamori's lovemaking. He wouldn't come to her tonight. Not now that her lady had arrived.

"I'll make tea," said Okiko as she set her bag against the hearth.

"I don't mind making it. You're clearly exhausted."

Her lady hesitated. Standing a bit straighter, she said, "I'm being selfish and I'm sorry. You've suffered as much as I, yet I'm going on and on about my ordeal. I'm a sorry excuse for a lady-in-waiting." She executed a deep, formal bow.

Saiko returned the bow but shook her head. "You've tolerated unpleasant surprises and trying circumstances better than most. I consider you a friend. It would sadden me if I thought you couldn't speak honestly to me."

A slight smile softened her friend's visage. Her shoulders relaxed, and she pointed to a bright red cushion on the floor. "Please. I'll make tea. Now you tell me of *your* ordeal...if you want."

"I call it more of an adventure than an ordeal."

"Adventure. Ordeal. Epic tale?"

"Perhaps one day." Saiko laughed. She told of her dash across the grassy field and using her bow to help her flee with Takamori. Her lady-in-waiting offered wide-eyed glances and commiserating sounds while she boiled water and readied tools.

"Yagyu Munenori-sensei was a most gracious host. He provided tea and food. His home gave us a chance to thaw and rest." She smiled as Okiko nodded agreement.

Her lady set out her tea table and settled to a cushion. "Where'd you stay the night?"

Saiko lowered her eyes as a thrill heated her cheeks. "We arrived in Osaka near dusk. I slept here."

"In one day? I thought my samurai was too implacable. Did you plead for rest to no avail?"

She shook her head. "Our journey became a race for our lives. We couldn't stop."

"You were pursued the entire way?" Her friend's hands stopped.

"No, but my enemies knew where I traveled. They awaited me in Osaka's streets when we arrived."

"Not *your* enemies, Your Highness. Who can find fault with you?"

Everyone if she ever revealed the truth of her desire. She gripped a steadying hand around her upper arm. "You're correct. I'm a pawn in a political power bid. This doesn't lessen the threat to my life, however."

Her lady-in-waiting returned to her endeavor, pouring steaming water into a tea bowl. "Takamori-san protected you from rogue warriors waiting here to attack you?"

Her stomach tensed at the memory. "I'm using skills I learned in Mito while living with Yorifusa-san. We fought together. We saved each other."

Okiko's whisk stopped. "Epic tale, indeed. Is this why servants in this castle treat you with deference suited to an empress...or legendary Lady Samurai?"

Saiko chuckled. She told her friend about the dragonflies.

"You made a two-day journey in one, fought at the side of your shogun father's own marshal, and met mystical dragonflies in Osaka before gaining victory over *ronin*? Two of you against how many?" She handed over a serving of swirling tea.

Saiko accepted her cup. "Put that way, I sound legendary to be sure." It certainly hadn't seemed so at the time.

"I'm serious. How many did you face yesterday evening?"

She shrugged. "It was dark, and shadows made it difficult to tell. Maybe five."

"I can't believe so few met you."

"Believe it. I only saw three. Besides, we had the advantage on horseback since they fought on foot."

"The dragonflies surely brought you good fortune. No need for retreat. An omen of success sent by the gods."

Saiko sighed. "I can't forget them or pretend it was coincidental. The dragonfly is Shogun's symbol of victory. For so many to meet us at an ambush where we defeated our attackers is a portend I refuse to ignore."

"It explains why you're treated with such exuberant veneration." Okiko shifted from her cushion and stood. She lapsed to her knees and executed a bow of deepest esteem where she touched her forehead to her fingers splayed upon the floor. "You're blessed by the gods."

Saiko stiffened. "Please rise. Your honor is misplaced. I've done nothing extraordinary. I defended against those who sought to harm me. I'm still me, Saiko, the retired shogun's youngest daughter and pawn to all...including our precious gods." Gods who had seen fit in their cruel games to bend her admiration toward a man she couldn't have.

Her door slid, and Takamori stood at attention. He had shed his armor and wore a white *kosode* with white sash and socks. He bowed in courtesy and entered. "What's this?"

Her lady-in-waiting rose and offered him a bow identical to that bestowed upon Saiko. "You walk with the gods, noble warrior."

"Do I?" A glint of humor shined in his dark eyes.

Saiko raised a hand in surrender and inclined her head toward a blue silk pillow next to hers. "I tried to dissuade her. Join us for tea?"

"There's no need for this formality," he said to Okiko, answering her bow by offering a shallow one. He approached with the smooth power of a tiger, his socks quiet on softly rustling *tatami*. He sank with graceful strength into a cross-legged sit upon the cushion.

Saiko's stiffened at his proximity. Her soul reached out to him in a way her body was forbidden. When his eyes met hers, she bit her lip to prevent a smile of joy to have him near.

Her lady regained her seat. Her face rosy on a blush, she prepared a second batch of tea.

"Can you share with me what Hoshihiro-san had to report?" Saiko brought her cup to her lips to hide their trembling. How would she survive these nights, mindful of Takamori's presence and unable to lie in his arms? So close, and now, beyond her reach. She couldn't bear it.

"It's my pleasure. A small band follows a few hours behind, if my second-in-command was able to release them from yesterday morning's battle. Shosan-san sent a messenger to Sumpu to alert your father. The remainder of my contingent should arrive the day after tomorrow with the palanquin and emperor's representatives."

If they survived? She closed her eyes and shuddered.

"I see what you think. Those *ronin* came after *you*. I'm confident they withdrew when they discovered their target had escaped."

"If you're right, they know I'm here."

He gave a curt nod. "The ambush outside these castle walls yesterday tells us as much."

A clatter at her tea table let her know Okiko hadn't considered any of this. Her lady's face had gone two shades paler as she grasped her dropped tea scoop with quivering fingers.

"We're safe," she reassured her friend. "Osaka Castle is a fortress."

Okiko added tea to water in the *chawan*. "For now, but Suzuki Shosan sent word to Sumpu. Surely your father wants you in Kyōto to meet your obligation to the emperor. What'll happen to us when we continue your journey?"

Her father loved her, no matter his sense of honor. Surely he would delay her trip until her safety could be secured. Wouldn't he?

"We talked about this." Takamori looked directly at her, and a hardness set in at the outer edges of his eyes. "We may yet face our fiercest fight."

Chapter Thirteen

A sun ablaze at a lavender horizon marked an end to Takamori's day. He closed his window's shutter then added a log to his fire.

Osaka Jodai had provided him luxurious accommodations as befitted his position as Shogun's marshal. His chamber appeared a world away from a shared common room where he'd lived last year with two other ranking samurai a couple sections out from this castle center. Unfortunately, his tortured heart drained any enjoyment of visiting as an honored guest.

Much like Princess Saiko's chamber situated along the same hallway, his room boasted a large fireplace, premium *tatami* flooring, and fine lacquered furnishings. His bamboo-covered walls, however, gave an illusion of closeness despite his room's spaciousness.

He lit a lamp and set it on a waiting tray before his fire where a large bowl of rice beckoned to his grumbling stomach. He only managed to down half its contents when his restless nerves demanded he stand and move.

Pacing appeased him, but not for long. Soon, he left his room and strode the hallway. Women's voices softly emanated through rice paper panels in Saiko's door. Though he couldn't interpret their muffled words, he took comfort in listening. Out a window, the sun made its final, wavering descent.

Dusk cast the hallway into variant shadows until a servant arrived and lit wick boxes set on wall posts between each room. Still, Takamori remained. Her voice comforted him. Her tone and inflection had grown dear to him. He took satisfaction in knowing she remained safe within this fortress he had fought so long to hold.

Night pushed dusk's last light into oblivion, and he secured the window's shutter. Saiko's chamber had succumbed to silence. A flicker of firelight danced upon her door's white panels, but nothing else stirred within. Still, he couldn't bring himself to retire. He stood for long minutes, hoping against reality that she'd emerge.

After a time, he sighed and padded along the corridor's pristine hardwood floor to his door. A final glimpse of hers assured him all was well, and he reluctantly entered his chamber.

Inside, he stared at fluttering amber and China blue flames slowly eating at thick timber. He dreaded sleepless hours plagued by memories of his beautiful warrior princess wrapped around him.

His door slid, gently scraping its wooden runner. Takamori startled and put a hand to his sword's hilt.

"I'm sorry," whispered Saiko, clutching with slender, tapered fingers the silk-trimmed neckline of her loosely tied white robe. Her black hair hung loose from a center part, sweeping down her temples and delicate cheeks. Her eyes, soft and thoughtful, glanced toward her chamber. "I didn't mean to alarm you."

"Please come in," he urged. As she did, he stepped to her side and closed his door. He gripped his *katana* to keep from reaching for her. "Is something wrong?"

She ducked and chuckled. "Everything's wrong."

He ushered her to his fireplace and positioned two large pillows so they could sit. From his dinner tray, he poured *sake* into a small cup and handed it to her. Then he settled beside her. "Nothing's easy."

She sipped and winced then put a warm hand atop his. "In all my life, one thing has been easy. Effortless, in fact."

"What has?"

"Falling in love with you. I fought it, but not hard. Really, I couldn't help it."

He smiled. "Yes. It's the same for me."

"This afternoon, you said we face our fiercest battle." She set aside her *sake* and faced him. "You didn't speak of the emperor's supporters, did you?"

"No. I didn't."

"My father?"

"Saiko-san, my love. I go against my upbringing and training to even say so, but I begin to doubt if I can deliver you into the hands of another man. Perhaps at the end of this, *I'll* be a lordless *ronin*." Or dead.

"Then you're right." Her bottom lip quavered. "A fiercer battle you couldn't face. You go against Emperor Go-Mizunoo *and* Shogun in this. How can you hope to win?"

"I don't." His stomach twisted, but he stifled the weakness.

She leaned forward, placing her head on his chest and sagging against him. "I couldn't endure living a single day with the knowledge that you died for me."

"What else is there?" He hugged her close and touched his cheek to the top of her head. Returning her to Sumpu would only postpone these events already set in motion. With or without Takamori, Tokugawa Shogun would ensure Japan's peace by delivering her to Kyōto. He no longer had an option.

"We should leave." The desperation in her quiet voice touched his soul.

"And go where?" He searched his mind for a place - one place - they could live in peace.

"Korea."

What? "We can't escape to Korea."

"Why not?" She sat on her heels and scanned his face.

"I'm Shogun's marshal. I know nothing but warfare and those studies that refine my mind. I'm fit only to serve Korea's emperor."

"You can't. It would be a direct insult to my father and my brother, Hidetada. My brother may only be shogun in name right now, but one day he'll rule Japan."

"It would be an insult to Japan," he said with a nod. "I'm

willing to sacrifice much, but not our dignity. Not our people's honor."

"Can't you teach like Yagyu Munenori?"

"Who in Korea would want to learn our way? They learn their own." He schooled his expression to ensure fear and frustration didn't show.

"Then where can we go?" She straightened and searched his gaze.

He shook his head. China would reduce them to refugees – not a life for a warrior of standing and a princess of learning and great skill. The heathen country north of China offered only squalor and ignorance, both of which they abhorred. They had nowhere to run.

"No," she whispered, her eyes growing glassy.

Takamori's chest constricted under the weight of his limitation. He smoothed hair from her cheek and tucked it behind one ear. "Would the gods bind us this tightly without a plan to aid us toward a life together?"

"Yes," she answered. "You speak of gods who snatch the life of a babe after allowing his mother months to fall in love with him. Gods who send walls of water from the sea to wash away whole villages."

"Gods who taught us how to cultivate crops, work metal, and create fabric. Gods who balance harmony between nature and us. We can't think we're nothing to them."

Her eyes dried without a tear spilled. "I'm ungrateful."

"You're frightened," he said quietly, understanding better than he wanted her to suspect. "We have much to lose."

She nodded, her eyes downcast. "When the time comes, we'll both do what we must. I only hope what we must do is stay together."

*   *   *   *

His unsmiling lips drew Saiko's focus.

She inhaled sharply as her body quickened. "I've never had

more to lose."

He closed their short distance and claimed her mouth. He tilted his face over hers. A thrill sent her blood rushing like rivers during rainy season. Her pulse raced, and she throbbed in time to it. Her fingertips. Her throat. Swelling folds between her thighs. Everything.

He added pressure to his kiss, and she opened. Eager for his exploration, she touched her tongue to his. He moaned, sending fingers into her hair.

As food refreshed her body and sleep refreshed her mind, Takamori refreshed her soul. If only they could've remained on her bridge in Sumpu forever. If only she had a different father, a different life, and hope for happiness.

In his arms at this moment, she had a taste. She needed more, though. She needed to submerge herself in him. To soak him up and fill her emptiness with his completing love.

She shrugged from her robe, baring her breasts. Engulfed in his kiss, she eased off of her pillow and onto his lap. His weapons were absent, though she couldn't recall him removing them. Heat from his legs penetrated his kimono to warm her hips while the fire radiated hot air to her back.

She wrapped her legs around him, unable to get as close as she wanted. Their tongues danced. His flavor of sweet rice and dried cherries mixed with her *sake* to form an intoxicating savor.

His skin carried the fresh scent of outdoors. She reached up and freed his topknot's tie. His hair fell to his shoulders, adding the smell of wood smoke and a hint of incense to the air around them.

He skimmed his hands up the middle of her back then gathered her hair over one shoulder. He released their kiss and focused attention on working his lips along the exposed skin of her neck.

Moisture of excitement seeped into her folds, and her nipples hardened to acute awareness. She arched, granting him easier access to her throat.

"Love me tonight," she whispered, closing her eyes.

"Love you forever," he said against her skin.

She slid her fingers into the overlap of his cover, loosening his neckline. Then she reached between them and untied thin cords securing his sash. Her breathing grew faster as she let the cords fall behind him and pulled his sash from around his waist. She tossed it aside, anxious to have him against her, skin to skin.

His robe opened, and she removed it. He traveled to her shoulder, his lips smooth and firm. She delighted in his hard muscles and brown skin. Her hands tingled as she learned his planes and angles, dips and contours.

She inched fingertips over ridges of his abdomen and found his ready length amidst the tousled remnants of kimono covering his thighs. He groaned. Empowered by her ability to give him pleasure, she wrapped her fingers around him. She pressed her breasts to his unyielding chest and planted kisses along a firm sinew stretched taut at his neck.

He gently bit into her shoulder. It didn't hurt but heightened her senses. Her core tightened, and she clung to him. She thrummed with need.

"Wait here," he said, his voice deep and throaty. He let her go and located the sleeves of his kimono.

Unsure what he intended, she released his rigid heat and slid off of his lap to her pillow. She tucked her legs under her hips while he shrugged into his garment and stood.

He strode to a far corner and collected his rolled bed. His member, ready and glistening with a pearl of dew at its tip, jutted past the gaping trim of his open robe.

She couldn't take her eyes from it, so badly did she want him inside her. Over her. Straining above her.

He unrolled his futon in front of the fire then let his kimono fall to the floor. Saiko admired his warrior's body in flickering light of flames. In his armor, he left no doubt of his power. But here before her like this, his strength was apparent rather than implied.

Takamori settled to his knees on the mattress and held out

his arms to her. She didn't hesitate. In an instant, she slid into his bed. Into his embrace and paradise on earth.

Their lips met as she let him lower her. The fire's warmth didn't compare to his inferno, and she combusted under his passionate stare when he broke their kiss to position his body atop hers. Her blood ran like molten lava.

She spread her legs, and he settled between, pressing his tip pressed to her turgid opening. She breathed deeply and relaxed. His intensity held her enthralled. Hiking her knees to his hips, she tilted her pelvis. Her slick opening brought him an inch inside.

The skin across his high cheekbones stretched taut, and he briefly closed his eyes. Then he took her in an open-mouthed kiss and plunged deep.

Her body quivered. Seated fully, he held steady a moment before withdrawing and thrusting. Pleasure sliced into a spiraling coil in her abdomen.

Her entire body thrummed. She closed her eyes as he set a gradually increasing rhythm. Tilting her pelvis, she kept pace. The coil tightened. It clenched her stomach muscles and constricted her lungs.

Each pump of his hips drew her walls into a tighter grip around his steely length. He drew her closer to orgasm's abysmal edge, into a bond more inextricable than she'd ever comprehended possible.

"Yes," he said against her mouth.

"Yes," she answered, meeting each thrust with a rock of her hips.

She grasped his flexing buttocks, needing him to maintain this rhythm. Fearing he would cease. More. More. Almost there.

She approached the pinnacle edge. The pleasure coil tugged insistently at her core. "Now, my love."

He doubled his pace. Unable to match it, Saiko let go of his backside and gripped his shoulders. He pushed her pleasure. Drove her hard.

The coil released.

Pure ecstasy ripped through her.

She arched as she slipped into the abyss, dropping weightless and spinning into a vortex of pure sensation. She hung suspended in pleasure until Takamori's moan of release lifted her out and into his arms. She opened her lids to find him tensed, his head back and his teeth bared. He shook violently then relaxed.

His slight frown stirred a surge of worry. It soon gave way to a peaceful smile, however. Caressing his jaw, she marveled at his male beauty. Melancholia settled a heavy hand into her chest at the idea that she may have to say goodbye to him one day soon, but she would never regret this time. She would treasure it forever.

He withdrew, and she mewled in protest but scooted to give him room to lie next to her. For a long minute, they embraced while recovering.

"You scare me," he said, gathering her close.

"How?" Closing her eyes, she surrendered to the moment, refusing to contemplate a tomorrow without promise. She trailed her fingertips along the lean muscles of his arm.

"I've always understood that as a samurai, I'd likely live a short life. I've never allowed myself to grow attached to anyone or anything. Before I met you, I could let go of everything without regret."

"But I scare you?" She snuggled close. She didn't want to consider a short life for either of them in her current state of bliss.

"Yes. Because you're the one person I couldn't lose. Against my will, you've made a home in my heart. When I lose you, my heart will be ripped out, and I'll never recover."

She sank her teeth into her bottom lip and squeezed her eyes closed. If only she could wish reality away.

He gathered her into his protective embrace. "If I survive. I hope they kill me, though. A life without you will be no life at all."

They. He meant her father's samurai.

Chapter Fourteen

"Two riders approach," shouted a sentry atop the wall-walk that ran adjacent to the road.

Takamori ran the stairs two at a time and joined him. Folding his fingers, he created a tiny hole and looked through. It brought the foremost rider into pinpoint clarity. A Tokugawa dragonfly emblazoned a shoulder plate on the man's armor. He identified their unique custom helmets as belonging to Ryuku and Makoto. "They're mine. Let them in."

He met them inside the gate as the morning grew to full brightness. Their horses stomped and snorted, so he stayed near a stable wall until the samurai had their impatient animals calmed. An Osaka man neared and collected reins, and the warriors dismounted.

"Shosan-san only sent two of you?" asked Takamori.

Makoto doffed his helmet and bowed. A bloody welt marred his cheek from mouth to ear. "No, Marshal. We were five when Shosan-san sent us."

Ryuku unfastened his chinstrap and joined Makoto. "Marshal. *Ronin* are moving toward Osaka in force."

Takamori had feared they'd come, but in force? That meant an army. "What of the remainder of our battalion?"

"Intact and coming this way." Ryuku took off his helmet and waved Makoto toward an outer barracks.

The samurai set off at a limping jog, and Takamori shook his head. "I hadn't expected war when I formed our company to escort Princess Saiko. How close is the *ronin* force?"

"Two days. Perhaps less. Shosan-san organized our men's

course change toward Osaka before Emperor Go-Mizunoo's supporters even realized Princess Saiko had escaped. We're ahead of them, but not by much."

Takamori gave a curt nod. "Go bathe then come to my quarters. You must be hungry. We can eat in my chamber and I'll hear the rest there."

Ryuku bowed and followed Makoto.

At the castle's center, Takamori located a servant and requested a late breakfast delivered to his room. He strode inside and found the jodai taking an accounting of a duty payable to the shogunate in Edo. After providing him a summary, he promised to meet later for a strategy session.

Then he raced upstairs. Outside Saiko's chamber, he hesitated. He'd kept her awake most of the night...a night beyond compare. Did she sleep now? Would her lady-in-waiting give him grief for asking his princess to rise? He rapped lightly upon her door and cleared his throat.

Saiko opened it. Evidence of their sleepless hours showed in purple smudges under her lovely eyes. In spite of her obvious fatigue, she looked beautiful. Her lady had arranged her hair into an intricate design of loops, swags, and weaves that shined with health. Brown and pink cherry tree branches formed a stunning print on her pale blue kimono, and layers of pink and white at her neckline revealed fine robes underneath.

He glanced past her.

"Okiko-san has gone to the laundry to oversee the care of our robes." Her lips curved into a sweet smile. "I hoped you'd visit this morning."

"A visit would delight me but I come on business. Only two of my rear patrol survived. One's injured. The other is to join me in my chamber to finish his report and eat. I want you to join us." He assumed a wide stance and rested a hand at his sash where his *wakizashi's* hilt met the hilt of his *katana*.

"You honor me. Yes, I'll come." She folded her hands together low in an appealing, womanly manner and followed him to his chamber.

Though he appreciated her demure countenance, he regarded it as strangely out of place for her. Of course, it wasn't. As a princess and a lady, such a posture was appropriate. Expected, even.

He knew her, however. He'd fought by her side. He'd connected with her on an infinitely intimate level and respected her intellect and opinion. Like Tomoe Gozen, the woman samurai of renown, she ought to wear *kamishimo* and a samurai sword. She ought to walk by his side, her head held high. Saiko was a warrior worthy of distinction.

Ushering her into his room, he left his door open. He arranged pillows on the floor.

"Have you ordered a screen for me to sit behind?" she asked, moving to his fireplace and reaching toward the heat.

He lost all sense in a vision of her upon his futon, naked and wanting, his fire at her back. He rubbed tired eyes then shook his head. "Until your father either kills me or strips me of my authority, you're my equal. Together, we'll weigh our options and form our plans. No hiding behind a screen. My men need know they can rely on you, too. For that, you must sit before them at my side, open in your opinions and decision-making."

"What of the jodai?" Saiko stepped near. "My situation hasn't changed in anyone's eyes but yours."

"It soon will." He couldn't explain further since servants entered carrying platters and bowls of food, so he told her what he'd learned from Ryuku, instead.

The samurai joined them shortly thereafter, dressed in a plain beige kimono. His still wet hair presented well in a neat topknot. He sank to his knees and touched his forehead to *tatami* matting first in Takamori's direction then to Princess Saiko.

Pleased by the samurai's show of honor to his princess, Takamori indicated they should sit and eat.

"You survived a dangerous run," said Saiko, pouring water in all three cups.

"As did you." Ryuku sat and positioned chopsticks in his

fingers. "We passed the bodies you two left in your wake."

Takamori offered a proud nod toward his princess. "Our high lady here must take credit for our escape. Her skill with the bow is remarkable."

Ryuku's eyebrows lifted, and he offered a slight bow to her. "Remarkable *and* commendable."

"You lost three in your patrol, and Makoto arrived with injuries. Tell us of your ordeal," she said, inclining her head in elegant acknowledgement.

"Suzuki Shosan pulled us from the rear defense as you escaped into the field. He told us you rode for Osaka and instructed us to give chase to defend your back. By the time we organized, Hoshihiro-san had taken Okiko-san onto his horse and followed you. They made it across the grassy flat without incident, but twelve *ronin* beset us halfway across."

Saiko shared a knowing look with Takamori. He nodded. Those additional *ronin* had come after *her*.

"They were upon us before we realized. Otherwise, we would've used bow and arrows to lessen their numbers. Boku-san fell under two swords. Makoto-san and I defeated six before we could turn around and help our remaining men. By then, Jimoshi-san had lost his seat and fought on foot. He killed two then died valiantly from a pike through his chest. Makoto-san and I joined Masashige-san to battle the last four. One, a samurai in red armor and horns on his helmet, was too fierce. We fled, hoping to outride him. He caught us on a rocky ridge at the field's edge. He killed Masashige-san and struck two blows on Makoto-san before I managed a fortunate attack. I sent my short blade into his throat."

"Five against twelve in hand-to-hand combat," said Taka-mori. He truly had the best fighters in the land. "Makoto-san will heal?"

"Yes, Marshal. Bearing scars to make him more fearsome on the battlefield."

"Indeed." Takamori nodded. "I'm impressed by the number of *ronin* gathered in this campaign. An enormous amount of money has paid these mercenaries – enough to form an army."

Saiko set her chopsticks onto a stand beside her bowl. Her graceful eyebrows approached one another, bunching her porcelain skin above her fine nose. "It can't be a daimyo. My brother keeps their duties high to prevent such independent wealth. Even a group of daimyo wouldn't have resources sufficient to amass such a force."

"I agree. This effort is based in Kyōto."

She nodded. "Yes. Someone close to the emperor. Though we must also consider they may act on their own. If they raid farms as they travel, they wouldn't need financial backing."

"All to prevent you from entering Emperor Go-Mizunoo's household?" asked Ryuku. "I understand your move is political, but this seems too extreme."

"In theory, the emperor and Shogun will unite through association when our princess enters Go-Mizunoo's bed." Takamori swallowed water to clear his tongue of rice and vegetables and to hide the fact that he had nearly choked on his last words.

"Such a unity would not bind our leaders beyond a social one," said Saiko, a sour twist of her lips telling him she found the arrangement as distasteful as he did. "I believe there are those who fear I could conceive a son with the emperor."

"I see." Ryuku's features grew stern. "A male child shared by blood between the shogunate and the royal seat would cement the two ruling forces. But why not suspect the emperor himself?"

Takamori set his chopsticks aside then tossed wood on his fire. "The emperor has no motive. In fact, he stands to benefit by this association by receiving concessions from Shogun. We can't negotiate this offensive to a peaceful end, however. Our only course is defense. Was Shosan-san able to estimate their army's size?"

"No, Marshal."

"We have to assume they are more than our numbers," said Saiko. "Every daimyo who had supported the emperor before the Battle of Sekigahara and surrendered his lands and samurai by force have left *ronin* to wander Japan. I identified samurai markings from several different daimyo on the armor of those who attacked us. I suspect far more houses are represented in their number than that."

"Agreed." Takamori rubbed suddenly burning eyes. "I'm preparing to wage battle against the world, it seems."

"My lord?" asked Ryuku.

He didn't miss a loss of color in Saiko's naturally pale face. "We'll have little time to prepare. I can't guess how many wounded we have and how many can still fight."

"Surely Ieyasu-shogun received our message and sends more men." Ryuku scraped the last of his rice to the lip of his bowl and used his chopsticks to shovel it into his mouth.

"We have a day," said Saiko. "Two at most. We can't wait for reinforcements that may not reach Osaka in time. We need to plan now."

Takamori stood. "Seek your rest, honorable samurai. You've fought bravely and served Lord Tokugawa well."

Ryuku stood and bowed deeply at the waist.

"When the remainder of our company arrives, we'll meet again to go over a strategy for defense."

"Yes, Marshal."

Ryuku left, and Takamori fetched a box of writing tools and took it to the table. His extensive experience with warfare hadn't prepared him for the screaming turmoil stabbing his gut at the thought of his gorgeous lady as the sole target of an encroaching army. Saiko stacked dishes out of the way. After spreading a parchment, he set out ink, stone, and brushes.

"This is Osaka's outer castle wall," he said, sending bristles of a brush in an irregular circle in the center.

She dipped another brush in ink and created random lines and blotches around half. "We have streets, buildings, and congested access along these walls."

"And this is where they'll likely attack." He formed a tree line in ink, which edged an open area at the castle's far side.

She strolled around the table and perused the sheet. She

pointed a tapered finger to three street outlets. "Here, here, and here. If we place patrols of twenty each in and around these buildings with archers atop the city-side wall for reinforcement, we can prevent *ronin* from entering the town."

Tracing a fingertip around the outer edge of her drawing, he followed the path they'd likely take after failing to gain entry. He tapped the open space. "We'll focus our main defense at this point. A double row of archers atop that wall. Pike bearers on the ground along the wall facing this tree line."

"If we position additional archers in a complete west-northeast lookout, opposite of that field, we can protect the castle's two main exits and feed horseback samurai into battle." She questioned with a glance.

He nodded. "Two hundred samurai in Osaka's streets. All archers on the walls. Every pike soldier in battle in this field. That only leaves two thousand samurai, including the jodai's, to drive this battle to victory. We'll have no ancillary forces."

She studied his parchment, and he admired penetrating intelligence shining in her eyes. She had a sharp mind, and her brilliant capacity for strategy showed in her astute assessments.

"If we had seven more days...five even..." He crossed his arms and paced to the far end of his chamber.

"True. There's no time for reinforcements to reach us from Edo. By the time my father's forces arrive, I think this'll be finished."

He strode to his makeshift map and tapped his forehead as if it would release the answer he sought.

"Munenori-sensei," she said and sank to the cushion Ryuku had occupied.

"Master Yagyu?" The sword master *had* fought by his side during both Osaka sieges. "He knows Osaka as well as I, but he has a school now. Students. A wife."

She nodded slowly. "Students proficient in *nihonto* – the way of the sword. His school is only hours away."

Munenori *had* offered to help. After two years providing sword instruction and enjoying a peaceful life, he surely grew restless. This would give him the excitement he sought. "I question how many he can bring. Students? Instructors? Men will die."

"If you send a messenger today, and he accepts this challenge, he and his students might have time to prepare and still arrive before the *ronin* reach us. Do we have scouts on watch?"

He nodded. "East, north, and west. I doubt they'll come from the northeast. Too obvious to approach in a straight, frontal attack."

"And they won't come from the south. They'd have to circle the entire way around. It would cost them time and any element of surprise."

He couldn't fight a smile. Beautiful. Brilliant. Highly skilled. Princess Saiko was worthy of an emperor's love, but not as the concubine Go-Mizunoo would make her. She deserved a voice. A chance to affect a difference for Japan and her people beyond a mere association of family.

"Do I amuse you?" she asked, her brow furrowing.

"No." He sank to a squat. He reached across the table and smoothed his thumb over the wrinkle. "Not you. Never will you be a target of ridicule."

One corner of her mouth lifted. "You speak of respect?"

"You've earned it in great measure." He devoured the sight of her lips. He didn't want her to believe his admiration stemmed from their intimate nights, but he had an irresistible need to kiss her.

With his foot, he slid the low table out from between them. He wrapped fingers around the warm, round nape of her neck and urged her near.

"I kiss you *despite* my respect for you," he said quietly, his nose nearly touching hers.

Her dark eyes blinked, emphasizing their stunning slant and laying her black lashes upon her white cheeks for the briefest of touches.

"I kiss you because I *must*."

A closed-mouthed chuckle bubbled a moment before her

lips parted on a lazy smile. "I'm glad you must." She leaned forward and achieved first contact.

Takamori immediately wanted to take her to bed but couldn't, making him grateful for their two delicious nights of lovemaking. She'd honored him, still honored him, and he cherished the memories. Especially since he may never have another opportunity to love her this way again.

Her kiss was sweet, gentle, a butterfly's wings beating softly upon a flower petal. He liked it, but passion stole his patience. He dropped to his knees and pressed deeper into a more intense kiss, pleased she didn't retreat.

She moaned quietly against his mouth a moment before she opened. Welcoming her inside, he met her warm tongue with his. His staff hardened as they began a sensual dance, their lips locked, their breaths mingling.

They had to stop. He groaned. Nobody lingered in his open doorway, but anyone could come any time. He issued a growl and withdrew. He couldn't resist caressing the backs of his fingers along her silken cheek before settling upon his heels.

"I should go," she said. Her gaze held his a moment before descending to her lap.

"You should," he whispered.

"I can't."

He stood and went to her side. His hand on her shoulder, he studied the top of her elaborate coiffure. If she were free of family and political obligations, their life would have much different prospects.

"Have you been practicing?"

She nodded. "The *yawara* forms are comforting in their familiarity."

"Go practice now. Archery, *nihonto*, and *yawara*. We can't guess what'll happen, so we should prepare for anything." Takamori closed his eyes, wishing he could spare her this but unable to dismiss her from it. She brought skills to battle. Besides, he suspected she wouldn't hide if he asked. He slid a hand under her arm and helped her rise.

"This'll be worse than the ambush at Kameyama."

"Yes." He tilted her chin with his finger, urging her to meet his eyes. "But we'll be ready this time. They no longer have surprise on their side."

As she glided to his doorway, silk threads shimmered in her kimono and decorations glittered in her hair. Anyone catching a glimpse of her would recognize her position as princess. Few, however, would guess at the warrior lurking within her fine and gentle countenance.

Chapter Fifteen

"I wish I had my own weapon." Saiko gave her borrowed bow a shake and rubbed her red, stinging forearm. "And I need an armguard."

"I don't think this activity befits a princess readying to join the emperor's household." Okiko took the bow and let loose an invisible arrow.

"Nonsense. If I don't practice, how will I perform in archery contests? The finest ladies compete in Kyōto."

"Harrumph. Your time would be better spent on music or painting or practicing your writing."

"Forming characters or composing poetry?"

"Both."

"You sound like Master Hayashi." Saiko planted a hand on her hip. She closed her eyes and turned her face to the warm sun, enjoying its heat on her skin.

"You need something here." Okiko turned the bow. She pointed to the too-round handhold.

"It's a new weapon. I'd be surprised if it's been used more than five times. There's no time to wear the wood, and my arm's already suffering abuse." Saiko massaged the sore spot. "If it were colder, I could wear my coat and protect my arm that way.

"I know what you need."

"A new arm? Or my own bow?"

Her maid bent in courtesy, humor tugging the corners of her thin lips. She headed toward a wall arch leading to the tradesmen's section.

"Where are you going?" asked Saiko. Okiko didn't answer, so she shrugged and returned to her practice. The bowstring struck her sore arm, and she sucked hissing air between her pursed lips as her skin smarted. She gripped the bow, her knuckles white, until the pain subsided. Glaring at the offending weapon, she said, "This is never going to work."

"Princess, try this." Okiko approached, a piece of suede in one hand and two leather cords in another.

"It's too soft for an armguard."

"I thought you might use this as a grip for the bow. To keep it from turning after you shoot."

"Ah, yes." She helped her lady-in-waiting tie the suede grip on with the cords. Then she sent an arrow into her target. Unfortunately, the string still smarted against her arm, though not as badly. "Better."

"I saw the tanner had hard leather armguards in his workshop. They looked too big, but I wonder if perhaps he could trim one to fit you."

Saiko didn't hesitate. "Let's go see if he's acquired the skill."

The tanner, an ancient little man with white hair so thin his topknot drooped, smiled and bowed in greeting. He set aside his work and graciously agreed to customize a guard for her. "I'm truly honored to serve you, Princess Saiko."

The workmen's huts blocked sunlight, leaving the walkway chilly in shadow. If she'd known the shadowed areas were so cold, she'd have practiced against the shelter of the castle wall and worn her jacket. Better to learn now of this problem, though, than in the heat of battle.

"I've heard of your skill," he said. "My reputation will grow once people learn I've fitted you for this battle."

Her lady-in-waiting shot her an accusing, horrified look, eyes wide and nostrils flared. Ignoring it, she chuckled at the old man. "Your reputation will grow if you do well fitting this armguard. I'm small compared to your warrior patrons."

"I understand *you're* a warrior patron," he said with a low bow. "Don't fear, Your Highness. I apprenticed under the very best master tanner. I'm prepared for this challenge." He skimmed a hand over his round forehead, considering a group of guards lined along a shelf. He chose a red-brown sheath guard decorated with endless swirls etched into its surface. "If I may...?"

Inside, a work fire created almost too much warmth. She held out her left arm and pulled the opening of her sleeve to her elbow. Okiko huffed and stood at the open doorway, her back to them.

Putting a hand to his apron-covered chest, he made a sad pout. "Yes, I see where your bow is stinging you." He slid the guard over her reddened skin. Like a tube, its smooth, cool leather encased her from wrist to elbow. He made scores in its firm surface with a sharp tool. At a workbench, he trimmed along the score marks to shorten its length and used a rough file to round the new edges. With impressive speed, he unlaced it, trimmed off the old holes, cut new holes, and laced it anew.

As he slid the modified leather into place, she smiled. Pleased by its excellent shape, she said, "It's as if you made this just for me."

"I did," he said, a humorous glint reflecting orange from his shop fire.

While he trimmed excess lacing at her wrist, a commotion arose at the outer gate. Men shouted. Soldiers raced atop nearby wall-walks.

"What is it?" shrieked Okiko, scurrying inside.

"The rest of Takamori-san's men have arrived." Saiko shared a knowing glance with the tanner. Tension stiffened her neck and shoulders. "There's very little time."

"Yes," agreed the man. He patted the guard. "This should do very well." He hesitated, pointing a staying finger at the ceiling. "I have something..." At a cabinet, he fetched a square of white fabric. "This'll prevent your armguard from irritating until your rub burn has a chance to heal." He inserted the incredibly soft material into the armguard. "I have much to ready, but if you have any difficulties with this, Your Highness, come see me."

"I will." Saiko offered him a coin, but he shook his head before bowing and retreating a step. "I can't accept payment, Princess. Your presence in my shop does me great honor and is reward enough."

"Thank you." Humbled by his generosity, she bowed low. She took her friend's hand, grasped her bow, and hurried for the castle's outermost wall.

"Princess—"

"Not now, Okiko."

Men and horses poured in, filling the castle's outer defense ring that housed stables and barracks. Archers and pike bearers stood at the ready atop thick stone walkways, but no enemy pursued...yet.

"They look tired," said Okiko, pulling Saiko's hand to inch her toward the second castle ring and away from the organized chaos.

"I can help," said Saiko. She spotted Takamori directing cavalry to the stables.

Her friend drew her lips into a thin line. "I'm sure you can. Perhaps it's best to let your father's officers see to their soldiers. Takamori-san will report to you when he has their news. He always does."

True. He'd involved her in every decision and plan. He wouldn't exclude her now. She studied the influx of forces where soldiers hauled in her hole-ridden palanquin. Her trunks followed, as well as the emperor's two officials in dust-laden black silk.

Okiko was right. Stepping in would likely cause confusion and misdirection. She stayed put.

"I should return to my target practice and test this new armguard." She tapped the leather hidden beneath her sleeve, reassured by its hard protection. "Now that my retinue's come, we could be attacked at any time."

Okiko issued a nervous sniff. "About that. Why did you tell me you were practicing for contests?"

Saiko sighed. "I didn't want you to worry. You haven't been your usual calm self since you arrived yesterday."

"You're part of all this." Her lady-in-waiting gestured to the rush of men. "Of course I'm upset."

"I'm the *cause* of this."

"You'll fight." Okiko waved wildly, her hands in a flutter as they climbed toward the sky.

Saiko didn't dare answer since Okiko appeared ready to spin into a panic. "Take a deep breath."

"May we go on the wall and see if the rogue samurai are coming?" Her friend's voice quavered.

She put a reassuring hand on her lady's shoulder. "I don't believe that would be a good idea, but know that if the *ronin* approached, those watchmen would give the alarm. Still, there could be scouts in the city, and my appearance on the wall might initiate a premature attack we're not yet prepared to defend against."

"I want to see them coming. From our room, we can only see in one direction. Here within the wall defense, we see nothing. I want to watch for the threat."

Saiko shook her head. "It's not our responsibility. Let the wall guards monitor and warn us when the time comes. I understand what heads our way. They hunt me."

"Princess, why does this have to happen? Why do you have to be their target? You're worthy of love and respect, not hatred and violence." Okiko released a sob as a tear slipped from her lashes to slide down the round of her cheek. She covered her eyes and slumped while her shoulders shuddered.

Saiko put a hand to her lady's arm. "You've been through a lot. This would be difficult to deal with for anyone."

Okiko sniffed and nodded.

"They don't hate me. They seek to prevent a political maneuver that'll strengthen the shogunate. Violence is their only recourse. It isn't about me. I'm only a pawn."

"It's not fair."

Saiko shrugged. "No, it's not."

She sought Takamori and found him staring at her, his

arms extended at odd angles as if he'd been gesturing then stopped in mid-motion. His dark gaze ensnared her, making awareness bloom, hot and heavy, low in her belly.

He loved her as much as she loved him.

Her face heated from within. Takamori. He had become as much a part of her as her hands or her eyes. Parting from him would be the same as lobbing her wrists or tearing out her eyes.

She had hoped for love but without an understanding of what it meant. This overwhelming joy suffused her with warmth and stirred her very soul to life. Her heart beat for him now. If her father understood the depth of her feelings for Takamori, would he reconsider sending her to the imperial city?

He blinked, releasing her from his spell. Once again, she stood at Osaka Castle where her lady-in-waiting hugged herself and whimpered softly. If only she'd *some* sense that she'd survive this. Some sense that their love had a chance.

*　　*　　*　　*

"The gods need to keep those *ronin* from Osaka through the night." Just one night. Takamori wiped a stiff hand over his fatigued face and surveyed the bustling activity filling the second court.

Hoshihiro offered a stern nod, his thick eyebrows slanting over his shadowed eyes. "Our men are too tired."

"Too brave." Takamori let his eyes follow Saiko's retreating back as she headed for the innermost court. "These men are exhausted, but they would fight."

"To their deaths," agreed the samurai.

"This is my point. One night would see them fed and rested."

Hoshihiro placed fingers on the handle of his *wakizashi* where it protruded from his sash. "I'll go to the castle temple with a few of jodai's samurai."

"Prayers and incense can only help. Do you want me to take

over direction of the men? Meals and baths still need to be arranged."

"Of course." Takamori studied his dusty boots and ran a quick massage over the back of his neck. "See to the injured, first."

Hoshihiro bowed then strode toward the armory.

Takamori wondered that Osaka Jodai hadn't come yet. Maybe he'd grown accustomed to his quiet, secure life under Shogun's iron-fisted rule. Surely he found it easier to let Ieyasu-shogun's marshal manage the warfare brought to this castle by beautiful Princess Saiko. This was, after all, just a post assignment – not the jodai's home.

Weary, he issued a few remaining orders then sought his chambers. A low fire greeted him from the hearth, but he sank onto a pillow in a shadowed corner. He wanted to hide, to melt into the darkness and lose himself for a time. Sitting cross-legged, he settled elbows onto his knees and took his head in his palms.

Years ago, before the shogunate began shifting power from the emperor, daimyo and their samurai had battled with respect and restraint. Each samurai had a family and retainers. Mouths to feed. To kill a samurai was to condemn the man's estate to potential starvation. The battlefield rarely saw the death of such warriors. Everything changed when honor meant fighting to the death for a lord's political position.

When he had reported to Sumpu, he'd hoped never to see this place again. He'd hoped never to face the brutal, deadly combat only samurai wreaked upon one another. Now, both this place of death and its promise of more senseless slaughter dragged him into an angry sadness that smothered him.

He slid his hands from the tight hair at the sides of head and covered his face. Honor and duty demanded he tackle this task with bravery. Love forbade him from failing.

As if summoned by his thoughts, the princess opened his chamber door and stepped inside. "Takamori-san?"

He sat straighter, enjoying her lovely silhouette against the yellow light of hallway lanterns. She stood still as a statue, and he burned the sight into his memory.

She released a soft sigh and made to go.

"I'm here," he said low.

"I can't see you."

He stood and left the shadows. As she closed his door, the unsteady orange glow from his fireplace brought her worried expression into view.

"What brings you?" he asked, not caring about her reason so much as trying to mask his joy at having her come to him when he needed her most.

"I... You..." She took a step closer. Her adorable hesitation had him wanting to take her in his arms. "There was something in your eyes as your men entered the castle gate. You appeared..."

"Tired?"

"Yes."

He rubbed a callus-hardened palm over his stiff face. "I am tired. I'm war-weary, and now I face a battle I don't want to fight, with travel-worn samurai and a jodai who refuses to do more than stand by and watch."

"How long do we have?"

"Days? Hours? I don't know." He put a hand on a red silk cushion atop a stack. "Can you stay?"

She nodded. "Okiko's napping."

He tossed the cushion before the hearth and gestured for her to sit. He put his black one next to it then added a log to the fire and settled. "Are you excited for battle?"

"No." Shifting her hips off of her folded legs and onto the edge of her cushion, she planted a hand on *tatami* matting between them. "I'm scared."

"Then you're wise."

"Takamori-san, we have nowhere to run. Your men must meet the enemy outside the walls, while those of us inside will try to keep *ronin* from breaching. If we fail—"

"We won't." He studied her large eyes glistening with reflected flames that grew taller around the fresh wood. "We can't."

"Tell me that what we face won't be worse than the Summer Siege."

"There's no comparison. This'll end quickly. A massacre." He sagged under the weight of his knowledge, the weight of his memories of tragedy and horror.

"A massacre of them or us?"

He shook his head, afraid the answer was both. "I can't guess. The gods must decide. We can only fight hard."

Chapter Sixteen

Night descended with an air of expectation that had Saiko
on edge. Any minute, an attack could change her world, take
Takamori from her, or take her life.

"I can't leave you tonight," she said, not caring if her lady-
in-waiting disapproved. "We may not have tomorrow. Neither
of us."

His features tightened to uncompromising lines. "Don't say
that. I plan to fight so you will have a tomorrow. Many
tomorrows."

"What are these tomorrows worth without you? If you
don't survive, I'm left in Kyōto, serving an emperor I despise
and spending the remainder of my life missing you. Takamori-
san, you're my love. You're my heart. There's so much I want to
do, but without you, it means nothing."

He took her hand and pulled until her head rested upon his
thigh. "I want a peaceful life with you by my side. Your father
has a fire in his belly that makes him want to fight, even in his
old age. I'm not like him." He peered into wavering, leaping
flames in the fireplace. "We live in an already hostile world.
Why do we seek our death on the battlefield?"

"The world is full of beauty and harmony, too," she said.

"Am I wrong in wanting to spend the rest of my days
searching for this beauty? Studying this harmony?"

"You see it already. It shows in your poetry and paintings."

"Maybe. For now, the way of war is my life. The way of

beauty is only something I glimpse in brief bits...and when I'm with you."

Saiko ached to her soul. She sat up and touched fingers to his solid jaw. "We can't stop this. We couldn't have prevented it. What tomorrow holds, we can't guess, but tonight is ours."

His eyes softened, and his shoulders eased some. "Yes. Tonight is ours. For these hours, you're mine as much as I'm yours."

"Are you mine?" She held her breath.

"For eternity. No matter what results from this battle. No matter our fates, I'm yours."

The ache grew. "And I'm yours. No matter what duty demands of us, my heart and soul will forever belong to you."

The black of his eyes drew her in, surrounded her, and refused to release her. He leaned near, and his lips captured hers. She inhaled sharply through her nostrils, adoring the fragrance of leather and outdoors that clung to his skin. Closing her eyes, she burned his scent into her brain.

Without releasing the kiss, he took her in his strong arms and eased onto his back so she lay atop him. His insistent mouth reassured her and reminded her of their strength and vitality. She had so many reasons to live. So much to appreciate. She relaxed into him and surrendered to passion. They made love as though this night, this moment, were their last.

"Princess Saiko," came a fervent whisper from the hall.

She blinked and lifted her head from Takamori's shoulder. When had she fallen asleep? The still-bright fire let her know she hadn't slept long.

"Princess." Okiko sounded desperate.

Takamori's countenance looked peaceful, and she placed fingers on his ribs as they expanded around his sleep-deepened lungs. Her heart felt full with love.

She rolled from his warmth and grabbed a white wrap from the many piled amongst her ensemble's numerous elements. She held it closed with one hand while padding across his *tatami* floor to the door.

"Shh," she hissed after sliding it aside. "Are you trying to wake everyone?"

"Your Highness, you weren't on your futon when I woke. I didn't know what to think." Her lady-in-waiting peered into the recesses of Takamori's chamber then at Saiko's scant cover. "This won't go well for any of us."

She sighed. "This isn't the place or time to talk."

Okiko stared at Saiko's hand where it clutched her wrap. Her eyes widened while her lips formed an O. "The man on the bridge. He's the marshal?"

Saiko simply nodded, her grip remaining on his door.

"I don't know what to say."

"Say nothing."

Her lady relaxed. "Yes. I understand. I'm glad, I really am."

"Then go to bed. We can talk in the morning over a bowl of rice."

Okiko turned on a bare foot, though her eyes never left Saiko. She headed toward their chamber, and a slight smile touched her lips as she stared over her shoulder.

Saiko didn't wait for her lady to traverse the length of the hall. She backed into Takamori's room and slid the door closed.

"Are we discovered?" he asked from where he lay.

"By Lady Okiko. It was going to happen." She shrugged, removing her wrap. Completely comfortable in her nudity with him, she crossed to his welcoming arms.

"I admire your bravery." He placed a soft kiss to her forehead and urged her cheek to his shoulder.

Settling against his firm, scarred body, she slid a leg atop his. "This requires no bravery. Being with you like this is right. I've never done anything so right in my life. Besides my lady-in-waiting is loyal to a fault. She won't tell."

She closed her eyes and focused on the rise and fall of his chest. She didn't dare sleep, however. Morning would come too soon, and she wanted to cherish every second.

A moment after his arm sagged at her back, a cry arose from the castle wall below his window. As her pulse leapt in dread, she swallowed hard and sat up. Their reprieve had ended.

*　　*　　*　　*

Takamori's heart hammered against his ribs. Saiko fastened a final tie on his armor then handed him his helmet and sword. She appeared calm, which only increased his unease. "You'll stay upon the wall."

"Yes, and I'll wear this." She held up a square, lacquered leather *haramaki* bound together in horizontal layers and ornamented with painted dragonflies. It would wrap her entire torso and included a skirt. Made of eight thick leather segments, it would protect her from her chest to her knees without hampering her ability to walk or run.

Outside the castle walls, the clacking of spears and ringing of swords echoed through dawn's coral glow. Osaka Jodai's soldiers and samurai already fought hard.

"Go," shouted Takamori. He sent an urgent wave toward his horse guard.

Archers above the main entrance sent a barrage of arrows down a moment before the gate opened and the riding samurai thundered out.

"Secure the inner perimeters," he yelled when the gate closed.

Saiko yanked excess material from her kimono's length up through her simple *obi*, ensuring she wouldn't trip over the material. He wrapped her in armor and tied it under her left arm. "I'm going out. Get to the wall before they lock the inner gates."

"I'm scared," she admitted, her hand trembling where it strapped on her armguard.

He was too. He feared now in a way he never had before because she'd face this battle without him to protect her. Without him at her side. "Use caution at all times."

He didn't wait for a response. He couldn't stay a moment longer for fear of finding it impossible to leave her. Spinning on his heel, he mounted his horse then rallied his remaining samurai with an up-thrust arm. Careful not to glance back, he galloped for the exit, his men prodding their horses to follow. Any sight of Saiko would have him hesitating – something he couldn't afford.

A war cry on his lips, he rode out the main gate. Accompanying cries of the men behind him deafened him at the same time they infused him with added strength.

Ronin bodies littered the roadway, arrows and pikes protruding at every angle. He'd expected a limited number since they comprised the initial attack. More than a hundred enemy samurai lay bleeding into the soil amongst the jodai's downed men. It told him they had far more than he'd thought.

Refusing to let it slow him, he galloped along the castle's outer wall and led his men toward the sound of screaming horses and clashing weapons. An occasional gunshot cracked through the cacophony.

When he rounded the final curve and onto the field, the sheer size of the *ronin* force caused him to reel backward in his saddle. For an instant, he forgot to breathe.

Thousands. Thousands of opposing samurai surged across the field toward the slanted castle wall. They had more than double his numbers. This army surely represented more than half of the samurai who'd served fallen daimyo and had survived Tokugawa Ieyasu's onslaught over the past years.

This was nothing compared to the sea of samurai Tokugawa Ieyasu had led against this castle nine months earlier, but this unplanned battle surely promised as much, if not more, violence and death.

His blood seemed to stop flowing for a second, sending a dull chill through him. How could he defeat so many? He had no choice. If they reached Osaka Castle, they would kill Saiko.

All the rage and protectiveness in him exploded into a burst of destructive energy. He raced past his engaged horse guard and into the center of the field. A number of his samurai rode in his wake, entering the fray with him. Enemies on foot came for them. He used the momentum of his horse and the added momentum of pulling his sword from its scabbard to decapitate the nearest.

Another footman thrust a polearm at him. Takamori blocked the swipe with the armor covering his arm, grasped the blade by the dull edge, and yanked. His attacker lost balance and sprawled upon the grass. As always happened in combat, a pulse throbbed in him. His heartbeat synced with the filling of his lungs to help him find a rhythm of response to attacks.

He brought his horse around, thrusting his sword tip between two armor plates of a third *ronin,* then returned to finish off the second by burying the polearm in his neck.

An arrow whizzed past. It landed in the armpit of an enemy who stood ready to strike with a *katana* overhead. The man screamed, and another arrow entered his gaping maw. He crumpled where he stood. All around, *ronin* increased their fighting frenzy.

Atop the castle wall, Saiko ran along the stone barrier. As she sprinted, she loaded another arrow into her bow, her pale kimono flaring and billowing beneath the swaying leather of her *harakami's* skirt. She leapt high, sending her arrow deep into the fighting. No shields protected her or any of the other archers on the wall.

He would've worried that the jodai hadn't arranged for standing shields, but what was the point of such protection when the archers moved freely? He didn't like it, but he couldn't return to the castle, either.

Below her, pike bearers protected the slanted wall while his horse guard continued to decimate the front line. Still, *ronin* surged forward. They wanted her dead.

His men fought hard, holding their own and protecting each other. The swarm of enemies had them surrounded, however. He had to get them advancing.

Shouting to summon his power, he whirled about and began hacking a path. These *ronin* had might, but nothing compared to his skill and battle experience. His instincts guided him through immediate threats, but he continuously calculated and maneuvered to work his way in the direction of the rear flanks where this army's leaders directed the assault.

He didn't make it anywhere close. Halfway across the field, three *ronin* attacked simultaneously. While he fended off a spear and sword, the third swung a staff that caught him across the chest.

As he fought to keep his seat, an arrow flew at his face. He swayed, but not enough. The tip grazed his forehead in a fiery slice before hitting the side guard of his helmet. The arrow fell to his lap. Blood coursed into his eye.

He wiped at the blood to clear his sight, swung his sword wide in a block, and grabbed the arrow. Howling his determination, he jabbed the arrow into the hollow between the spearman's collarbones.

His attack forced him to bend. Off balance, he had no chance to recover when the staff whacked his back. He tumbled from his horse, landing atop the gurgling, wide-eyed spearman. Before he could roll, the sharp, icy blade of a sword slid beneath the neck guard of his helmet and bit into his skin.

*   *   *   *

Arrows flew her way, but from her vantage point above the battle, she saw them coming and easily swayed in avoidance. It was nothing new. She'd used *yawara* to evade arrows since her first arrival atop the wall.

Guns were another matter, however. She couldn't evade bullets. Rifles at the tree line fired out of range, but she kept a check on them from time to time. If they advanced, she'd have to consider leaving the fight.

Takamori dropped out of sight. Saiko screamed. Staggering a step as lights exploded behind her eyes, she gripped her bow as if it served as a lifeline.

"My fault. My fault," she muttered.

He was so far. With his men fighting near him, she couldn't fire an arrow until she knew for certain it would hit an attacker and not one of their own. On instinct, she sidestepped an oncoming arrow then resumed her position.

Fear provided a renewed surge of energy as she frantically searched the sea of thrashing men and rearing horses. She shot a few arrows into the chaos at the front line, taking out enemies on the attack, but always her eyes returned to where Takamori had fallen.

He'd seemed invincible. Fierce. Powerful. Nobody could stop him...until now. She whimpered but bit her lip. She had no time for weakness.

Her mind screamed in worry. She cocked her bow and aimed carefully. Letting her arrow fly, she experienced a satisfaction like nothing else as its metal tip pierced the armor of the samurai who had knocked Takamori from his horse. The man jerked then whirled. He pointed toward her, his lips moving rapidly.

She drew her last arrow from her quiver and shouted, "More arrows!"

She would take that *ronin* down, determined to make it happen.

She pulled the string of her bow and aimed carefully. Two more arrows flew toward her, but she calculated they'd miss. Focusing on the *ronin* holding the staff, she slowly exhaled and let the string slip from her fingertips. Her arrow arced.

"Don't move," she said but needn't have worried. The *ronin* appeared engrossed in the spot where Takamori had toppled.

The swordsman on the other side of Takamori's horse fell for no apparent reason. A second later, her arrow found its target, striking the staff wielder in a vulnerable place at the back of one arm. He straightened, reaching for the arrow.

Through the madness, Takamori emerged, slashing with his sword. Saiko's stifled a sob of relief. He lived but his bleeding head wound was obvious even at such a distance.

He struck down a *ronin* who ran at him with a polearm at a deadly angle. As he turned to reclaim his horse, however, his mount took an arrow in the rump. It reared then bolted.

He was stranded on foot.

"More arrows," she shrieked. He needed her.

A boy ran across the wall, three thick bundles of arrows dangling from his thin hands. His topknot bobbing, he dropped a bundle at her feet with a bow and sliced through its binding. After handing her one, he put a handful in her quiver then raced to the next archer.

Her armor rubbed a sore spot under her arm, but she didn't care. She spent a moment locating Takamori. When she had him in sight, she aimed.

He fought two *ronin* using a solid two-handed grip on his *katana*. She aimed high, picturing the necessary arc and sending her arrow toward the sky so it could make the distance.

One of his opponents collapsed when her arrow sank into the rogue samurai's face. Takamori didn't miss a step. He continued his deadly dance – each swing and step fluid into the next, his sword acting as an extension of his arms.

Rogue samurai on horseback arrived at the fore, and Osaka's defenders began to lose what little ground they'd gained. The jodai's men were falling and not recovering.

At this rate, it would quickly turn into a massacre – as Takamori had predicted. Their planning accomplished nothing against these overwhelming numbers. Saiko fired arrows as fast as she could, but fear slowed her shaking fingers.

On the wind, a hum of distant male shouts carried to the castle wall. Everyone atop the walkway hesitated. She stilled, willing her thrumming nerves to quiet.

The rear enemy flank erupted in a flurry of activity as fresh fighters spilled from the trees and onto the field to engage the *ronin*. Swords sliced and swung, their metal blades glinting in early morning light. Rifles fired but didn't seem to lessen the new offensive.

Rogue warriors everywhere began moving in that direction. Takamori, however, waved his men back toward the castle. She knew exactly what he intended.

"Hoshihiro-san," Saiko shouted downward, gaining the attention of the samurai overseeing the pike bearers protecting the wall's base. "Advance your men. Join the marshal."

Hoshihiro offered a swift nod and led the pikemen onto the field. It wasn't much, but the added men allowed Takamori to form a line and press his advantage.

The *ronin* discovered too late that they were sandwiched. Fighting escalated to a deafening pitch.

Saiko could fairly smell the enemy's panic. She couldn't lower her guard, however. Takamori had suffered a head wound, and she had no idea how bad. Despite his vigor in battle, he could collapse without warning at any time.

She desperately wanted to join him on the field and fight at his side. He was right, though. It would only place her within reach of the men who sought her death – the very reason for this battle in the first place. Also, her presence would distract Takamori and put him at unnecessary risk.

"More arrows!" She scooped the last of her bundle from the stone walkway at her feet and loaded one in her bow.

Chapter Seventeen

The *ronin* had nowhere to go. Takamori recognized Yagyu Munenori's armor among the samurai who raced to help. The sensei had brought his students unbidden. It didn't surprise him and made him love and respect his friend even more.

It amazed him that Munenori's soldiers – mere students – defeated rogue samurai at the rear flank, which consisted of the oldest, most experienced warriors. Their element of surprise proved a more powerful weapon than he would've supposed. It also spoke to Munenori's success as a teacher of elite sword skill.

Takamori's men, combined with Munenori's efforts, overcame the dwindled *ronin* army. Takamori had lost too many of his own men, but not so many that they couldn't finish the enemy. Some rogue samurai fled, to his disappointment, though less than twenty he was sure.

Sparing *ronin* who fought to the end wasn't a consideration. These warriors battled to avenge their fallen daimyo masters and to take Princess Saiko's life. They lacked the honor and respect of previous battles and wouldn't stop, if spared.

He, however, still lived by the code and respected life in battle. Death in warfare ensured them honor. Letting any live would only serve to strip them of their dignity. He had to afford them this courtesy, as he would've expected the same had the circumstances been reversed. Rogue or not, they understood the samurai code.

Sometime during the fight, his injury stopped bleeding. He had no idea when, but was glad for it. From time to time, he glanced to the wall. Princess Saiko kept to her word and remained out of the fray. Each time he checked, she still fired arrows into the enemy forces, and he took courage.

When the sun nearly reached its zenith, he killed his toughest *ronin* of the day - a leader he'd first had to drag from the saddle – and spun to face his next only to discover none remained. Throughout the field, his men dealt final blows or began their migration around bodies toward the castle.

He removed his helmet and wiped sweat from his face then sagged. He hadn't witnessed this level of carnage since the Summer Siege. By the number of samurai left standing, he estimated he'd lost two-thirds of his men. The sheer waste and senselessness of this kind of destruction struck him. It caused a terrible ache of loss.

Hoshihiro approached at a jog then performed a deep bow. "I sent my pike bearers and five archers on horseback to chase the *ronin* who ran, my lord. I instructed they return by sunset if they have no success."

Takamori sighed. "They won't find them. Those samurai wouldn't have run from this fight, which tells me they have a mission to fulfill. Besides, it's been too long, and these *ronin* have been hiding for more than a year. They know where to go and how to disappear."

"Then this isn't over."

"I don't think so. We don't dishonor our families by running from death, so I must believe they have some alternative purpose. A secondary strategy, maybe. We need to continue in our vigilance to protect the princess." He searched the wall-walk, but Saiko had gone. The idea that she may be hurt gave him a new burst of energy, and he broke into a run. He called over his shoulder, "Begin preparations to clear this field."

Once inside, he ordered the inner gates opened. He took a brief moment to evaluate the castle's state. Arrows had killed some of his wall archers, but not nearly as many as he'd expected. The castle structure didn't show any damage thanks to the absence of war machines.

Perhaps he'd misjudged the amount of backing their army had from Kyōto's nobility. He had originally thought the *ronin* army under the authority of someone in the emperor's service. Now, he accepted the possibility that they'd organized on their own. Still, money had to support their effort to feed and outfit so many.

When the innermost gate opened and he stepped through, he discovered why his men on the walls had survived so well. Thousands of arrows covered the ground here, so many he couldn't see the soil beneath them. They'd shot everything at Saiko.

His lungs constricted. Where was she? He began to tremble.

"Takamori-san!" She ran from a doorway on the right, still wearing her armor.

Relief hit him, threatening to take his knees out from under him.

She stopped short of hugging him. Her lips quivered, and she made to touch his forehead. She didn't, though. "You're hurt."

Not caring who saw, he closed the distance between them and gathered her close. "And you're alive and uninjured."

"Only because of you." She placed gentle fingertips to his forehead.

"I'm filthy," he said, though he didn't pull away. He clung to her with every fiber of his being.

"What happens now?" She cupped his cheek, her gaze finding his mouth.

Instantly, his loins tightened. He said in a low voice, "We wait for your father."

Okiko cleared her throat, emerging from hiding. "Yagyu Munenori comes."

He reluctantly released Saiko and faced his friend who approached through the inner middle gate. Behind marched nearly a hundred students, blood-spattered and weary, none appearing younger than fourteen.

"I can't offer enough thanks," said Takamori. He bowed deeply and held it an extra three seconds.

"I'm honored to be of use," said his friend. Grinning, he extended an arm to the rear of his group. "This is yours, I believe."

Students parted to reveal the horse he had left at the school during his run to Osaka with Saiko.

"My gratitude grows by the second. Thank you, Sensei." He waived a soldier to take his horse to the stable. "I rode yours into battle, and I'm sorry to report that it took an arrow in the rump."

"It's fine. My son tends it now." Munenori grinned. "You know it's my pleasure to do right by you, Marshal. I'm actually glad for this rare opportunity to test my students' skills in genuine battle."

Takamori grew somber. "How many did you lose?"

"None," said his friend. "I believe we fought under heavenly protection."

Saiko came to Takamori's side. Munenori bowed low, and she returned it with a shallower one as befitted their stations. "Were you sent by the gods? Because your arrival was most auspiciously timed."

He straightened and chuckled. "I wish I could claim such exalted connections, *Princess*." He grinned. "Okiko told me who you are." He indicated three young men sporting strong faces and sturdy shoulders who bowed in deference. "My sons witnessed a group of *ronin* pass the school yesterday. Among them were samurai from the Owari daimyo's domain. I knew you had come to Osaka after having trouble with them, so we decided to help."

"I'm very glad you did. I'll speak to the Osaka Jodai about providing you and your students with accommodations worthy of your generous contribution to our victory." Her lovely face pinked a bit, giving her an ethereal loveliness that stole Takamori's breath.

"That won't be necessary, Your Highness. My students will return to the school within the hour, as soon as their mounts have a chance to rest." Munenori faced him, his features settling into serious lines. "I only wish we could've come sooner. Perhaps Ieyasu-shogun wouldn't have lost so many men."

Takamori only offered a brief nod. What could he say? They had won the day, but at great expense.

"I'll stay the night. Try to spare me a few minutes," his friend said and waved his students to follow a waiting retainer. "I would share some ideas with you."

"Of course. I'll join you for *sake* after dinner." Takamori bowed, and Munenori responded with one in farewell." To Saiko, he said, "There's much to be done."

"I'll come with you to make your reports to the jodai, if you wish. I had a different perspective from the wall."

He shook his head, resisting an urge to take her hand and draw her nearer. "Lady Okiko waits to assist you. Go with her. I don't expect Osaka Jodai will be pleasant after this blow to his ranks. As senior military officer for this central region, he'll have to hire and train new samurai in order to maintain Osaka Castle's strength for Shogun. He'll be in a foul mood, I expect. Plus, I need to personally see that the sword master receives a room in our quarter."

"Perhaps if you point out that Osaka's forces were diminished in the protection of a Tokugawa princess, he may cool. No doubt my brother will help him rebuild his numbers. Who has access to more samurai than Shogun?"

Pulling his mouth tight in distaste over having to listen to the official complain, he offered a single nod. "I agree. There doesn't seem much left of the warrior Jodai used to be. He's become a bureaucrat more concerned with reporting loss and expense to Shogun."

She touched his wrist. "You might also point out that Shogun won't mind the loss when tempered with the knowledge that he suffered such to save me and rid Japan of a terrible threat."

He smiled, liking the way she thought. "Indeed. We're all heroes today."

"What official doesn't dream of Shogun thinking him a hero?"

He pictured the jodai suddenly eager to write his report after Takamori finished with him. "Thank you, Princess."

Her lips curved slightly. "I'll see you later?"

"If I have any say in the matter," he agreed.

*   *   *   *

"You didn't see Hosokawa Takamori last night?" Okiko asked, setting a tray on a rosewood stand before the fireplace. Steam wisped from cups of tea and bowls of rice and soup.

Saiko buried her face in her futon and groaned then sat. How long had she slept? As stiff as her limbs felt, she'd believe days had passed. "No, and I don't blame him. By the time he finished with the demands of his position, he probably dropped right to sleep."

"Dropped, ha!" Her lady slid aside the shutters covering her window and let in gray light. A fine mist fell, shrouding the view and creating a fresh scent in the air. "He only fought through one morning yesterday. That man could go for days. His men tell me so. Hasn't he told you about his part in the Sekigahara and Osaka battles?"

"Some. He doesn't speak much about his exploits." She stretched then joined Okiko at the hearth. "How do *you* know?"

"Hoshihiro-san told me. We had a lot of time to talk on our ride here."

"Ah. Yesterday seems like a dream. Like a nightmare that didn't really happen."

"It happened. Don't doubt it. You saved so many lives with your well-placed arrows. Everyone's talking about it." Okiko sank to her knees onto a square cushion and arranged the dishes on the tray. "You know what they're talking about even more? How you avoided all those arrows. They're out there counting them right now."

"In the rain?" Saiko shook her head. "I did nothing extraordinary. Not like Takamori-san and Hoshihiro-san. They fought with swords and faced our enemy hand-to-hand."

"Harrumph. Don't reduce your contribution's worth. It's unbecoming."

Saiko laughed. "Have I slept the entire day away?"

Did Takamori still sleep? Or had he come for a visit and found her slumbering?

"No, Your Highness. It's only midday." Okiko handed her a damp cloth.

Saiko stifled a smile and cleaned her hands. After breaking her fast, she would dress with care then seek him out.

Halfway through the meal, the sound of many men and horses reached her window from the direction of the main gate. She shared a worried glance with her lady then scrambled to her feet.

"It could be anyone," Saiko said. Based on the size of the party, however, she suspected her father had arrived.

"It could just be a retinue from the emperor," said Okiko, but she wrung her hands and glared at the door. "I'll go see who it is."

Saiko combed her hair and changed into clean, white-lined first-layer robes. While she tied a wide red and gold damask belt to secure her third layer, Okiko returned.

"Your father's here," she said, struggling for air and clutching her side. "I ran...the whole way...up the stairs."

"How much do you think he knows?" Saiko's heart shuddered.

Okiko paused, staring as if Saiko had sprouted a second head. "Everything, of course. He *is* the retired shogun."

"He's not a god."

"Might as well be. Nothing ever escapes him." Her lady shrugged. At a cupboard, she lifted three large, thin boxes from a drawer and spread them on the floor. Removing a lid, she revealed a bright kimono of plain, supple silk. "White with red chrysanthemums?"

"Too cheerful. We're surrounded by death. Plus, I'm seeing my father, and he's sure to be mad. If not directly at me, then at the situation."

Okiko grunted on a nod. She lifted another lid. "Ocean waves?"

"Too festive."

"Festive? These are storm waves."

Saiko shook her head. "What's in the other?"

Her lady lifted the lid and showed a pale plum damask. Threads in its raised pattern formed drooping bud-filled branches of a single willow tree.

"Perfect."

"But, Princess—"

"Find me an *obi* for semi-mourning – white with black edging. I need to appeal to his affection. To remind him that I'm his beloved daughter and that he could've lost me at any time this past week."

Okiko sighed. "I don't see how such an *obi* will do that."

Saiko kneeled next to the kimono's storage box. Tracing a branch pattern with her fingertip, she said, "I love my father. I know better than any how I've betrayed him."

"Your Highness, you were prepared to do your duty. Is it your fault a *ronin* army attacked and stopped you from going to Kyōto? That they came here because they wanted you dead?"

"Don't be obtuse."

"Fine. This is about Takamori-san. How can you hold yourself distant when love insists on having its way? I know how impossible it is. I tried to hate Hoshihiro-san."

"You love him?"

"I can't help it. It's as if I have no choice." Okiko's mouth softened into a sort of secret smile.

Saiko, however, didn't love against her will. She hadn't been pulled by the gods to place her affections where she didn't wish. On her own, she'd willingly sought love, real love, with Takamori. She reveled in it without regret. Would it make a difference to her father? She hoped so.

It took her an hour to finish dressing and arranging her hair. She insisted on moving slowly, stressing the importance of striving for perfection. As Okiko fitted a final decorative comb of silver and plum into Saiko's hair, a knock sounded on the door.

Takamori? She had spent the entire time hoping he'd come and frustrated that he didn't.

"Princess Saiko," a gruff voice said through the paper panels.

Not Takamori. She swallowed a lump of disappointment. Gaining her feet, she called, "I'm here."

"His Excellency requests your presence."

She took a deep breath and slowly released it. "I'm ready to see my father."

Her lady slid open the door, and a guard bowed low. "Please follow me."

Assuming a discreet posture, her chin down and shoulders rounded, she left Okiko. He led her down two flights of stairs and to the end of a long corridor, which seemed like the longest walk of her life. The guard opened a solid, swinging door and bowed. She passed inside, her knees weak and her throat tight.

High windows filled the immense white room with light. Her father sat near the far wall at the end of a narrow, Chinese runner. Osaka Jodai sat at his side, and a table bearing *sake* and cups stood before them.

He appeared old, which struck her as alarming. Despite his age, he'd never carried the looks or bearing of an aged man. He still bore a gray tinge that had worried her before she left Sumpu, and the skin above his eyes sagged, as did his cheeks and the corners of his mouth. He'd grown thinner, bringing his cheekbones and chin into sharp prominence. He'd changed a great deal in so little time, and worry made her throat even tighter.

"Daughter," he greeted. "You look well, which is quite an accomplishment, considering. I'm pleased by your somber colors. You honor the samurai who gave their lives for you yesterday."

She reached the table. Keeping her eyes lowered, she descended to her knees and pressed her forehead to the runner.

"I don't miss your symbolism. Rise and talk to me, Saiko." His voice still held strength and authority, despite the change in his appearance.

"Yes, Father," she managed past the constriction. "It *is* quite an accomplishment. Marshal Hosokawa has done a remarkable service in protecting my life. We'd hoped you'd come sooner. We could've used the help yesterday."

He blasted a gust through his nose. "I traveled as fast as the roads allowed. You had a hand in defending your own safety, I understand."

"Yes, Father." Why should she deny it? "I'm more like you perhaps than I thought."

"I'm a warrior in *every* way, Saiko. You're not. I'm not surprised by your skill and fighting spirit, however. You'll bring our family great honor in your association with Emperor Go-Mizunoo."

Disappointment sank a weight into her gut. "I love you dearly, Father. You've always been fair and kind with me. This is why I'm not afraid to ask you to reconsider."

"Reconsider?" His eyes narrowed.

"I won't make a good courtesan. I'm too headstrong."

"You'll make a good consort because I say you must!" His voice shook as his fist hit the table. *Sake* and cups jumped then landed with a rattle.

The jodai stiffened. "If you'll excuse me, I have business to attend."

Her father waved a dismissive hand. He waited until the man left then said, "You are no longer a child learning the ways of the world. As a woman, you need to understand sacrifice."

"I understand sacrifice very well, but the sacrifice you ask is too great."

He trembled, whether in anger or weakness she couldn't tell. "Any sacrifice you make for family or country is never too great. This sacrifice is for both."

Anger and fear of losing Takamori, fed by her lack of control over her own life, caused her to fist her hands in her lap. Her fingernails bit into her palms. She whispered, "I love him. Please, Father."

He sighed and slouched a bit. "Saiko, if I could, I would. I cannot void the contract. To withdraw it would dishonor both our family and the shogunate under your brother. I think you forget who you are. I'd never have agreed to let your brother bind you in this way if I suspected for an instant that you were any less the woman than you are. Shogun believes in you. I believe in you."

Without this connection, the shogunate would have to continue in its struggle to maintain its ruling power. This wasn't about her. It was about easing tensions and reducing the number and frequency of uprisings. She understood well but had lost sight of this. Knowing it didn't lessen the pain, however. Tears smarting, she nodded. "I must fulfill the terms of their agreement."

"Yes. You're a woman of birth and quality. I wish you could have the freedoms some lesser women enjoy, but this is bigger than any of that. Bigger than you or your love. Bigger than me, or Shogun, or the emperor by ourselves. You comprehend this, don't you?"

"I do." Never mind her heart shredding. Never mind the loss of any dreams she had for her future. He was right. Her love for Takamori had blinded her and made her forget. "I won't be selfish, Father. I'll leave for Kyōto in the morning."

Pushing at the tabletop, he eased to his feet on a wheezing groan. "You'll leave for Kyōto in an hour."

"An hour?" But she had hoped for a final night in Takamori's arms. She had hoped for the chance to explain why she had to leave him. A crushing weight pressed air from her lungs.

"Even now, your retinue forms at the gate."

"Lady Okiko can't be ready to leave so quickly." How would Okiko face leaving Hoshihiro? How would she find Takamori in time?

"She does not accompany you. I understand she seeks permission to marry. Osaka Jodai sent a messenger to her uncle just before you came to me."

"She didn't tell me."

"You didn't suspect?" He stepped around the table and offered her a hand.

She accepted, not liking the boniness of the hand that had once been substantial. "Of course I suspected. I just hadn't considered she'd stay behind. She's a dear friend. She's been afraid for me."

Part of her was relieved Okiko wouldn't have to leave Hoshihiro, and part of her dreaded the idea of facing entry into the emperor's household alone without a single friendly face to ease her suffering.

He offered a curt nod. "It's best for her to stay. Hoshihiro-san is up for promotion, which will put him in a desirable position. Her uncle would be a fool to pass up this opportunity, and well she knows it."

"It would be difficult to extricate her from the emperor's palace once she enters service. I'm told ladies can never come and go from Kyōto with ease. She's wise to stay and await her uncle's response." Loneliness hollowed her chest, emptying her soul.

"You'll make new friends."

She found him frowning. They both knew she was more likely to make enemies than friends. How could it be any other way among women who competed for the time and affection of one man?

Chapter Eighteen

"Is there a call to arms at the castle?" asked Shosan, urging his horse next to Takamori's as they approached the castle road from the town.

On the wall-walk, bowman increased their number. Pike bearers also ran the length of the northern side. He frowned. "It can't be another attack."

"I doubt Tokugawa-shogun's leaving so soon. We just got here."

Leaving. Yes, someone prepared to leave. "Saiko-san."

"My lord?"

Takamori shook his head. He kicked his horse, abandoning his friend and the other men in their surveillance party. Ieyasu had tricked him. He'd sent him to scout the city knowing he planned to send Saiko away. But to where? Surely not to Kyōto. Not after everything she'd endured.

Inside, he couldn't mistake her travel retinue. Her palanquin had received repairs – or at least patches enough to withstand a couple days' travel. The emperor's dignitaries, dressed entirely in black silk and wearing the tall headpieces of their stations, climbed into an ox-drawn carriage ahead of it. He pulled his horse to a skidding halt and slid from the saddle. Halfway along the organizing line, he spotted the old man.

"Don't give me grief," said Ieyasu upon his approach. "This is just as much her decision as it is mine."

Takamori refused to believe it. "Where is she?"

"Right behind me."

Saiko emerged from the main building, her fine lavender and blue checked kimono extra-long where it trailed after her sandals and from the sleeves of her white quilted jacket. Her features appeared tight, as if from pain or distress.

"Princess," he said, taking three long strides to stand before her. "Tell me you don't want to go. I swear to the gods, I'll fight for your honor. For our love."

Her bottom lip quivered, her sweet face pointed at his chest. "My honor demands that I complete my journey to Kyōto. I want to go, Takamori-san."

"I can't believe it," he whispered. His mind reeled from the pain of losing her.

Beside her, Okiko sniffled and wiped a tear. "It's true."

Saiko pressed her lips together and headed for her palanquin. "It's more a matter of needing to go than wanting to."

How could she walk away? She loved him. He didn't doubt it. So how did she find the strength to do this? He followed her, fighting a desire to take her hand and make her stop. "You don't need to go. There are other Tokugawa women who can take your place. Why must it be you?"

"None with her learning and presence." Her father opened her palanquin's door. He said on a scowl, "Don't challenge me on this Takamori-san."

Saiko halted at the door but didn't enter. She faced Takamori, her eyes moist and sorry. "Only Shogun's daughter has the characteristics necessary to take a place of honor in the emperor's household, but my niece won't be old enough for two more years. I have to go *now*. For peace."

"Two more years of uprisings could send Japan into a revolution." Ieyasu's mouth straightened into a stern line. "Neither Go-Mizunoo nor my son is prepared to manage that. You had a taste of it yesterday. It'll only continue."

Takamori wanted to shout his pain and displeasure because they spoke the truth. He had nothing to convince either that she should stay. For Japan, she should go, but it didn't ease his hopelessness. "I'll gather my things and prepare to go."

"That won't be necessary." Her father gave her a helping hand into the palanquin while Okiko assisted with her trailing kimono. "Shosan-san will lead this retinue."

"I will?" Shosan, still upon his horse, thrust his chin Takamori's way.

"I need to go," said Takamori, suddenly drowning in the realization that he was losing her this very second.

Ieyasu closed the door, and Saiko sent a hand out the window to his shoulder. Her voice caught on a sob as she said, "I need you to stay."

"Princess—"

"This is already nearly impossible." She tugged at him, and he leaned to the opening. "You're everything to me, and going without you makes me wish I could die. But having you come on the journey would be a hundred times worse."

"Why?" He searched her lovely, sorrow-darkened visage. They were two days from Kyōto. They could have that time together.

"Because every moment more with you makes me yearn for what I can't have. It would be unbearable, and I'd fight temptation to betray my family and country."

"You meet the needs of your duty but deny the needs of your heart." His chest ached so badly he thought he might vomit. How could love hurt so much?

"I'm sorry, friend," said his second-in-command. A soldier ran from the barracks and handed belongings in a neat roll to Shosan who reined his horse around and trotted to the front of the line.

Saiko gave his shoulder a squeeze then withdrew her hand. Her voice sounded strangled when she said, "I'll love you, only you, for all of my life."

Shosan raised a fist, and the line of soldiers advanced through the gate.

"There must be a way," Takamori said, his stomach lurching in alarm. She was leaving. Now.

"To avert revolution? To guarantee peace without uniting

the ruling families?"

Her palanquin shifted forward, and he took a step. Panic twisted in his gut. He'd never thought to find a woman like her. A love like hers. But he had, and now it sifted through his fingers like sand. "By the gods, there must be a way out of this. We just can't see it."

As the palanquin traveled toward the gate, her voice grew weaker. "I'll never love another."

The retinue picked up speed, and Takamori stepped away. He stood as her box passed through the gate then disappeared around the first bend in the castle road. The weight of the world crashed down on him, suffocating him.

She was gone.

*   *   *   *

In the meeting hall of the main compound tower, Takamori somehow managed to force past his constricting throat, "Before we begin preparations to return to Sumpu, I would beg a moment of your time."

Ieyasu glared up at him from where he sat. "You dishonored my daughter. Our family faces great shame if Go-Mizunoo rejects her."

Takamori bowed respectfully. "I'm sorry for any disgrace I've caused, but I'm not sorry for my time with Saiko-san." He stood upright, keeping his gaze lowered in courtesy. "I love her. With everything in me, with everything I am, I love her."

A hand placed on the floor to aid his ascent, revealing a frailty not otherwise apparent, Ieyasu stood. He grunted then sighed. "Saiko is dearest to me. Besides my oldest son who is now Shogun, it's my youngest daughter who inherited my warrior's skill. My warrior's spirit. Like me, when she loves, it'll be with only one, and it'll be forever."

A terrible pain twisted in Takamori's chest. "It's this way with me, as well."

Ieyasu waved him in then collected *sake* and two ceramic cups from a shelf. He set everything down on *tatami* matting before his blue silk cushion. "You're young. You've loved before, and you'll love again."

Takamori stepped quickly until he stood behind a brown cushion opposite to the retired shogun's. "I've never loved before Saiko-san, and I can never love another. She completes me. Where she is, I am."

The old man stared, a fierce scowl upon his sagging features.

"You could've ordered my death."

"I *should* have ordered your death." Ieyasu's voice held none of the anger his face had shown. He sank to his blue silk cushion with a moan. "I'm dying."

Takamori startled. The great and powerful Tokugawa Ieyasu was dying? It didn't seem possible. Then again, nobody lived forever. Most never reached Ieyasu's age. He studied the old man. "You're so easy about it."

Ieyasu shrugged and indicated the brown cushion. "I have nothing to fear from death. The gods have blessed me in this rich life. Sit."

"I don't fear death, either. In fact, I'm prepared to have you take my life. It would end my suffering." He pictured Saiko in the emperor's arms, her expression blank and her soul crying out to him. His head wound began to throb, and he pushed fingertips against it as he settled to the floor.

"You suffer for my daughter." Ieyasu handed him a cup.

Takamori accepted but didn't drink. He poured *sake* into the dying samurai's cup. "I suffer for the loss of her. For the knowledge that she's duty-bound to leave me, and I'm duty-bound not to follow. I suffer for the idea that I may never see her again." His voice broke. He took a sip of *sake* and closed his eyes, welcoming its burn down his throat and into his stomach. "Am I less of a man for loving her so much?"

Ieyasu slowly shook his head. "I love her mother this way still. My wife died years ago, but she was and still is my one. Despite the concubines in my household, there was never another. Not even casually."

"Part of me thinks it would hurt worse if she'd died, and I should take consolation in that she lives and shares this world with me, though we can't be together. Part of me despairs that she lives but I can't be with her. It takes all my strength to stay when I think only about how much I want to take a horse and run to her."

"You seek to leave my service?"

Takamori closed his eyes. "You're like family to me. Like a father. I don't seek to leave your service before you're ready to release me."

"But your heart breaks."

"My heart breaks." He set down his cup and looked at his sword's hilt where it protruded from his belt. He rubbed his thumb across his family crest. Saiko's face filled his mind, and he drowned in her liquid eyes. "I'm tired of war."

Ieyasu said nothing for a long time. "When I die, you and my retainers will relocate to Edo and into service to my son, Shogun. Unless I release you ahead of time..."

Takamori held his breath. If Ieyasu-shogun released him, would he go to Kyōto, instead? Should he? What would he accomplish? To exist in that city only to live for a chance at a momentary glimpse of his love? To lay at night in a city where she lay with another?

"What will you do?" asked Saiko's father. "Become a monk?"

"No. That's Shosan-san's calling, I think. I'd like to teach."

Ieyasu offered a curt nod and sipped his *sake*. "You'd do very well to open your own *bushido* school. You have the reputation and tremendous skill necessary to attract the best students, but you'd need help, I think."

"The only help I ever wanted or needed has gone to Kyōto."

"Then it's settled. You'll return with me to Sumpu. I can't undo this vital union. Hidetada-shogun's daughter will join Saiko as Go-Mizunoo's consort in a couple years and make the union between Kyōto and Edo even stronger. Finish your service to me. Then I'll release you to go start your school."

Takamori died inside. Ieyasu wouldn't withdraw Saiko's

consignment to Go-Mizunoo's household. If only he'd taken a deathblow in battle. What had Saiko saved him for? A life of missing her? A life of loneliness? How would he bear this?

*   *   *   *

In the comfort of an April evening, Saiko undressed down to her closest three layers of thin silk under-robes and dismissed her maids. She wiped a tear. When would the pain lessen? Would she ever come to a day when she didn't miss Takamori every waking minute? She settled to a cushion, tucking her feet next to her hip.

Life in Kyōto hadn't met with her expectations. The emperor hadn't greeted her upon her arrival. It had taken him two days simply to send her a note that contained one word: Welcome. She received nothing since. No visits. No gifts. Not even a chance to see him. She had no idea what the man looked like.

To make matters worse, servants had made her aware that guards had thwarted two rebel attempts to break into the palace grounds and assassinate her. Only servants spoke to her, and what few encounters she had with ladies in the household left her cold. They openly scorned her, and she couldn't blame them because she represented both competition and enemy.

She released a light laugh. "Competition. Ha! The man hasn't spared me five seconds. They shouldn't worry a wink."

She preferred it this way. She betrayed her love for Takamori by simply residing in this place. To win the emperor's favor and affection would betray him a thousand times worse. She shuddered. "Better I commit *harakiri* and restore every-one's honor."

The moment the words left her lips, she recognized she couldn't truly mean them. Like her mother, she loved life.

"Excuse me?" Her door slid aside to reveal a young man resplendent in a red Chinese-style robe with gold embroidered dragons and a matching cap. "Did you say *harakiri*?"

The emperor. She took in his kind eyes before lowering her lashes. She smoothly swiveled and, shifting her hips onto her heels, faced him. Touching her forehead to *tatami* matting covering her bedroom floor, she said, "Your Majesty."

He entered unbidden and touched her shoulder.

"You do me great honor in this visit." She straightened from her bow, wondering what his presence tonight would bring her from the other ladies in the morning.

"You do me great honor in agreeing to come live with me, Princess. I am the envy of all to have such a famous warrior princess of renowned beauty in my household."

Famous warrior princess? Renowned beauty? "Please forgive me, but do you refer to the story people began telling a few weeks ago?"

"Stories or reports?" He sank gracefully to an emerald satin cushion a comfortable distance from hers. "Are you implying they are not accurate?"

"Stories? There's more than one story about me?" She glanced quickly at him then away. He appeared relaxed, even amused, though his shoulders belied his tension. It occurred to her she made him nervous. Why?

He chuckled. "We began receiving word of an attack by rogue samurai on your travel party. Reports said you personally fought by the side of your father's marshal. Is that wrong?"

"Not entirely. I wasn't by his side, exactly. More like sharing his horse."

He laughed. "Then the report is accurate and not a story. A day before you arrived, I heard another *report*. This one said you fought in a great battle at Osaka Castle. Refute this."

Saiko sighed. "I stayed atop the castle wall and sent arrows down from the walkway."

"You wanted to be on that battlefield, I would wager."

"We can't always have what we want. Sacrifice for the greater good seems to be the theme of my life."

"Sacrifice? So something happened that made you especially want to leave that wall?"

"Yes." Nausea surfaced at the memory of Takamori fighting

a losing battle, blood mixing with sweat to form red lines down his face. She swallowed past a lump and took a deep, calming breath.

The emperor cleared his throat. "I am proud to have a courageous and loyal woman in my house. You are rare. The women of my experience are neither courageous nor loyal."

"Then I'm sorry for you. The women of mine have these qualities and more." She studied him through her lashes. "You should know I suspect a faction is based here in Kyōto. In your very court. It takes a great deal of rice to pay such a large army of *ronin*."

He stared at her, his features melting slowly into a mild scowl. After a time, he said, "You suspect me."

"I don't, no. Do you have any idea who might be behind the attacks?"

His eyes narrowed and his mouth tightened. "I will concede an investigation might be in order."

"My duty requires I live here, but my love and loyalty lie elsewhere. It's only fair you know this."

He studied her a moment longer.

She dropped her gaze to her lap.

"I do not require your love," he said quietly.

She gathered a handful of silk from her thigh and clenched her fist around it. "What is it you do require, if you don't mind my asking?"

He sniffed and parted his lips, but a squeal from the maid's rooms at the other end of her suite stopped him from speaking. They shared a questioning look, then Saiko turned her attention to her still-open doorway.

Quiet footfalls on hardwood told her an enemy approached along the hallway. A maid's steps would shuffle, and a retainer's walk would proudly announce. This was an invader.

She pointed toward the nearest corner and whispered, "You should hide. Danger's coming."

Without waiting to see if he took her advice, she rolled backward off of her cushion and slid her hands under her fluffy futon. The second her fingers connected with hard, wrapped leather, she leapt to her feet. Her two short swords slid free.

Weapons in hand, she spun into ready stance in time to block a strike as a samurai in a red-brown monk's robe rushed inside. She sliced her other blade at chest high. He blocked, which ceased his forward progression.

Saiko's heart pounded as she lunged for him. The confined space offered limited room to maneuver, so in order to gain speed and momentum enough to strike a disabling blow, she executed a reverse turn. She sent one sword in a circle around her head while using the second to protect her chest. When she finished her turn, her high blade sliced into his shoulder right as his weapon made contact with the one blocking her chest. He cried out and took an evading slide backward.

A second *ronin* arrived and leaped to his cohort's side. His russet hood fell to his back, revealing an older face twisted in hatred. They met her, long samurai swords at the ready. She jumped over her cushion in a double attack, hoping to force the two out.

From the corner, a red blur caught her attention. She landed in a defensive stance, facing the sudden movement. Issuing a cry, Go-Mizunoo lunged at the nearest samurai with a dagger. His grip and posture clearly evidenced his lack of training.

She fought panic. If he died during an attack on her, a conflict against Shogun and his government would no longer consist of an underground initiative manned by lordless samurai. His death here in her room would be the impetus for a full-scale war funded by Kyōto's nobles and commanded by daimyo who had lost their lands after losing against her father years ago. She couldn't let that happen.

The samurai turned in a split second, swinging his weapon in a low upward slice meant to cut her inner thigh. Saiko barely had time to respond. She sprang high, bringing one sword blade down in a block that deflected the attack while sending the hilt of the other into the emperor's chest. Go-Mizunoo stumbled into the corner, issuing a loud grunt.

Saiko landed on her *tatami* matting and kicked into a spin. She slammed the samurai in the head, her under-robes parting easily to allow her roundhouse kick. Continuing in her spin, she crouched low. She positioned one blade at an angle to block her head, forcing the second *ronin's* chop to ricochet off of it, and cut his ankles with her other. He toppled on an agonized cry.

She recovered quickly, blinked a trickle of perspiration from her eye, and checked the corner to make sure Go-Mizunoo didn't prepare to attempt another assault. He slumped against the wall, fingers at his sternum where she'd thumped him.

The first samurai bounced off of her doorway then gave his head a vigorous shake. He snarled. Without taking his eyes from her, he glided forward in the beginnings of a step-spin-slice.

He underestimated her. Did they never learn? On a relieved exhale, she lunged and stabbed while his long blade still made its downward rotation at his side. His blocking arm at his chest lowered too slowly to stop her weapon from sliding smoothing into his gut. For power, she bellowed a fierce war cry and wrenched her sword sideways. It slit his abdomen deep enough to kill.

His eyes widened right before he dropped where he stood. His sword hit the floor a second before he did.

Saiko didn't clean her sword, however. She swiped a trickle of perspiration from her hairline using the back of her wrist then strode three steps to stand over the second samurai who tried to claw his way on his belly to her doorway.

"This is done," she said, holding the slanted tip of her bloodied blade to his throat.

He stilled. He tipped his chin to meet her stare in a show of disrespectful defiance. "This will never be done."

Chapter Nineteen

"This *is* done, and so are you." She thrust her sword point into his windpipe and yanked her weapon's sharp edge through, severing the thick blood vessel at the side of his neck. His life poured from him, and she said a silent prayer to the gods to somehow let this senseless loss of life mean something.

She withdrew her weapon and gave it a flick to send the blood from its blade. Sighing, she planted the hilts of her swords at her hips, setting the blades behind her – safe but ready for use. Not sparing the emperor a glance, she said, "Stay here, Your Majesty."

Heavy, running footfalls pounded wooden floorboards. The emperor's guards approached. She met the captain at the end of her corridor. He stopped with a few of his men, and the rest jogged toward her bedroom, swords drawn.

"How many were there?" she asked quietly, taking in blood spatters on his uniform.

"We defeated sixteen outside." He studied her destroyed robes. "How many made it inside?"

"Only two."

The captain marched to her door where a guard waved the okay.

A second later, the emperor emerged and stood next to her. "You saved my life."

Saiko only nodded. She wouldn't have needed to if he'd stayed out of the way. "They were after *me*, Your Majesty."

He directed a hard stare at his captain. "This threat is

unacceptable. Everyone in my household was in danger tonight because of these so-called supporters of the empire. I want to know who is behind this. It has to be a daimyo, and I will have his name."

"Yes, Your Majesty," said the captain with a deep bow.

Go-Mizunoo took two steps as if to leave then halted. He faced Saiko. "Perhaps we would do well to involve your brother, the shogun. It can only help if we combine our efforts."

"You're most wise," she agreed, though she doubted a daimyo had plotted this.

"I will send him my request in the morning." He rubbed his chest. "I will have an audience with you in a week or two."

"Of course," she said, bowing low. Did he mean to see her punished for assaulting him? She wished she knew.

He waved a hand, and she noticed for the first time that her entire staff clustered, waiting and watching in her drawing room. Servants belonging to other ladies in the household swelled their number, no doubt come at their mistresses' bidding to gather information about the night's disturbance. Tonight would provide grand fodder for their gossip. She frowned at the intruding servants, but it did no good. They had eyes only for the emperor.

Her two maids shuffled into the hall, their foreheads nearly at their knees, so deeply did they bow.

"See to the care of my princess," said Go-Mizunoo. "She is most precious to me."

Saiko shuddered. Never would she be *his* princess. No matter how much he showed her favor, she'd only ever belong to Takamori.

*   *   *   *

Late spring heat threatened to cook Takamori as he leaned over his horse's neck and gave it an encouraging pat. Dirt and grass flew to the sky as his mount's hind hooves dug into the earth. Still, they didn't go fast enough. In his opinion, they wouldn't achieve a satisfying speed until his horse sprang wings and flew.

He didn't know what kind of greeting he expected in Kyōto, but he would speak to Saiko. He would see her. Considering the news he brought, nobody dared deny him. A thick knot in his throat, he urged his horse faster.

*   *   *   *

In an antechamber gleaming with pristine burgundy and ebony lacquered walls, Saiko shuffled sock-enshrouded feet across smooth hardwood to a bright window. She slid its panel aside and inhaled scents of oncoming summer. She longed to go out and enjoy the sunshine.

The last profusion of blossoms bedecking tree limbs gave way to leaves, and tiny ground flowers decorated thick green grass. Last night, she had denied Go-Mizunoo access to her bed. Had she called his honor into question by refusing him her body, and thus his authority over her? Would he allow her to live to welcome summer's beauty?

"Princess," said a man, his voice mingling in the grating of wood on wood as he slid open the door. "The emperor summons you."

She pivoted on the balls of her feet and offered a cursory inclination of her head toward an elderly chancellor. She followed him along a dim hallway, his stark indigo kimono and slippers in sharp contrast to the formal white and ruby of her attire. It surprised her how much, in his gait, posture, and attire, he resembled her would-be tutor, Master Hayashi. It made her uncomfortable, though she didn't know why.

Her maids had approved the austere white for such an occasion, but severely showed their dislike for the red. Saiko had insisted. If he ordered her to commit suicide, it fit that she wore the color of her death. She also found it poetic how the crimson of her under-robe showing at neck and overlong sleeve and the matching hue of her *obi* seemed to symbolize spilled blood – the very reason for this audience, in her opinion.

His chancellor led her into a spacious room where thick golden columns supported an impossibly high ceiling. When she reached the halfway point, a servant in a black and white checkered knee-length kimono appeared in the far doorway. His topknot quivered in agitation, and he wrung his hands as his eyes darted from the administrator to Saiko and back.

The chancellor halted and waved the servant near. They whispered, heads bent.

Saiko sighed. She just wanted this audience finished. Her stomach lurched, and she closed her eyes. Takamori's strong, handsome features consumed her memory. A life with him would've meant no more of this court intrigue. None of the silly jealousies that made ladies hate each other. None of those secrets. A life with Takamori could've been honest. Real. Meaningful. A life filled with love. Not this empty semblance here in Kyōto.

The administrator sent her a worried look, his slanted eyes more open under raised lines passing for eyebrows. "You have a guest."

A guest. Had Okiko changed her mind and left Hoshihiro? No. Her last letter sounded too content. Perhaps she only visited and planned some wedding shopping in the old capitol. "Will she wait?"

The servant made a high-pitched squeak and stumbled over his own feet in his hurry to escape.

The administrator scowled, and his flat nose lifted into the air. "Your visitor has no choice but to wait. The emperor expects you, and we have kept him too long already."

She wanted to scream, or better yet, trip the self-important peacock. Few things would satisfy her more in that moment than seeing this pompous aristocrat fall on his face. She stifled a wave of nausea and fell in step behind him.

She passed through the far doorway where the flustered servant had gone and entered a long corridor lit by glowing lanterns and lined on one side by gold doors equally spaced. Ink drawings and finely worked scrolls provided decoration on wall sections between the doors.

Her guide led her to the last door. He rapped a single knock, and the door immediately opened.

This was it. This would either go very well or mark the beginning of her end. She took a deep breath. If only she hadn't been so bound to the honor of her duty.

The administrator waved her in but didn't follow. Instead, he closed the door. A boy on the verge of manhood offered her a tight-lipped smile and indicated she should follow a row of fancy, painted single-panel screens.

As she passed scenes of flying cranes and ancient noblewomen playing instruments, natural light increased apace with the size of the stone forming in her belly.

Her guard up, she stepped into a wide audience chamber that overlooked a perfect garden. Bamboo blinds hung in rolls at ceiling level, making it possible to simply step outside with no impediment. A warm breeze billowed a few hairs that had come loose from her elaborate coiffure, and their ends wrapped the nape of her neck.

Emperor Go-Mizunoo sat cross-legged atop a long platform at the back of the chamber. A dozen aristocratic advisors wearing varying shades of gray and black sat in a neat cluster facing the platform. Nobody appeared pleased.

She was doomed.

She gulped, suddenly staggering under the idea that she may never see Takamori again. She hadn't realized until this moment how much she'd clung to the hope.

"Princess Saiko," acknowledged the emperor.

Keeping her eyes downcast, she chose a pillow at the foot of the dais and settled to her knees before touching her forehead to the floor. "Your Majesty, I'm at your mercy."

He laughed. "It may be that I am at yours. Please be comfortable."

She lifted her forehead and set her hips onto her feet. "I don't understand."

Low murmurs passed through the assembled gentlemen.

The emperor rose, placed his hands behind his back, and

inclined his head toward her in a token bow. "You saved my life. I acknowledge you before my advisors."

"But, last night..."

"That was nothing. I am not so insecure that I cannot be considerate of an aching heart." He paused then paced once to the far end of the dais and back. "My advisors agree with me that you must be rewarded for your willingness to risk your life to protect me, but we have a problem."

She waited, unsure if he wanted her to speak. She no longer feared for her life, but what did he expect of her now? Until this moment, she thought he had chosen to let the incident go without an audience. The attack had been weeks ago.

"We are well aware that you are unlike any lady in Kyōto. Perhaps, unlike any lady in Japan. We could not offer you silks or jewels or any of the fine things women usually want. What if you were not duly impressed? What if these things do not properly reward you?"

She schooled her features, fighting a frown. Where did he go with his confusing ramble?

"We have, therefore, decided to grant you one request. Anything you desire. What is the one thing I can give you that will let you feel my deep gratitude?"

Her mind spun. Did she dream? His advisors appeared worried, some downright scared. What did they think she would ask? Or was it not knowing the magnitude of her demand that had them concerned?

The only questions holding her attention, however, was whether or not he would grant her request, and whether or not she should ask. She wanted one thing. She faced Go-Mizunoo but planted her gaze on the edge of the platform under his elegant golden slippers.

"Freedom," she said simply. She braced for his anger.

"Freedom?" His voice sounded high and feminine in his surprise.

The advisors skipped their murmuring and talked openly among themselves.

"Quiet!" The emperor stood a minute in the suddenly silent room.

Birdsong and breeze rustling bright garden fauna provided the sole relief from the room's tense quiet.

"I offer you anything," he said after a time. "Miles of silks, trunks full of jewels, your own property...whatever you want."

"I want the freedom to leave. I want to be released from my duty to serve you. I know I can't have it, though. I'm told my residence here has quieted the uprisings and brought true peace to Japan. I won't compromise that."

The advisors exchanged questioning looks, and she sensed relief in their ranks. What price would they have paid had she asked for riches? Something told her the cost would have exceeded any monetary value and included political ramifications.

"Then you have not heard." Go-Mizunoo stepped to the edge of his dais and squatted.

"Heard what, Your Majesty?" She tensed, afraid he'd speak of revolution or worse. She hated her seclusion in this place.

"I shouldn't tell you. I enjoy your presence in my palace too much." He chuckled, shaking his head, then grew sober. He shot a weighted look toward an advisor sitting in front who offered a nod in response. "Your niece has come to live here. She arrived last week."

"She's too young, Emperor."

"Hmm. Yes, I understand this. She did not undergo her ceremony before coming, as you did. She came to study our ways and live among our nobles. She will conduct her ceremony here in Kyōto to become my consort when she is of a better age. Shogun and I both agree this will make life here more bearable for her."

"Yes. She's young." Saiko relaxed a bit. Shogun's daughter in the palace would ensure continued peace, however. Why had nobody told her? Keeping her eyes from his face, she said, "I would've liked to welcome my brother's daughter with a visit, but under the circumstances, I ask for my freedom in earnest."

"I do not care to lose you," said Go-Mizunoo.

"You cannot lose what you never had, Your Majesty. I may physically exist in your household, but my mind and spirit reside elsewhere."

He backed from the edge and sat upon his cushion in thoughtful ease. "Are you saying you cannot develop affection for me? It hardly seems fair to make such an assumption when you do not know me. We have spent almost no time together. Will you not give me a chance?"

Saiko shifted her gaze to his chest then hazarded a peek at his face. "I'm here only out of obligation to family and country. If we're completely honest, perhaps you might admit that you only want me as a prize. There's no affection lost. No opportunity for affection lost."

His eyebrows shifted upward out of a pensive frown, and humor replaced a hard glint. "Well, I might admit it."

"Will you deny me my request?"

"After I already granted you your any desire in front of so many witnesses?" He chuckled and indicated his crowd of advisors with an outstretched arm. "Would you have me appear selfish and hard?"

She contemplated her thumb sweeping the silk covering her thigh. She prayed he would let her go.

"What if I demanded you alter your request and ask for anything else?"

"Please."

The silence grew oppressive.

"Very well. With you, Princess, I cannot ignore the sensation that I cage a bird meant to fly free and that you will lose your strength and purpose in this luxurious imprisonment to which your father has consigned you."

Her hope soared. She bit her lip to prevent a smile as her stomach performed a rejoicing somersault.

"Shall I make arrangements to caravan you to your father's castle?"

She placed her forehead upon the floor then rocked back and stood. This was really happening. "You're most gracious and generous. An entourage won't be necessary, however. I'm told I have a visitor. I'll return with her. If you'd kindly agree to spare a wagon and driver to ship my belongings to Sumpu, I'd be appreciative."

"It is the least I can do. The very least, indeed." As she offered another bow, he descended from the dais and stood before her. "Will you not reconsider?"

"I can't," she whispered. "My heart isn't in Kyōto."

"Ah. Now I understand." He studied her a moment longer then retreated a step. "I hope one day we will meet again."

Perhaps they would. She inclined her head then forced her feet to a stately pace despite their urge to run. She was free and ready to burst with joy. Finally, she had a chance to find Takamori. A chance for true happiness.

"Please show me to my guest," she told the attendant outside the door, glad to sound so much more composed than she felt.

She grasped shaking hands in front of her stiff *obi* and hurried after the young man. He showed her to an antechamber near the palace's main entrance. Without a word, he bowed and slid open the door.

Saiko froze in terrified delight as Takamori spun from a window, his expression difficult to read. She prayed she didn't dream. His eyes reflected a hint of happiness then a dark sadness. Did she also sense hope, or mistake despair?

"Princess Saiko," he said with a bow.

"Marshal." She offered a bow equal in depth and length. When she stepped inside, the boy closed the door, leaving her alone with the man who possessed her. She wanted to fly into his arms and soar on his kiss. "I'm so surprised and overjoyed to see you."

A brief light shone in his gaze. "I missed you more than I can put into words."

"I missed you, too." Tension whooshed out of her, and she stumbled to him on trembling legs. Wrapping her arms around his middle, she pressed her cheek to his chest. "I feel like I've just been brought back from death."

His sword hilt pressed into her belly, but she didn't care. He wore a dusting of travel grime, letting her know he had come to her immediately upon arriving. It meant everything.

"I have news," he said, his voice deep and quiet. He rested his hand on her hip while grazing fingertips along the nape of her neck.

She sighed. "I had hoped you'd only used that as an excuse to come."

His fingers made another pass across her nape, sending chills down her spine. Then he put a hand on her shoulder and took a step backward, out of her embrace. "It's your father."

His dark eyes, sad and full of worry, told her so much. The bottom fell out of her stomach. "Something's happened."

"Yes. I'm sorry."

"You're sorry? He died?" Shock sent icy fingers into her chest. "I knew he wasn't well. He suffered before I left Sumpu, not that he would've admitted it."

The sad lines around his eyes still offered an edge of strength, but he said nothing.

The shock faded, and a heat that caused perspiration to moisten her upper lip replaced the cold. She began to tremble. "But dead? It's strange how I always thought he'd live forever."

Takamori nodded solemnly. "We all did. He had lived so long already."

Her vision blurred a moment before tears spilled past her lashes. She hugged herself and searched Takamori's face. "Did he have pain?"

He shook his head and gathered her close. "He had returned to his home, Suruga. He took us on a hawking tour, but it took the last of his strength, I think. He grew very ill. I ate with him that evening, and he passed in his sleep."

"When?" Her father's face came to mind, and she closed her eyes to savor it.

"Three days ago."

He had ridden hard, turning a five-day trip into three. No wonder word hadn't yet reached Kyōto.

"He loved you best," said Takamori.

"Yes," she whispered, barely managing with a throat gone tight. "He takes his place among the most honored of my family's ancients."

He gathered her in his arms and held her until her tears ceased and her feet ached. "I can stay a day, but they are moving him to Sumpu as we speak. I must return for his final procession."

"I'm coming."

"You can't without—"

"I'm released from my service by the emperor himself. This very day. I'm free."

He eased her to arm's length but didn't let her go and searched her eyes. "Truly?"

"Truly."

Hope and longing lifted the angles of his handsome face.

"One hour," she said, hugging him with all her might. "I'll change," she said, lifting an arm to show its floor-length sleeve, "into something more suitable for traveling, and arrange for the packing of my belongings. I'll meet you in the courtyard."

"My love." He placed a finger under her chin and tipped her face upward. His lips lowered to hers, and her grieving melted.

It amazed her how she could experience such sadness and such joy at the same time.

*　*　*　*

As the sun approached its zenith, Saiko strode from the emperor's palatial compound. She wore a purple raw silk trouser skirt under a steel-blue jacket and matching damask sash. In her sash she had secured two *wakizashi*, their black leather hilts in stark contrast against the white of her *kosode*, which fitted to her torso and emphasized her grace and strength. Here came the warrior princess he knew her to be, and he smiled his approval.

Without a word, she strapped a satchel to the saddle of a gift horse from the emperor's stables and mounted. She rode out at his side.

Just outside the city walls, Takamori cleared his throat. "Are you okay? Do you want to talk about your father?"

"No. I was thinking that I haven't learned yet if a nobleman here in Kyōto organized the *ronin* attacks." Saiko shook her head, her lips pulled in frustrated tightness. "The more I think about it, the more I'm convinced the samurai didn't act on their own. They scattered when their masters lost their domains, and I haven't heard of a single raid by rogue warriors, which would support the theory that they had no financial support. Not that I heard much inside the walls of the palace."

He frowned. "True. We would've had word of raids well before we had left Sumpu."

"So someone brought them together. Someone directed their forces and managed their provisions."

"You're certain the emperor's not behind it?"

"I'm positive. He ordered an investigation, but I doubt he's learned anything."

"Why? Because you suspect as I do?" If she did, he would have validation of his suspicion.

She halted her horse and turned to him. "Do you suspect someone active on both sides?"

"I do." Why had he doubted? Why had he hesitated to begin looking? "Someone who spends time in both Kyōto and Edo."

She nodded, her eyes deepening to obsidian in their intensity. "Yes. Someone in a government position with Shogun, and who has loyalties in the old aristocracy."

"I can think of a few." But who? He put a hand on the smooth sleeve of her jacket where it covered her arm. "When your father died, two men who fit this description immediately departed. Fujiwara left for Edo. He said he needed to offer his service and condolence to your brother. The other, Hayashi, left for Kyōto. He said nothing to anyone about his purpose. He simply left."

"Hayashi oversaw my activities in Sumpu. He knew my

agenda and our traveling schedule."

They stared at each other a long moment then said simultaneously, "Hayashi!"

Chapter Twenty

"That traitor!" spat Saiko. "There he was, tutoring me as though he readied me for the imperial court when the entire time, he plotted my death. He didn't go to Kotu on business shortly after my arrival. He traveled to tell his *ronin* army where and when to attack me." She fisted her hands on her horse's reins. "But how? He lived and worked in Sumpu. How could a traitor accomplish so much while under the constant scrutiny of the shogunate?"

"Easy." He'd kill him! He tamped his outrage by sending a fist into his palm. "Your father ruled from Sumpu, which has a steady coming and going of messengers and resources. As a trusted advisor, Hayashi's dispatch of messages and supplies would've gone unquestioned. Nobody would've known an unofficial messenger came and went, or where."

"How did we not see before? We should've figured this out in Osaka." Saiko closed her eyes and pressed on her eyelids.

"We saw what everyone else did," he said gently, unsure if he could handle it if she cried.

"We have to do something." She glanced at the wall gate they had come through.

"Yes." He wanted to wrap protective arms around her. He let go of her sleeve and took a double grip on his reins. "He raised an army once. He can do it again."

Her eyes darted down the road, back to the gate, and down the road once more. "Now that I've left the emperor's palace,

I'm no longer his target. He'll go after my niece. She has no one and no way to defend against such malevolence. We have to protect her."

"Not by staying in Kyōto." He nudged his horse into motion away from the old capitol.

"But—"

"Princess, we have to find him while he travels."

She drew her mount alongside, and her questioning expression melted into comprehension. The time had come to hunt a monster.

*   *   *   *

They traveled hard, making remarkable progress. By sundown, Takamori led the way into the castle town of Okazaki, approaching the Tokaido Road outpost station from the rear.

Saiko urged her horse toward a packed dirt yard in front of an inn. "He once admitted that he only travels by his own carriage. I think this is the farthest he could've traveled in four days. I'll check if there's a carriage here that bears his family crest."

"Be careful. I'll meet you inside." He dismounted and left his horse, trusting it to stay put.

Inside, the entire first floor served as a restaurant. Nearly every table had diners, and the place buzzed with conversation while servers rushed back and forth. Takamori signaled an older woman who tried to hurry past with a couple of empty bowls. Her fine patterned silk kimono proclaimed her either the proprietress or the proprietor's wife.

"Excuse me," he said.

An irritated expression pinched her full features as she stopped. She eyed the crest at the end of his *katana*, and her demeanor immediately changed. "Marshal Hosokawa, what an honor it is to have you visit our establishment. May I show you to a table? Or perhaps you'd like a room, and I can bring a meal to you there?"

"Not yet." He scanned the vast, bustling restaurant. "I'm

looking for someone. An aristocrat traveling under the seal of Shogun."

Saiko neared and whispered, "He's here."

His senses alert, Takamori placed a wary hand on the hilt of his long sword.

"Well, Marshal, we have three noblemen matching that description. They arrived together and took a single room upstairs." The woman's gaze shifted to his hand on the sword. "Will there be trouble? We don't want trouble here."

Saiko placed a slender hand on her shoulder. "Where are they?"

The woman took in the princess' clothing and *wakizashi*. "A woman samurai?" She shrank, took two steps back, and pointed. "Top of the stairs, third door on the right. Please, it's our nicest room."

As Saiko headed for the stairs at a jog, Takamori took a small sack of copper and silver coins from the folds of his *kosode* and handed them to the woman. "Then I apologize in advance. Give those to the innkeeper."

Sprinting, he took the steps three at a time and joined Saiko before she reached the traitor's door. He whispered, "Three noblemen. It makes more sense than thinking he acted alone."

She thrust open the door and leaped inside, drawing both swords.

Master Hayashi sat with two aristocrats older than he. A lavish meal sat before them upon a wide tatami mat, and opposite them kneeled a fierce samurai, a scar sealing one indented eye permanently closed.

"*Ronin*," said Takamori with disgust. He drew his *katana*, strode into the room, and slammed the door with his foot.

"Kill them!" cried Master Hayashi, hatred rampant in his drooping sneer.

The rogue samurai slowly stood. On a dry, grating voice, he said, "They promise us new masters, new homes, and renewed purpose. They give us an alternative to wandering hungry and homeless. I can't let you interfere with that."

"They can offer you nothing if they're dead," said Saiko.

"Kill them," screeched the nobleman, his voice an octave higher.

The *ronin* advanced with a jump, his long sword drawn and ready in a split second. Takamori withdrew his *wakizashi* and used it to block. Metal met metal, sending a resounding clang reverberating off of the walls. He made to strike at the rogue's back with his *katana*, but the scarred warrior spun, avoiding his attack.

The aristocrats screamed like women, scooting toward the corners while Takamori took the offensive. He had never wanted anyone's blood like he wanted this samurai's. As their long blades clashed, he felt his opponent's strength. The *ronin* had agility too, but Takamori had speed.

In the corner of his eye, he caught a flash of purple as Saiko pursued the noblemen. She let out a war cry, but he didn't take his eyes from the *ronin*.

Takamori took a sliding step back to evade a slash toward his middle. The samurai expected him to come right back and dropped into a crouch to cut Takamori down at the ankles. He knew this maneuver, however, and instead let his thigh muscles bunch. Then he sprang on a lunging step, sending him sailing over his enemy's head. He sent his sword down, cleaving the man's skull open. Not a sound issued from the rogue warrior's lips as he slumped, lifeless.

In the corner, a small blade clattered on the floor. An agonized scream joined a coughing sound a moment before the room went silent. At least the aristocrats had enough honor to offer a fight rather than subjecting Saiko to outright murder.

Takamori met her gaze. They shared an unspoken appreciation and respect of one another. When they turned on Master Hayashi hunched in the far corner, the old man began to scream. He kept screaming, his eyes as wide as his heavy, sagging lids allowed.

"Have you no pride?" asked Saiko, her lip curled in disgust. She took a threatening step toward him, her swords at the ready.

Without warning, Hayashi drew a blade from the folds of his black robes and thrust it at Saiko. "Die!"

Takamori dove for the traitor, long sword first.

She used *yawara* to avoid Hayashi's strike. Her steel caught the traitor in the throat at the same time Takamori's entered between two ribs. The old nobleman let out a gurgling moan then collapsed into the corner. Life leeched from his eyes.

Panting, Takamori withdrew his blade and flicked it clean. Saiko took a step back and did the same, taking in the death they had wrought. He wished he could read her thoughts. Her hands trembled as they sent her cleaned swords into the sash at her waist.

"Let's get out of here," she said, her voice thick.

*   *   *   *

Saiko couldn't ignore the fearful stares of those on the first floor who'd abandoned their meals and now stood as Takamori led her out. More had apparently run outside at the sound of their fight, and stood in whispering groups about the inn's front yard.

Takamori paid them no mind as he strode for his horse. "Mount up. We'll stay at the castle."

Of course. Where better for Shogun's marshal and a princess to stay? Though, she was ready to give up her title and privilege. Before swinging onto the saddle, she whispered to her horse, "I just want to be happy like I was in Mito."

She took off at a gallop, and he followed. With the traitor dispatched, her heart now sought to mourn her father. On edge and about to lose her composure, she needed to secret away, and soon.

She wound her way through the town, barely slowing for corners, and climbed to the castle. She thundered across the Okazaki Castle's moat bridge and through the gate. Takamori pounded across seconds after.

She gently pulled the reins, and her horse's hooves skidded a bit on pale gravel. Pebbles flew. Guards hurried out of the way as a shout sounded. Moments later, a tall, thin samurai approached from the direction of the main tower.

He recognized Takamori and bowed. "Marshal Hosokawa. Welcome."

"Thank you. Honda Oribe, please meet Tokugawa Saiko."

The samurai's eyes widened a fraction before he offered a lower bow. "Princess. We're honored. Please come inside and find comfort. I'll let the daimyo know you've arrived." He waved a couple guards forward to take the horses then turned on his heel and stalked away.

Grateful for the generous welcome, she dismounted and unfastened her satchel from the saddle. Takamori held out a hand, and she gladly took it. His warmth surrounded her fingers as they headed for the white tower.

The castle compound was impressive. It sprawled, so unlike the other castles that utilized defensive rings. Outbuildings, pristine in their whitewash, glowed orange in the evening sun. Ahead, the tower stood four stories high with grayish-black metal eaves over windows at each level.

The emotion of the day overwhelmed her, and she rapidly blinked at tears. She inhaled a deep, shaky breath that helped. Still, she wouldn't hold her composure much longer. She needed to cry – to release the tightness in her chest and to mourn her loss.

At the tower entrance, a servant opened the door and bowed.

Takamori stopped her with a tug on her hand before she could enter. "Your bravery and skill do your family great honor."

Somehow hearing him say so meant more than it would have coming from her father. A wave of sadness washed over her. This time, she couldn't stop a tear from falling. She swiped a wayward strand of hair from her forehead. "Then it's truly over."

"Yes." He brought her hand to the crisscross neckline of his *kosode*. "There's a small but beautiful garden at the south side of the tower. After you bathe, meet me there and we'll go to dinner together."

"Of course." Saiko rubbed her thumb across the back of his hand, enjoying the feel of his thick skin and strong tendons. When he made to pull away, she grasped his fingers. "Thank you for coming to Kyōto in person. Thank you for telling me about my father when you could've sent the news in a missive."

"I can never be so casual with you. You mean too much."

* * * *

A fragrant breeze cooled Takamori's hot cheeks while he stood under the last blooms of a maple tree. Saiko had gone to her room an hour ago, and he began to wonder if she'd come. He imagined her weeping for the loss of her father and refused to intrude upon that. No, he would wait the night through under this tree if she needed.

The cloudless sky allowed him an unencumbered view of a nearly full moon resting on a glittering bed of stars. Did the gods plan to grant him the happiness he envisioned, or would they deny him his dream?

He removed *Whisperings* from his sleeve and traced the thin book's edge. It belonged to her, and he needed to see it returned.

A scuffling footstep made him turn. Princess Saiko stood in a bird's-egg blue kimono and solid black *obi*, her freshly washed hair still wet and drawn atop her head in an intricate twist. Lantern light shone orange upon her shoulders, and her skin appeared to glow in its warm circle.

"You look well," he offered, afraid to move for fear she'd evaporate like a mist as she'd done in his dreams every night since they'd parted.

"You expected me red-eyed and pale?"

"Perhaps." He longed for her to come into his embrace so he could have reassurance that she was real.

"I was," she said with a faint smile. "But I couldn't meet you like that. I want to look beautiful for you."

"I've seen you afraid and worried. I've seen you battle-beaten. Sleep-mussed. Miserable with grief. I've also seen you serene. Happy. In my arms in the throes of passion. Always I see your beauty. It's not in what you wear or how pleasant you set your expression. It's in who you are. What you mean to me. Where you've been and where you're going."

She took a step forward.

The lantern's light fell behind her, casting her lovely face in an interesting pattern of half shadow, half orange glow. "And where am I going?"

His very soul yearned for her, but he refused to go to her. She had to take the last few steps of her own volition.

"For the first time, I have no one telling me where I must go and what I must do." She bowed her head, hesitating a heavy moment. "I can live under my brother's authority..."

"But?"

She inched forward on a halting step, passing out of the orange light and into the clean illumination of the moon. "Now that I have the chance to make my own choices, there's only one thing I want."

He tensed. The uncertainty in her eyes worried him. He'd never seen her insecure. "What is it you want, Princess Saiko?"

She closed the distance between them and landed fingertips upon his bare wrist. "A life with you."

His love for her grew, but so did his anxiety. He placed his hand atop hers, adoring how she'd come to him without his asking. He no longer feared she'd evaporate. Instead, he feared her reaction to the words he had to speak.

He trailed a fingertip along her smooth cheek. "You've only known luxury. I can't give you that."

She kept her eyes lowered, and her face revealed nothing. He wished she'd show some indication of how she took his statement.

"Your father released me from duty. He presented me his proclamation a week ago. It states that, upon his death, I'm free to live where I choose and do as I decide."

"Have you chosen?"

He nodded. "After the battle at Osaka, Yagyu Munenori offered me an opportunity. I'm opening a samurai school in partnership with him. I've already purchased a portion of his lands."

She released a shaky breath. "Are you trying to tell me that you have no place for me in your future?"

He urged her chin upward and met her dark, glistening gaze. "I'm trying to tell you that this is the future I've made. A life of teaching and learning. Though you'd honor me by agreeing to share this future with me, I'll understand if such a simple existence doesn't appeal to you."

He closed his eyes a moment, the idea of parting with her once more almost more than he could bear. He tried to press the book into her hand, but she glanced at it then gave it a gentle push toward him.

"Doesn't appeal to me?" Moisture pooled along her lower eyelids. "Nothing could appeal to me more. A quiet life at your side where we decide *together* what's best? Takamori-san, I want nothing more."

He caught a tear from her lashes before it slipped to her skin. He massaged it between thumb and forefinger. "I love you."

She offered him a watery smile. "I love you, too."

His heart soared. "Then honor me and my family and become my wife?"

Her smile grew, reaching her eyes. "Yes. Marrying you is all I've wanted since we met on my bridge in Sumpu."

"Marrying you is all I've wanted my entire life."

His worry and anxiety fled. In the pure light of a lover's moon, he lowered his lips to hers and sealed his promise of a life worth living. The promise of a life of their own making, a life together, loving always.

The End

Chapter One

Kyō, Japan
March 31, 1001

"I don't want a house full of women." Yūkan drained his cup of *sake*, smoothing an appreciative finger along his friend's porcelain. He'd traded some of the finest dishes throughout the eastern world and recognized that Lord Yoki had acquired the best. "As it is, I'm not used to this aristocratic life you *good people* live. What makes you think I want to infect my home with the arguing and cackling of women?"

"You only think that because you've never experienced the pleasure of having lovely ladies at your beck and call," said Lord Yoki from across a low, beautifully wrought black pine table. His effeminate features thoughtful and still smooth despite his thirty-one years, he gestured toward his servant who stood at the far side of the vast common area of his mansion's main building. "Ladies ready and willing. Eager to please. Working hard to gain your favor above the others."

It only showed how little this dandy of a gentleman knew. Yūkan naïve? Ha! Annoyance nudging him, he returned, "You're naïve. You've been doing business with me for years. Both of you. Can you imagine me with a bevy of women? I can barely manage one at a time." He shuddered, not having to fake his horror.

Shizuka, the too-thin minister of trade in his staid robe of office and his face bearing his thirty years far less gracefully than Yoki's, snuffled his mirth. He took the *sake* bottle and refilled Yūkan's cup. "Don't blame the ideal for the fact that you've never wished to add to your household. All those women you've bedded, and you're trying to tell me you never wanted to make a single one a permanent part of your life?"

"Not one." Yūkan made a derisory snort then thrust his hands from inside his sleeves and pressed warm palms to his stiff, ice-cold cheeks. A servant stoked a brazier, but the heat it emitted didn't begin to warm the room's massive area. "You've both done well. Minister, you've taken a wife who represents what a wife should be. I've no interest whatsoever in meeting any of your consorts. And you, Yoki, don't have a single permanent lover in your house, so you can't criticize. Believe me, though. I wouldn't want to trade places with either of you. You're suited to this life. Even though we share an age, I'm not interested in making any woman a part of my household."

"So you've not found a wife because of your own skittishness then?" Yoki sipped his rice wine and ran a hand down the glittering peacock blue damask of his rich array.

"Skittishness? You compare me with a lamb or doe?" Yūkan sniffed with disdain then laughed at the idea. "I haven't married partly in dread and partly in kindness. Dread of marrying the wrong woman and having to live with a harridan, or worse, a mindless, uneducated dolt. Kindness in sparing a woman, or women as you'd have me take, the unfortunate fate of having to live with my unrefined, manly ways."

"As an import shipper, you've traveled the world. You can't claim ignorance of women. I suspect your knowledge is in pleasuring, however. A lady of this fine city can enhance your life. Bring beauty and culture into your home."

Shizuka plunked his empty cup upon the table. "I imagine we wouldn't even be having this conversation if you'd gotten your meeting with the emperor, but I'm glad we're talking. Will you spend the rest of your days wasting away with drink and common one-night rendezvous, never begetting an heir or achieving enlightenment through love? I won't have it. You're a son of the finest of our families. A Minamoto."

"You say this to me but not Lord Yoki? You describe his life better than mine." The *sake* began to cloud his thinking, and Yūkan gave his head a vigorous shake. "I didn't come to Kyō to find a wife or consort, and I certainly didn't come to argue. I need to meet with Emperor Ichijō. Despite our family name, now that my brother, Fudōno, has taken over our family shipping business, I have to ensure he has rights to the trade agreement my father set in place with the former emperor."

Shizuka shook his head. "Even so, I'm determined to help you see the error of your ways. Now that you've retired from trade, you're free to stay. You may not have our friend's ideal roundness of face, and you'd do well to grow a bit of hair on that bare, brown chin of yours, but I think there are ladies in our fair city who would find you attractive."

Yoki nodded then slapped the table and barked a drunken laugh. "You're ugly. It's true, but I've seen worse. Listen, the emperor's schedule is relentless. It could be three months before I can arrange a time for you to meet. There's time to make you appealing."

"Three months?" asked Yūkan in dismay. "What am I to do for three months in this city?"

"Ichijō knows you're in Kyō. I told him this morning while I went over his day's agenda. He invites you to stay at the palace. I'll sponsor you in society. He's found you a tutor to teach you the way of this city's *good people*, and we'll see if you don't come to embrace our lifestyle."

"Three months of you and some tutor preaching to me the benefits of aristocratic morality and ideals of domesticity?" Yūkan rolled his eyes. "My aunt has already tried. You waste your time."

His friends shared a glance. He'd known them for ten years, before any of them had achieved anywhere the greatness they now enjoyed. Yūkan's father had brought him to Kyō right before he took over the family trading business and introduced him to Ichijō's father, the previous emperor. Shizuka had just been appointed as an apprentice to the ministry of trade and complained often about the humiliation of his Seventh Rank robes of office. Now he ran the ministry and had no shame in his apparel. In the trade district those many years ago, he'd met Lord Yoki who had recently accepted a promotion that earned him a mansion, and he shopped for items to fill this home where they sat tonight. Now Yoki served the emperor directly as Supreme Minister of Personal Affairs.

Every time he had brought wares to the city through the years, they had met to dine and drink. He knew them well, and he understood that look. They were about to counsel him. If he weren't so set on paving the way for his brother to trade with ease in Kyō, as their father had done for him, he'd return to his home province.

"Let's get serious," said Yoki, filling the minister's cup. "What do you think you're doing?"

Shizuka leaned against a wide, elaborately carved ceiling support column and arched anemic eyebrows. "Yes. Tell us, what do you think you're doing?"

"What do you mean?" Yūkan blinked. Had he consumed too much *sake*? He could usually read these two like a scroll.

"You're set on retiring, and I understand. I really do. But this is an uncertain world we live in. Fudōno is sailing the seas."

"So? He's been doing that for years with me."

Shizuka leaned forward, causing his tall, skinny black hat to tip forward and pull at his shiny, ebony topknot. "And the gods have granted you safety and good fortune. Don't be so complacent that you think it may not change. What happens if you lose your brother? If you have no heirs, who will continue? Fudōno is eight years younger, only twenty-three and in no mind or position to start a family. It's on you."

Interesting. He hadn't expected them to come at him from the perspective of family. It showed how well they knew him, too. Family meant everything to him.

Yoki nodded. "You're acting careless. Heedless. Rash."

"Rash!" Yūkan threw back his head and laughed. "And I thought *I'd* had too much wine. My not taking a wife is acting rash? That's ridiculous."

The minister's lips formed a moue then slowly widened into a sly smile. "You're ready."

"For what?"

Shizuka leaned nearer still, his stiff robe puffing above the edge of the table. "Oh, yes. I see it now. When you see her, you'll know."

"What are you talking about?" Yūkan didn't even try to hide his irritation.

"You protest the same way I did right before I was introduced to Izumi. The moment I met her, I knew she'd be my wife."

"Then how come I haven't met my wife yet?" asked Yoki, his voice a bit whiny. "I protest all the time."

The minister sat back and grinned.

"Look," said Yūkan, crossing his arms. "My prospects are different from yours. You're both happy, and that works for you."

"I'm not happy," cut in Yoki, a slight pout pulling the edges of his small mouth downward.

Yūkan sent him a dismissive glance. "As for me, I don't want a proper and fine life in Kyō." He signaled to the servant to bring another bottle. "And I think I've been very generous in my willingness to listen to the two of you prattle on about the supposed virtues of surrounding oneself with women galore—"

"Three months," cut in Shizuka. "Honestly, what have you got to lose?"

That gave him pause. He had nothing waiting for him on his country estate but servants and workers who functioned quite well under the guidance of his manager. Without acquisition trips and sales contracts, what did he have to do? Time was the one thing of which he had plenty.

He studied his friends. They'd always been good for a diversion. Their attempts to win him to their way of thinking could only prove entertaining in the extreme.

"Fine. Three months. But don't hope too hard. I'm me, after all."

Shizuka beamed, making his too-wide mouth appear garish, and brought his hands together in a single clap of delight. "Excellent. We'll start tonight."

*   *   *   *

"It'll be fun. Come with me tonight," Amai said, a hopeful smile upon her delicate face while she stepped as light as a cherry blossom petal floating on a garden pond. She emerged from the hallway that led to individual bedchambers and came into the common area of the wing her father had built onto his mansion especially for her. "Everyone will be disappointed if you don't."

Kirei adored her sweet cousin's youthful enthusiasm. Excitement colored the young woman's round face a becoming pink. She almost envied her. Almost.

Amai had beauty and taste ladies would envy if they didn't like her so well. Her thick, glossy hair fell heavy and straight to pool upon the outermost layer of her many silk robes in shades of maroon, pink, and white. The color combination, a tribute to winter with a nod toward the coming change in season, complimented her cousin's delicate youth and ideal face. Her narrow eyes gleamed with anticipation.

Kirei had also enjoyed this kind of excitement her first year in high society. Now, she had spent too much time with Kyō's jaded and fickle aristocrats to eagerly seek their company. Well, with the exception of a few. Fingering the soft silk of her innermost layer of robes, a pale green chemise that spilled at sleeves and hem, she allowed a brief smile. "I can't. It takes weeks to prepare for an incense contest. I haven't blended anything new or chosen an elaborate bowl or burner."

"You don't need to and you know it." Amai's soft brown eyes widened a fraction. "You always create new scents."

Sometimes having a person know her so well was *not* a

good thing.

"You're the best smelling lady in the city. Besides, you use the very best containers and burners. Nothing but the finest for you."

Kirei plucked at the heavy flower-patterned burgundy silk of her outermost layer, her dress garment, and changed tactics. "But I have to wash my hair tonight. My usual washing night won't be auspicious. I might get sick."

"Nonsense. We both wash our hair the day after tomorrow. It's a most auspicious day for it. Nobody follows the celestial calendar as closely as I." Amai laughed and rolled her eyes. "As if I have a choice. With my brother promoted at the Yin-Yang Bureau, is it any wonder? It's all he talks about these days."

Too true, unfortunately. "Can I give you any reason not to go to this party that you'll accept?"

"No." The young woman stood in a single, fluid motion. Her maroon and pink silk layers swayed in glimmering loveliness as her floor-length hair spooled off of her cushion. Like a dancer, she threw her arms wide and spun. The polished dark wood floor offered no resistance to her white socks. She hugged her arms across the front of her multi-layered *uchigi* robes. "Yours will be the most beguiling fragrance, and you'll surely win the contest. I must go choose what to wear."

"Indeed," Kirei said under her breath as Amai shuffled away. The gods forbid she should appear with any less than twelve colors showing at her neckline. In frustration, she gently kicked her six-foot portable *kichō*, its two opaque curtains fluttering.

She hated the screen of state and the restrictive life it represented. In the country, she'd been free to come and go as she pleased. She could wear far fewer layers of silk and didn't have to hide from every man around. Here in the imperial city, if she didn't demure behind a fan, she was tied to the *kichō*.

She fell onto her back, her head landing on a yellow silk pillow, and gazed out at delicate pink cherry blossoms shining in a rare beam of afternoon sunlight cheating its way through a gray sky. Morning rain had left the ground wet, and a cool breeze blowing in had a rich, loamy quality.

The recent rain caused aches where broken bones had healed. The more time that passed since her injuries, the more she ached when rain and snow fell. It offered an inescapable reminder of her suffering. An inescapable reminder of her guilt. Of the pain in her heart. Warui. She would never forget his name and what he had done to her and her brother.

She had been glad when her father sent her to Kyō because she wanted to leave the horrors of Shinano Province behind. In recent weeks, however, her uncle's behavior had indicated he moved to make a match for her.

She had never intended to find a gentleman. Perhaps her father had. Certainly her uncle did. She only wanted peace, though.

Perhaps if she had a chance to marry, to meet a gentleman she could respect and love, she might not resist. Were she to love, she wouldn't easily share him with a wife and multiple concubines.

She gave her head a vigorous shake and covered her eyes with a hand. This line of thinking could only lead to deeper unhappiness. A true lady of Kyō wasn't to harbor such selfish ideas. Not that she'd ever be considered a true lady of the imperial city. Her country upbringing made her unsuitable for marriage. She could only hope to become a consort. Shivering with distaste, she removed her hand and stared up into the pale blossoms of the cherry tree.

City life had its benefits. Art. Religious choice. Stimulating conversation. She had even managed to make associations with people she genuinely called friends. Country life would always be her preference, however. Unfortunately, her home province held too many painful memories to return. She'd nearly lost her sanity to grief before her father sent her to his brother's house. If only she had a relative in another province. Lately, her lack of freedom in this city suffocated her.

She was trapped. With her uncle's intentions growing

clearer, she now stood to become a pawn, as well.

"Have you no correspondence to write?" came a deep, guttural voice from the main house.

"Ojisan." Kirei sat up like a shot. She smoothed a hand over her ruffled hair and peeked through her screen of state's loose strips of curtain. "Um, no. I wrote my notes and responses this morning. No correspondence has come this afternoon."

"That's disappointing. You need to get out more." Her uncle stepped into the doorframe separating her and Amai's wing of rooms from the main part of his Fourth Ward mansion. "I might've suggested you spend your idle time in writing poetry or perfecting your drawing, but I understand you've been invited to Prince Hansamu's perfume party tonight."

His balding pate gleamed in white light filtering through rice paper. His hard eyes showed no kindness as he assessed what he could see of her past her *kichō*. To appease his curiosity, she extended her arm so he could admire the arrangement of colors showing at the end of her sleeve. His gaze fell upon her silks and he appeared to relax a fraction, so she rested her hand on her knee to keep her layers in his view. At his waist, he fingered a jeweled sword that he wore for show.

She fought a smirk at the thought of him trying to wield such a weapon in earnest. With his narrow shoulders and thin arms, she doubted he could lift the blade over his head. He was more likely to send robbers into peals of laughter rather than running for their lives.

Her voice tight from restrained humor, she said, "Yes, Ojisan. Amai has the party's particulars."

He grunted. "Then you should go speak with her. Prince Hansamu, it's rumored, has expressed an interest in you. I won't deny him if he seeks to take you as a consort, so you'd do well to encourage him. I want you looking your best tonight."

"Of course." Her fun evaporated, and when he left, she released a disgusted huff.

Prince Hansamu was entirely too aware of his good looks. She couldn't think of a more unfaithful gentleman in the capital city. Half the ladies she knew had shared a bed with him at one time or another. Encourage him, indeed. If anything, she'd spend her night protecting her naive cousin from his considerable charms.

A consort. She didn't want a man who would take her as less than a wife. Regardless of the fact that she came from the best family and shared the blood of the city's most powerful aristocrats, her childhood spent away from the imperial city's refinements automatically reduced her status to second class citizen. She fisted an angry hand in the heavy garments draping her trousers.

She stood with nowhere near the grace of Amai and moved toward their hallway as fast as her seven layers would allow. Despite the minutes of bright light reflecting off of polished wooden floors and round column supports, a chill cooled her nose and cheeks. Though she appreciated the warmth her thicker robes offered, she looked forward to Change of Dress Day when she could trade her heavy *uchigi* in winter colors for lightweight silk in spring hues.

If only she could've stayed in Shinano. Too many demons haunted her there, however. Kirei preferred a happy, peaceful life in the country, perhaps married to a governor like her father. Just not in her home province.

In her sparse chamber, her two maids met her in a flurry of activity. It took every bit of her self-control not to issue an irritated groan. In a corner, her caged birds twittered their agitation. She went and opened their door so they could fly about the room.

"My lady," said Uma, her plain features pinching into a frown. "They will poop."

"Then raise a blind. Let them gaze at the sunset and soil the sill."

The maid moved to do her bidding. "I don't understand why they don't simply fly away. I think they must love you very much."

Kirei scoffed. "Hardly. They were born and raised in captivity. It's more a matter of being too frightened to fly into that big, unknown world than to stay here where they feel safe."

In so many ways, the aristocracy were human versions of her tiny birds. Born and raised in the imperial city, they only ventured from the walls of their elaborate cage to visit the nearby Mount Hiei and its temples and breathtaking views. Their window ledge of sorts. To the *good people* of this city, the world was savage - large, coarse, and not meant for refined sensibilities. Even the rural vastness of their own country beyond the city walls was ventured into only by those cast from their society.

Uma stood a moment, her gaze blank as if Kirei's request that she consider a bird's perspective tasked her faculties too greatly. Smoothing a weathered hand down her simple but quality gray *kosode*, she cast the feathered creatures a fleeting glance. Then she gave herself a little shake and scurried past, indicating a rack draped with rich worked silk. "I've prepared three color combinations, my lady. You must choose quickly. We have so much to do."

Her other maid, Zo, lifted her sizable girth to reveal she held Kirei's hair accessories box on her limited lap. "I can't set out your decorations and dress your hair until you tell us what you'll wear."

Kirei moved to the rack and fingered a pale purple damask. Only her connection to her uncle allowed her to wear such fine fabrics, and still there would be some who'd dis-approve of a governor's daughter in finery reserved for the city's elite. As she traced a delicate crane sewn into the silk's texture, she wished she had a reason to care. "Ojisan says I have to look my best tonight."

Uma exchanged a wide-eyed glance with Zo. "You must wear the sky blue then." She slid a hand under a *mo* apron-skirt artfully weaved into a random floating of diaphanous white clouds amidst a sky that started in pale blue at the waist and gradually darkened to deepest indigo where the hem formed a train. "You'll appear as if a piece of the heavens settled to earth to move among the cherry blossoms."

"Will I?" She found it hard to believe. In her mood, she couldn't compare herself to heaven in any way.

"You will. You will." Zo set aside the box and grunted low while struggling to get her rotund body off the floor. When she heaved to her feet, she had a red face and breathed hard. It didn't stop her, though. She hurried over and began smoothing Kirei's hair. "Today's the last day you can wear it. Tomorrow is the first day of the fourth month. It's Change of Dress."

Uma lit incense near the open window where the two small birds hopped, fluffing their feathers against the chill, and happily sang. A cold breeze pushed the smoke throughout her room, infusing it with the sweet scent of white and pink cherry blossoms that grew just outside. Wisps of pale gray snaked through the air, and Kirei inhaled deeply while fingering a loosened length of hair. The flower's perfume mingled with her unique preparation of rich wood tones and exotic Chinese spices to soothe her nerves.

She relaxed her shoulders. "What will Amai wear?"

Uma shrugged then squatted, helping Kirei out of her socks. "Do you want me to ask?"

"Yes. She needs to shine brightly tonight. My uncle wants me matched well and quickly, but I'll put my effort into seeing my cousin wed for happiness."

Kirei swallowed a lump of jealousy. Amai's city upbringing and Fujiwara family connections made it possible for her to actually wed. Preferably as a primary wife. One day, she would be an official wife to a very important man.

Zo finished freeing Kirei's hair then went to work removing the many layers of her robes. "You'll wear your hair down and loose tonight? It's so thick and lovely."

And risk attracting attention away from Amai? Not tonight. "I think it would be better to fashion it gathered with a ribbon halfway down my back." Kirei drew the ebony length over one shoulder to clear the way for her maid to work. The ends tickled her bare toes, and she fed it like a thick rope through a fist to help dispel her nervous energy. "I wish I could think of some excuse to get out of going to this party."

"Why?" Zo removed the final robe, leaving Kirei in the faded jade chemise and her white *kosode* tucked into dark purple-red raw silk *hakama* skirt-trousers.

"I have a bad feeling."

Her maid went still then came around to face her, the multiple swaths of material draped over an arm. Pink drained from her cheeks, and her unfashionably round eyes widened. "Have you had a dream? Was there an omen?"

"No." She had a bad feeling Prince Hansamu would try to insinuate his way into her *hakama*. She was nobody's one-night of pleasure. Kirei put a hand on the good-natured young woman's arm, contrite for causing alarm. "Not at all. I don't like these gatherings. Simple as that."

She shivered, her single raw silk *kosode* offering no protection against the evening's chill. Stepping to the window, she shooed the adorable birds back to their cage and rolled the bamboo blind down to close the window.

Zo relaxed, her cheeks finding color once again and her lips puckering. She carefully folded each robe in plain paper and placed them into separate thin shelves built into a long black lacquered drawer. "You'll enjoy yourself. You'll see. When you get there and meet friends, you'll have stimulating conversation and discover your happiness. Why be bored in your uncle's house when you can enjoy society and entertainments?"

"Entertainment is subjective, I think. What amuses one may bore another." Not everyone could stay home and entertain themselves as she did. Though to be completely fair, she'd been hard pressed to amuse herself these last days of winter. Poor Amai had cried once in sheer boredom. Perhaps she shouldn't fight this outing so much. It might do them both good.

"Except for me." Zo laughed, her double chin jiggling in her mirth. "I'm amused by most anything."

"I envy you. I wish I could find joy like that." Did her father ruin her disposition by educating her on equal level with her brother? Kirei wouldn't trade her knowledge and thirst of learning for all the possibilities of joy, however. It was her secret delight.

"Why do you say you find no joy, my lady? Is there something you would rather do?"

"I would rather accomplish something worthwhile and meaningful. The people I'm expected to spend time with move through this life as if asleep. Their eyes only touch on each other and the beauty of nature and our surroundings. Their thoughts never seem to move past seeking the next pleasure or criticizing their peers."

"I think your dark mood is clouding your view," said Zo, sliding the drawer into a tall bureau against the far wall. "I see a lot of goodness in the *good people* of Kyō. Charity. Artwork. A constant striving for perfection. You are among the best, Lady Kirei, for your excellent taste and very high opinions, and for your skill with a brush and your rare ability to turn a phrase. I hear what the *good people* say about you."

It reassured Kirei to hear of her acceptance and admiration by the aristocracy, but that had never been her goal. She was herself, true to her upbringing and beliefs. "You sound like Ojisan."

"You pay me a compliment." Zo laughed. "Fujiwara no Rikō is a wise and caring lord. I'm the luckiest of maids to have work in his house."

Her maid was right. If her uncle didn't care, he would've immediately matched her to whomever he deemed could best advance his career without a thought to her wants and desires. Since coming to live in the imperial city, Kirei had seen it happen again and again to ladies of her acquaintance. Ojisan insisted she seek a gentleman of high rank, but he'd already given her a year and the freedom to do so in her own way and time.

He wouldn't be so kind and generous if he learned of her and Uma's late-night forays into less pristine areas of the city. She refused to confine her charitable works to simple handouts when people in genuine crisis needed help.

"Why do you easily accept the place society says you must hold? The only obstacle between you and a birthright like mine is one marriage." Kirei pulled her chemise closed over her *kosode*, as if the flimsy material could offer any added warmth.

Zo's smile widened as she stoked a brazier under the birdcage then moved to a hairbrush waiting next to the accessories box. "Yes, my mother came from an aristocratic family, but I wouldn't be a lady for anything if it meant she had to marry a man other than my father. My parents *love*. Really love each other. And I rejoice in my position because I'm free to love where I will. A governor's son. A soldier. Even a gentleman could have me as a consort if I loved him."

"You would do that?"

"For love, yes. My mother was ostracized for her choice. Her mother disowned her. She lost all of her friends. She was no longer welcome among Kyō's *good people*, but she lives a life filled with joy and told me how glad she is that her children have a chance at the same. Were I a lady like you, I might not. In fact, with my looks, I'd practically be guaranteed not to." She patted her generous hip and chuckled.

Love. In her circles, love was only talked of in terms of clandestine meetings and extra-marital affairs. Rarely was love associated with a spouse. Her own father had loved her mother, his primary and only wife, and had refused to take other women into his bed. His 'unnatural' love had cost him his brilliant career as a Fifth Rank official in the emperor's court. When it became clear he wouldn't add women to his household, the emperor took *some* pity on him by assigning him a wealthy and prestigious governorship. It was banishment nonetheless.

"You feel sorry for me?" asked Kirei with a teasing grin. "A moment ago, you expounded on the entertainments I should pursue."

Zo shrugged and set down the hairbrush unused. Settling to the floor, she released a heavy breath. "We have to make the best of our situations. I'm trying to help you see the good in yours."

"Am I wrong to want more?"

Her maid didn't respond, her eyes on the box of accessories she moved to her knees.

She did want more. Was she being selfish?

Uma hurried in and quickly bowed then scurried to the displayed *uwagi* over-robes and *mo*. "Amai wears plum layers – plum and red robes with a blue-green chemise. They're all lined, so she'll have twelve colors showing under her *uwagi*."

Kirei shook her head. "She'll be stunning in the forbidden colors, but she's a tiny woman. After she dons an *uwagi*, *mo*, and *karaginu* jacket over her lined robes and *kosode*, how will she walk?"

Uma laughed. "Why does she need to walk? She will only be sitting, anyway."

"Embarrassing," Kirei said under her breath. "Well, the colors will make her skin glow. She's chosen wisely."

Uma placed fingertips on the purple damask. "This over-robe, I think, is the best choice."

"Maybe so, but the colors will be too striking next to Amai's. I don't want to draw attention." She moved, her feet cold on the bare wood floor. She stepped lightly to the third *uwagi* – a pale yellow confection with red lanterns applied in watered dye that made them blur at their edges and gave an abstract impression. "This one, with only five *uchigi* layers – all dark golden yellow – and this green chemise I already wear. No *mo*. No *karaginu*."

"But—"

"No. I don't go to court tonight, so I have no need or desire to dress formally. It's just a party in the Sixth Ward."

Uma's countenance drooped with disappointment. "You'll pale in comparison."

Kirei shook her head. "I'll compliment her. This is what I want."

Zo frowned but drew a plain yellow ribbon from the box and waved Kirei to turn around. "Very well. I'll dress your hair."

COMING IN 2016

Lady of the Shadows

What happens when a ninja saves the very man she's hired to assassinate?

ABOUT THE AUTHOR

Laura Kitchell lives in Virginia. She is a member of Romance Writers of America and Chesapeake Romance Writers. She lived in Japan as a child and has a love and respect for Japanese history and culture. Contact her at laurakitchell@cox.net, visit her website for events, excerpts, and upcoming projects at www.laurakitchell.vpweb.com, and follow her at laura.kitchell.1@facebook.com.

CPSIA information can be obtained
at www.ICGtesting.com
Printed in the USA
LVOW04s2113180117
521395LV00014BA/1247/P